THE HUNTER KING

THE HUNTED DUET: BOOK 1

JAGGER COLE

The Hunter King
Jagger Cole © 2022
All rights reserved.
Cover and interior design by Plan 9 Book Design
Photography by Wander Aguiar
Editing by MJ Edits | Proofing by Jessie Stafford, Teshia Elborne

This is a literary work of fiction. Any names, places, or incidents are the product of the author's imagination. Similarities or resemblance to actual persons, living or dead, or events or establishments, are solely coincidental. No part of this book may be reproduced, scanned, or distributed in any printed or electronic form without prior written permission from the author, except for the use of brief quotations in a book review.
The unauthorized reproduction, transmission, or distribution of this copyrighted work is illegal and a violation of US copyright law.

❦ Created with Vellum

PLAYLIST

Nightcall - Kavinsky
Gravedigger - MXMS
Bed Head - Manchester Orchestra
Trigger - Mississippi Twilight
Roman Holiday - Fontaines D.C.
Running Up That Hill (A Deal With God) - Kate Bush
Zero - The Smashing Pumpkins
Want Want - Maggie Rogers
Feral Love - Chelsea Wolfe
Hold Back The River - James Bay
This Is It - Ryan Adams
The Silence - Manchester Orchestra
Here She Comes Again - Röyksopp
Spitting Off the Edge of the World - Yeah Yeah Yeahs, Perfume Genius
All Comes Crashing - Metric
September - Ryan Adams & The Cardinals
A Rush of Blood to the Head - Coldplay
Slow Motion - Charlotte Lawrence

PLAYLIST

Forget Myself - Third Eye Blind
New Person, Old Place - Madi Diaz
Gimme Shelter - The Rolling Stones
Bang Bang (My Baby Shot Me Down) - Nancy Sinatra

Listen to the playlist on Spotify.

TRIGGER WARNING

This book contains darker themes involving a chase kink, CNC, and breath-play, as well as graphic depictions of past trauma. While these scenes were written to create a more vivid, in-depth story, they may be triggering to some readers. Please read with that in mind.

1

The darkness of night swirls around me, clawing at my peripherals and snarling at my pounding feet. Branches catch at my hair and ankles, raking my skin and leaving whip-marks I can't feel over the thudding, heaving pressure in my chest.

My breathing is ragged as I race barefoot and naked though the black woods. The thud-thud-thudding of my pulse roaring like a dragon in my ears drowns out everything—the sting of sticks and pine needles under my feet. The branches whipping at my exposed skin. The raised root that slams my shin as I vault over it. The screaming violence of fear, and the dark rush of excitement that comes hand-in-hand with it.

The thudding, pounding sound of heavy, masculine feet on the path behind me grow louder. The low grunt of his breath as he chases me… rhythmically, ceaselessly, sleeplessly. An animalistic, unyielding, utterly driven force inches away from capturing me.

The adrenaline screams through my body as I hear him pull closer. His breath, hot on my neck; his fingertips barely brushing the ends of my long hair, milliseconds away from tangling in my locks and yanking me to the ground like the prey I am.

I scream, my throat haggard and raw, my skin both recoiling and shivering for his touch and that single moment where I'll go from hunted to caught. From fleeing to pinned.

From free to *his*.

The fear spikes through me, shoving energy into my limbs and igniting the last few drops of fuel I have left in the tank. A wrenching sound breaks through my lips as I surge ahead, dodging left and then right through the black trees and swirling shadows. Branches slice at my face, cutting at my nakedness—clawing me back as if the very woods I run through are bent to his bidding, determined to deliver me into his grasp.

Faceless. Furious. Ceaseless.

My venomous fear, and my dark excitement.

The shadow that chases me screaming through the night and leaves me shivering and aching for more when it's over.

I lurch between two trees and jerk to the left, bolting for an opening in the woods. The pounding of his footsteps draws closer, and closer, and *closer*. My heart roars, my muscles scream, and my core clenches as I dig deep for the very last of my reserves, pushing myself to just *get to the clearing*.

If I get to the clearing, I'll be safe. I'll be free from his poisonous, all-consuming need for me.

Until next time.

With a choking, gasping sound from my throat, I surge forward.

Eyes on the prize.

Don't look back.

Swallow the fear.

Run.

Something sharp slices the arch of my bare foot. I scream, stumbling but catching myself. It's only a quarter second… but it's enough.

I feel the ephemeral throb of his power against my back before I feel the very physical grip of his hands circling my neck from behind.

Oh God…

My eyes bulge, my throat closes off the scream. Hot, iron-corded muscles wrap around my body, yanking me against his bare skin before he brings me forward to the ground beneath him, the weight of him pinning me to the dirt and pine needles.

Every molecule in my body explodes. Every nerve ending howls. My breath chokes, my muscles scream, and the horrible ache in my core engulfs me in fire.

Hand on my neck. Skin on my skin. Lips rasping against my ear as he prepares to claim his prey.

"Mine…"

I bolt upright in bed, gasping and choking, my hands flying to my neck as my legs kick and thrash the blankets away.

Silence hums in my ears.

I swallow dryness, and blink at the semi-light of daybreak coming through the window shades. My pulse still screaming in my veins as my eyes dart around the frilly white bedroom.

The woods are gone.

The darkness is faded.

The dream is gone.

The aching throb deep in my core and the shivering fear it leaves teasing over my skin, however, remain.

I swallow again and close my eyes, shivering as my hands slide from my neck to push the fiery tangles back from my face. Sweat slicks across my skin, even in the cool of the air-conditioned bedroom.

Gradually, my racing heart slows. The slick across my skin begins to cool to goosebumps. My clenched throat opens, and the knot throbbing in my core begins to unravel.

In the ephemeral half-light of day creeping over the horizon, my eyes slide to the clock on my nightstand. Four minutes until five in the morning.

Fucking nightmares.

I exhale again, my arms circling as I hug myself. It isn't the first time I've been chased through the woods in my dreams. Though, this is a newer direction than my usual nightmares.

Usually, they're about the accident. Usually, I'm drowning in the water, helpless to stop it. The man, or creature, or devil, or whatever it is that hunts me like prey through the darkness is a recent development.

But, if I'm going to have nightmares almost nightly, at least my brain is keeping things fresh, I suppose.

My brow furrows. My alarm was set for seven this morning—almost two hours from now. But I know from experience that there's no going back to sleep after a dream like the chase through the woods.

A dream that leaves me rattled.

And shivering.

And... *other* physical manifestations that frankly alarm me, considering the content of my nightmare.

The fear is rational.

The arousal is perverse.

I scoot back, leaning my shoulders against the headboard of the large queen-sized bed adorned with lacy frills and elegant details. My gaze sweeps the semi-dark room, slowly tracing over the equally frilly and entirely white aesthetic—like the whole bedroom suite is a white-washed showroom out of a Lillian August or Restoration Hardware catalog. Cold, sanitized, and completely depersonalized.

I have no idea who decided to redo my old bedroom in the two years I've been gone at college. Certainly not my father—interior design is *slightly* outside the purview of running a criminal empire. It could have been my stepmother, Jana—even if only to erase my own personal touches to the bedroom I left behind when I went off to Harvard. Because erasing my history seems to be a pastime of hers.

My musings move on to Senna, my father's head housekeeper and chief of household staff. But then they swing back to Jana.

Painting over the dark blues and ripping down my old punk and indie rock posters was almost certainly Jana's doing.

In the month I've been home, I've been tempting to make it look exactly like it did before, down to the smallest detail— the Sex Pistols and Nick Cave concert posters, the decoupage desk made from Rolling Stone magazine clippings; all of it.

But somehow, the last month has slipped by in a haze of uncertainty and mourning.

Coming back to your father's mansion after he dies unexpectedly will do that, I guess.

We were never close. And I always, *always* knew I came second to his work. I'm not sure he would've even bothered denying that if confronted with it. But still; losing a parent is still a process that takes time.

My gaze flits to the side table again, to the single piece of personalization I've brought back to this showroom of a bedroom. The framed photo of my parents was shot by me, age nine, while we were visiting Paris. In a rare, *rare* occurrence of my father actually appearing in public, he and my mother are standing beside the big glass pyramid that sits in the courtyard of the Louvre. My father, Peter, is unsmiling and cold—nothing outside the usual there. But my mother's smile lights up the photo for the both of them.

That's a loss that still stings four years later.

My phone lights up, yanking my head out of the memories of death. I reach for it, smiling when I see the text from Lyra, my roommate back at Harvard.

Happy birthday, roomie! I hope you enjoy the day. I'm here if you ever need a chat!

My lips curl into a grin.

Well, that's one person who'll remember the occasion today.

Lyra and I were junior year roommates for all of two weeks before the accident—before I had to come home and bury my second parent, and then try and process what comes next. But she's been checking in on me every few days since I left to make sure I'm okay.

Friends are a luxury I'm still getting used to. Or, *was* getting used to, before I was sucked back into this world, and this version of myself.

Not Tatiana Fairist the poli-sci major at Harvard University, lover of quirky indie rock, collector of vintage leather jackets, and drinker of strong black coffee.

No, this version—the version I've tried to bury in two years of college, is a darker version. Here, I'm Tatiana Fairist the Bratva princess. Tatiana who is about to get a deep-end lesson in mafia politics, because as of a month ago, with the death of my father, I am now officially the next in line for Balagula Bratva that was once helmed by my maternal grandfather. Much to the bitterness of my stepmother.

It's not official yet, of course. But it will be, and that's been hanging over me like a prison sentence since I watched them lower my father into the ground. The strict and very old-fashioned "high council" of advisors originally set up by my grandfather is hard at work with what comes next. Technically, pursuant with the laws of the Balagula family, I have to be *married* in order to helm the organization. Or rather, I have to be married so that my—chosen for me—*husband* can helm things.

It's why Peter Fairist, my father, was in charge after my grandfather passed, not Casmir's own daughter, Lisana.

"Bratva" and "old-school sexist patriarchy" are the same word in the Balagula organization. Not that I actually care in this case, since having anything to do with my family's criminal organization, or being forced to marry, or *any* of the current realities of my life are at the very bottom of my list.

I exhale, fully awake now as I smile at the birthday text from Lyra. I'm officially twenty. Though, I won't be celebrating with anyone but myself and maybe some of the household staff, since Jana's been in Paris for the last month on a shopping spree.

Grief works in mysterious ways.

I glance at the book I fell asleep reading last night; a gift from Lyra when I was packing up in a rush to get back home. It's a slightly embellished story of Harriet Quimby, the first female pilot to fly across the Thames river, and honestly, it's not bad.

I open to where I left off, where Harriet is faced with the choice between her aspirations of flying and the advances of the swoony and handsome Lord Buckmiller—that would be the wildly embellished part of the actual history of Harriet Quimby. But as the room grows lighter with morning, I close the book again.

I might as well get up.

In my closet, I pick out something fun to wear. It's fifty-fifty if anyone else in this house even remembers the day but screw it: it's my birthday and I'll wear what I want. So, my favorite ripped jeans and vintage The Clash t-shirt it is.

I drape them over the back of a chair and sit at the vanity. My eyes drop to the silver ring that sits on a small silver chain necklace—a gift from my father years ago for my sixteenth birthday right after my accident and right after my mom died. There's a little charm of a puzzle piece on it, and my father, in a *rare* blip of sentimentality, told me it was because I was the "final piece of his heart."

I smile wryly as I put it on, clasping it behind my neck and letting it fall across my chest. I exhale, pushing my red tangles back into a messy ponytail as I stand and turn for my clothes.

And that's when I hear the screaming.

I freeze, my pulse jangling as my heart lurches into my throat. A shot rings out, making me flinch as my eyes wrench to the door to my room. More gunshots pound out—a back and forth, closer this time—and I can hear more screaming from the staff.

I drop the clothes I've picked out and bolt for the bathroom door. Inside, my hands shaking and my pulse thudding in my ears, I lock the door behind and move to crank open the window. Barefoot in just sleep shorts and a baggie t-shirt, and ignoring the sounds of gunfire coming closer to my bedroom, I swing a leg over the sill. I find footing it the rose-covered lattice on the outside of the sprawling Tudor brick mansion and swing the other leg over.

Trembling, swallowing back the fear, I climb down as fast as I can, wincing at the sting of thorns and brambles. My feet touch grass, and I whirl to run. It's still barely light out as I bolt for the rose gardens at the back of the house.

There's no more gunshots.

No more screaming.

The only sound is my ragged breathing and my roaring pulse as I run. Just like the dream.

There's a gate at the far end of the property—a service driveway for staff and deliveries. If I can make it there, I can alert the guard on duty. Even if there's no one there, I can escape. I realize I've left my phone back in my room, but if I can get to the gate, I can run the three kilometers into town and—

The scream strangles in my throat as the hard, muscled arm wraps like iron around my neck. Another wraps around my torso, and my entire body spasms with fear. My lungs scream for air and my pulse spikes as I'm yanked back against a man's rock-hard body, his breath hot on my neck.

I'm caught; trapped. Just like my dream.

But I'm not going to wake up from this nightmare.

2

AT FIRST, the fear is paralyzing. I go rigid, shrinking in on myself like a cocoon as the muscled arms grip me tight to a firm, broad chest.

The man is silent, but we're moving quickly—or rather, he's carrying me through the gardens around to the front of the house. My eyes whip to the side, my face paling at the sight of two of the household guards face down on the front steps of the mansion, blood pooling and dripping over the granite.

My eyes slide back, and horror sets in as I realize my captor is carrying me towards an all-black Range Rover.

Suddenly, a survival instinct I wasn't even aware I had kicks in. Suddenly, I'm not prey.

I'm a caged fucking animal.

I scream as I suddenly wrench in his arms. The man seems like he's made out of pure iron, but the suddenness of my actions seems to stun him. I kick back hard, catching him in the shin with my heel, right before my elbow slams into his ribs. He hisses, swearing in Russian just before my other elbow jams into his other side. My foot thrashes back again, and I know I've hit his balls when he groans violently, and his iron grip loosens.

I don't waste the opportunity.

My elbows slam back again and again, finding his ribs over and over until suddenly, I'm twisting out of his grip. My feet hit the gravel of the driveway, my pulse so loud it's the only thing I can hear in my ears.

I whirl to run before suddenly, there's a very visceral clicking sound, and the heart-stopping sight of the morning sun cresting the trees to glint off the gleaming barrel of a gun.

Leveled at my forehead.

My breath catches as the world swims a little. My heart stops, and my eyes slide up the chrome instrument of my death. My gaze drags slowly up over metal, past it to tattooed knuckles, to more ink on a veined, muscled forearm with a dress-shirt rolled up crisply to the elbow.

The man towers over me, and my gaze slides higher up over the white dress shirt molded to bulging bicep and shoulder. Up to a chiseled jaw covered in dark scruff. To thinned but stunningly beautiful lips. To a regal nose, dark, furrowed brows, and then the most piercing, hauntingly ice blue eyes I've ever seen.

The world blurs to a stillness around me as he closes the distance between us, until the barrel of his gleaming gun is an inch from the space between my eyes.

My heart thuds powerfully, but seemingly in slow motion as my breath catches in my throat. His jaw grinds, those vicious eyes of his slide down over me, pausing at my neck as his brow furrows.

With the end of my life right there an inch away, it's like everything becomes clearer. I can hear his slow, measured breaths. I can feel the morning sun slowly creeping over the trees and warming my skin. I can smell the masculine, woodsy smell of leather and earth from his.

His eyes drag back up, locking with mine, and it's like that mere look incapacitates me. As if even without the threat of death or being chased, there's no way I could run right now anyway. He takes another measured breath and then slowly exhales as his eyes narrow.

"Get in the car."

His voice is warm and deep, a baritone that sends a shiver down my spine. And accented like my mother and grandfather's native Russian.

I swallow, still unable to move.

"Now, malen-kaya printsessa."

Little princess.

I shiver, my pulse beginning to thud once again at the reality unfolding in front of me.

"I—"

"I won't ask again."

I gasp as his other hand shoots out to grab a fist-full of my hair at the nape. I wince as he pulls me around, bringing me to the Range Rover before he lets go of my hair to open the backdoor.

"Turn around and face the car."

The pressure in my chest and the thudding of my heart begins to overwhelm me. The world spins, and I start to suck in air faster.

"Turn the fuck around," he snarls. "And face the goddamn car."

When I don't move, he does it for me. I whimper pathetically as he whips me around, presses me against the side of the SUV, and yanks my hands behind me to the small of my back.

"Please…" I choke. "Don't hurt—"

"If I was going to hurt you…"

I flinch at the nearness of his deep voice, his lips right by my ear.

"I would have by now."

Cold metal suddenly wraps around both wrists, and my pulse surges at the metallic clicking sound that follows.

Handcuffs. I'm being handcuffed.

But I barely have time to process it before a strip of fabric suddenly wraps across my eyes, pulling somewhat tight as he ties it firmly behind my head. I jolt, choking on my breath as those strong arms suddenly grab me again, lifting me and shoving me across the backseat of the Range Rover. The door slams shut with a click, and for a second, I'm in complete silence as my heart races in terror.

The driver's door opens, and in my blindfolded darkness, I'm aware of the car rocking slightly as he gets in and slams the door shut.

Then, we're driving.

It's my twentieth birthday, and I'm handcuffed, blindfolded and face-down in the backseat of a car driven by a stranger who's just shot his way into my home and abducted me, going God knows where.

So he can do God knows what to me.

With that second part of the thought process, the panic starts to rise. The fear begins to surge like a rogue wave, rushing faster and harder than even my sheer terror can hold back. The freshman orientation seminar they gave us all when I first got to college comes rushing back—the one about navigating a city, and keeping your wits. Where they told us—the female incoming students especially, about fighting as if your life depends on it if you're attacked. Because it might.

About yelling, and screaming, and making yourself as visible as possible so that anyone even remotely in earshot or eyesight of you is aware that something is wrong.

And suddenly, that's exactly what I'm doing.

I scream as loud as I fucking can. I thrash, kicking out, my bare feet pounding painfully off the armrest of the door. I kick again, aiming higher; this time feeling my heel connect with the window.

"*Stop it*," the man hisses.

He stomps on the gas, rolling me askew in the backseat as the car lurches faster. But I keep screaming, and I keep twisting and kicking until my feet find glass once again.

"I said *enough*," he snaps.

But it'll never be enough. And I tell myself I will *never* stop fighting and I will never stop screaming. Not when I'm bound in the backseat of this monster's car.

Finally, I hear him swear under his breath. Suddenly, the car lurches to the side of the road, thumping me around as the tires leave asphalt and crunch over rough rocks and grit. He slams on the brakes, almost tumbling me onto the floor before the engine shuts off.

My throat burns, but I keep screaming—I keep thrashing and kicking, hoping to God we've stopped someplace where someone might hear me, or see the car rocking and maybe wonder what the hell is going on.

I hear his car door open and slam shut. My pulse pounds maniacally, jolting again when the door by my feet yanks open.

"I *said*—"

I kick; *hard*. Both legs are bent at the knee, and when he opens the door, I kick out as hard as I can. Both feet catch him square in what feels like the neck and face, and I hear a gruff, strangled choke from him.

Somehow, through the fear that should be paralyzing me, I move. I lurch out of the SUV feet first, almost falling onto my face, but instead slamming against the side of the car. I right myself, whirling away from the vehicle as I start to bolt forward.

"*HELP!*" I scream, my throat raw and burning. "Help me! Help—"

The scream chokes off along with my breath as an arm wraps like metal around my throat. He yanks me back, another hand slamming over my mouth to silence me as I'm pinned back against that rock-hard chest again. I squirm and kick like this is life or death. But this time, he's prepared.

This time, I'm not going anywhere.

"There's a four-hundred foot cliff drop three feet in front of you."

I stiffen. As if on cue, a breeze wafts up over me, teasing over my skin and fluttering the hem of my baggy t-shirt.

I try to swallow, but the lump lodges against the muscled arm wrapped around my throat. My mind reels, trying to think through the topography around my father's mansion in the countryside outside Birmingham. But we only moved to this house when I was fifteen, and I spent most of the year in boarding school.

Point being: I have no idea where I am, or if there's an abyss three feet in front of me or not.

Also, I don't have the luxury of debating truth right now at all. Because that arm is still around my neck. That big, powerful hand is still clamped over my mouth. And I'm still blindfolded, handcuffed, and pinned against the monster at my back.

Suddenly, we're moving again. But this time, he's dragging me to the back of the SUV. I hear a door open, and then I gasp loudly as he pulls his arms from around me to lift me into the Range Rover.

Not the back seat. The trunk.

My panic surges. But I don't have time to fight this time. He's on me instantly, wrapping a rope of some kind around both ankles and tying them tight. He tugs it taut, binding me to the wall of the SUV trunk. Another rope slips around my handcuffed wrists, pulling me in an opposite direction; pinning me in place in the back of the vehicle.

Even though I doubt we're anywhere near other people, I open my mouth to scream again.

Which is exactly when the thick wad of fabric jams between my lips.

A gag. He's just gagged me. I scream anyway, but it's muffled and mumbled.

Then, without a word from him, the trunk door slams shut, cloaking me in silence. I hear and feel the driver's door open again. Then the Range Rover rumbles to life before pulling back onto the road.

I start to try and keep track of the lefts and rights we take. But I soon realize that without knowing where I was when we pulled off the road before, I have absolutely zero idea where we are. I also lose all track of time in my fear. Has it been an hour since we left my home? Ten minutes?

All I can do is try not to have a complete breakdown there in the trunk. All I can do is try to breathe and try to keep my heart from thundering out of my chest.

At a certain point, the car stops and turns off. When the trunk opens, I instinctively want to lash out again, but the ropes stop me. I even swear I hear him chuckle at my stymied attempt.

Powerful hands grab me, pinning me down tightly as he undoes the ropes.

"Try what you tried before, and I promise there will be consequences you are not prepared to deal with."

In another circumstance, the deep, masculine, honeyed voice right into my ear would bring a different kind of shiver up my spine. Circumstances where I'm not blindfolded, handcuffed, and gagged, maybe.

I jolt, gasping into the gag as he lifts me effortlessly and suddenly tosses me over his broad shoulder. I simmer, pulse thudding as this huge man carries me away from the car. We're outside, and there's the loud whine of some kind of machine or engine.

I stiffen.

It's the sound of a jet engine. It's the sound of a plane powering up, getting ready to fly.

It's the sound of me about to completely disappear.

I scream again, heedless of his last warning as I start to thrash and kick. But this time, again, he's ready for it, and his powerful arms pin me firm to his body as he climbs a staircase and ducks into the plane. I'm still kicking and screaming bloody murder as I fight my captor.

Words like "trafficked" or "sex slavery" explode in my mind, shaking me to my core as I fight and claw with everything I have. I get a few hits in, but it's useless. Before I can react, he's swinging me off his shoulder, slamming me into a padded seat, and wrapping a rope tight around my body over and over.

I kick and thrash, but the rope is tight, wrapped around my stomach, my upper chest, and both my arms. Another loops around my ankles, binding them together and to the seat I'm in.

I hear him sit near me and fasten a seatbelt. The tears I've desperately tried to hold back begin to well in my eyes, bleeding into the fabric tied around them. The plane begins to move, and the sob catches in my throat.

Engines whine as the plane shoots forward. I feel it begins to rise, lifting into the air as the clanking sound of the wheels tucking up make me shudder.

Time slips by. It's meaningless, because I have no way of keeping track of it. And my captor is silent—silent to the point where I wonder if he even stayed on the plane when it took off. Maybe his job was just to shoot his way into my home to kidnap me, and now I'm off to the whoever is going to sell my body to another monster.

That does it. I've been trying to keep it together and not lose control. But the horrible imagery of a scenario where I'm enslaved and raped or something is too much. I start to shake, choking on my sobs as the tears fall freely.

Suddenly, something brushes my hand. I gasp, jolting as I feel fingers pull at the gag in my mouth. I don't have to wonder who it is, though. I recognize the same woodsy, masculine scent of him.

So he did stay on the plane.

The man plucks the gag from my lips, and I shiver as I feel the heat of him as he leans close.

"If you scream, this will go back for the remainder of our journey. Nod if you understand that."

I nod stiffly.

"Good girl."

I swallow.

"Here. Drink this."

I flinch as a plastic straw dances against my lips. I purse them tightly, sinking back into the seat away from it. The man sighs heavily.

"It's water. And you're bound to a seat on my plane. Surely if I wanted to harm you, I wouldn't have to trick you."

I keep my mouth pursed tightly.

"Suit yourself."

The straw and the man move away from me, and I hear the sound of him sitting back in his chair, near mine. The hum of the plane is the only sound as more time slips by. More thoughts of what fate awaits me poison my thoughts. More evil, horrifying nightmares of what he might do to me seep into my very skin, until I'm trembling. I swallow, but it's like sand in my throat, and my dry lips rub painfully together.

"Let's try that water again."

The tone isn't jokey or warm. It's a command. It's a statement. He's not asking if I want some water. He's telling me I'm about to get some.

I hear him stand again and move to my side. But this time, his fingers tug the blindfold from my eyes. Instantly, those ice-blue orbs of his pierce into my very soul. I flinch back, taken aback with how close he is, looming over me.

Once again, I drink him in. The dark hair and stubble on his strong, defined jaw. The tattoo ink slipping out of the neck and rolled sleeves of his crisp dress shirt. The piercing blue eyes and beautiful mouth. The bulging muscles of his biceps and shoulders, the veins of his thick forearms.

The gun in a holster on his hip.

We're in a small private jet, seeped in opulence, and we're alone in the cabin. He's holding a cup of water with a straw in a tattooed hand. Without blinking or pulling his gaze from me, he brings the straw to his own mouth and wraps his lips around it, drinking. He swallows, arching a brow as if to say "see?".

Then he brings the same straw to my mouth. This time, even though I'm shaking, I take it between my lips and drink.

"Good girl."

I feel my face darken with heat when he rumbles the words out. My skin flushes, and I swallow a last gulp of water before he pulls the empty cup away.

"We'll be landing soon."

My brows knit, and my lips part.

"Where are we—"

I stiffen with a whimper as he suddenly pulls the blindfold back down over my eyes. The gag stays out, and he stays silent as he moves back to his seat and buckles his seatbelt with a click. My stomach flutters as I feel the plane begin to descend.

There's no announcement, we just keep descending until I bite back a gasp as I feel the wheels touch down. My pulse throbs, and my stomach aches in hunger. My head is swimming in a daze by the time we finally stop, and I hear him get out of his seat.

"Once again, I will remind you that not being gagged is a privilege I would not abuse if I were you."

He unties me, and I whimper when he yanks me out of my seat and throws me over his shoulder again. We descend a flight of stairs, and then suddenly, I'm being tossed across the back seat of a car or SUV again.

I'm scared out of my mind. Every part of me wants to cry or beg for mercy. I want to plead with him not to hurt me, and not to touch me like a horrible dark voice inside of me tells me he's going to.

But I keep my mouth shut. I stay silent, heeding his warnings.

We drive for what feels like forever before we stop. Once again, he easily lifts me out of the car and carries me over his shoulder as he walks—first across pavement, then gravel, and then an echoey wood.

He steps down heavily, and I feel whatever he's standing on rock slightly.

I shiver when I hear the lapping sound of water.

We're on a boat.

The man sets me on a bench of some kind and ties my wrists behind me to something. The engine thunders to life, and I bite my lip hard as we surge out into waves. More time slips by, my heart racing with the thudding of the boat against the surf. Until finally, the engine winds down and then off.

He lifts me again, and once again, I hear the sound of footsteps on a wooden dock. Then gravel. Then we pause as he punches in a beeping alarm code of some kind. A door unlocks, and we step through into a house or some other structure.

He's climbing stairs, and my body begins to tremble and quake.

We're where he's going to hurt me. Where he's going to take from me. Where he's going to use my body, or maybe just kill me.

I choke on a sob as he opens a doorway and steps through. And then suddenly, he's swinging me off his shoulder and putting me on my shaky feet. He grabs my wrists, making me flinch. Then there's a click, and the handcuffs fall away. The blindfold slips from my head, and I blink at the sudden light the floods my eyes.

Then I blink, my eyes focus, and my jaw drops.

I was excepting a creepy warehouse. Or a murder shack of some kind. But instead, I'm standing in one of the most stunning rooms I've ever been in, and I've been in some beautiful places before.

The Scandinavian aesthetic is almost like a hunting or ski lodge. But the lux factor has been dialed up through the roof. Across the huge, wide-plank wooden floor, a wall of black-iron-framed windows overlooks a stunning view of the forested edge of a misty lake on the brink of night. Across the wide water, there's more forest, and not another house in sight.

I shiver as my eyes slide back to focus on the room itself. A huge, vaulted beam ceiling. Crystal and white-wood accents everywhere. An enormous, elegant fireplace along one wall, flanked by shelves filled with books. An open doorway gives a glimpse of an all-white tile and black-iron fixtured en-suite bathroom.

I turn, and my heart suddenly lurches when my gaze lands on the big platformed bed against the far wall. I stiffen, every single fear that has been momentarily white-washed by elegance rushing back all at once.

"I'll be back with food."

He grunts the words behind me, making me flinch. I swallow a lump in my throat as I slowly force myself to turn back to him. I quiver under that piercing, icy-blue gaze once again as I drink him in.

He's tall, built, cold-looking, and yet hauntingly beautiful.

I cringe on the inside.

I just described the monster who kidnapped me and just brought me to a fucking bedroom as beautiful.

He turns to walk out of the room, and my mouth opens unbidden.

"Where..."

"You're at my home. And you will be staying here."

My stomach drops as he steps through the doorway into an elegant hallway.

"Wait," I blurt, shivering. "Wait, why am I—"

"Because you're mine."

The words hit me like a slap, and the arctic gaze that lances into me cuts me in two.

"Because you belong to me, now."

The door shuts with a click as he locks it behind him, leaving me alone with my racing, sinking heart and terrified thoughts.

I turn, shaking as my eyes land on the bed. My jaw sets.

I will not die here. I will not let him take from me here.

Not without a fight.

3

There's a monster inside of me.

I fill my lungs with air as I grip the edges of the porcelain sink. My knuckles go white with the tension, the corded muscles and ink of my forearms rippling as my teeth grit.

I can feel the demon I've locked up and buried deep in my soul snarling at his prison bars; prowling behind the iron before occasionally slamming violently against them, as if to test their strength.

Or his.

This wasn't supposed to go like this.

I exhale slowly as I reach for the faucet. I let the water run cold before I scoop up two handfuls to splash against my face. As if the shock of cold might stun my monster back into submission.

As if I actually believe that.

I splash more coldness against my face before I turn off the faucet and reach for a towel. I look up into the mirror—face dripping, eyes hardened, grip tightened on the edge of the sink.

I told myself I'd never do this again.

I don't mean the violence, or the actions I've done over the last few hours. I mean doing those things for *who* I'm doing them for. I walked away from the organization years ago and cut that cancer from my life.

And yet here it is. Metastasizing. Insidiously worming its way back into my world even with the years and miles I've put between my current life and the one I once lived.

When I was truly a monster. A demon. A beast. A killer. The boogeyman. The nightmare under your bed.

The *bukavac*, they once called me: a mythical demon king. Not to my face, of course. But I know it's a moniker that's trailed me from the shadows—one both feared and earned, through blood. Through killing. Through precise, unemotional savagery.

All in service to the Ghost Syndicate, and a man I'll hate to the ends of Hell itself.

They took me when I was fourteen. A punk, forgotten, nothing son of a work-visa Russian mother, slumming it on the streets of Liverpool. My mother was an old-school, drink-the-kool-aid Soviet supporter. So they told her they were the government—and they once *had* been, operating as a secret Soviet military training program called *Prizrak Proyekta*; Project Ghost.

But when the USSR fell, the man in charge of the program, a then young captain named Mikhail Arakas, saw opportunity.

Here he was running a completely black-ops, off-the-books assassin program. And when the ones writing the checks fell from power, he decided to start writing his own.

Mikhail is the one who took the program private, turning it into the world's most deadly, unknown, and vicious school for shadow assassins and spies. He's also the same man that took a hot-headed shit off the streets of Liverpool and turned him into the bukavac.

His prized demon. His ultimate killer. Until the day I left and never came back.

At the time, I was a captain in the Bratva-affiliated Tsavakov empire. Placed there, of course, by Mikhail for one of his many Machiavellian plots. But what started as me being a deep-plant to one day help Mik take over an empire, ended the day Nikita died. And after that, I was done with Mikhail and his bullshit. His lies. His endless sociopathic need for power, with me as the bullet used to topple kings.

So I walked away. I cut ties and I've stayed on as a top advisor to Boris Tsavakov. Now, I'm a man wearing a permanent mask.

On the outside, I'm the man people see me as: a top rank within a powerful business and criminal empire. A man who wears custom tailored suits and Patek Philippe watches. A man who graduated top of his class from the prestigious Lords College of Business, alongside peers that went on to become titans of the financial and political worlds.

But that's all surface. The mask I wear to bury the past. The one that keeps the monster in me chained, subdued, and hidden.

To keep the *bukavac* the children's imaginary nightmare he's supposed to be.

I've never once been tempted to go back to that life. And up until recently, Mikhail wasn't foolish enough to even ask me to.

Until he found my weak spot and pressed. Until he offered me something the ludicrous money I make now under Boris couldn't even buy.

When the man I swore I'd kill offered me the location of my sister's final resting place, so that I could finally, *finally* give her the peace she deserves, I broke my own rule.

I took another job for the devil himself.

Technically, Mik and I still haven't spoken since years ago. Even this entire exchange was through Jana, his second in command. Mikhail knows I won't speak to him directly—not after what he let happen to Nikita.

But still, I took the job. Well, the two jobs. Because after all of these years, Nikita *will* be laid to rest as she deserves. Even if it means me doing the bidding of the piece of shit who let her die in the first place.

The first was a simple assassination—a hit on a mid-level government official in Munich a month ago. The man was apparently pushing through some sort of law that would impact The Ghost Syndicate's operations in Germany. Nothing complicated, just a simple rooftop sniper shot through the windshield of his armored town car.

Then came the second and last job to fulfill our deal. A second easy, by-the-numbers hit on Peter Fairist's only living heir.

Simple. Quick. Efficient.

And yet, here I am, thousands of miles later in my sanctuary, with a captive I was supposed to kill. And a simple job has become very much complicated.

It's the ring that stopped me: the silver puzzle-piece ring hung on a thin chain around her neck. Tatiana's: the only person now that Peter himself is dead, who could take over the Balagula Bratva—otherwise known as Mikhail's *obsession*.

Of all his insidious, Machiavellian machinations, worming his way into power with the Balagula has stood above all else. Maybe it's because he's yet to succeed with that conquest, even after his own second in command, Jana, seduced and married Peter after his wife died.

But whatever the case, it was supposed to end with me shooting Tatiana in her late father's home this morning—all engineered to look like the messy work of a rival Bratva family, of course.

Obviously, things have played out differently.

I grit my teeth as I turn, striding from the bathroom back into my study. My target is the bar cart, and I splash a heavy pour of vodka into a tumbler before bringing it greedily to my lips.

I know it's not the same ring. It *can't* be the same ring I gave Nikita on one of the rare occasions our mother let me see her. Before Mik took her, too, into the training program like the cruel psychopath he is.

It's not the same ring. But it stopped me cold. It broke the trance I go into when I need to be the emotionless killing machine I have to be at times. And suddenly, for the first time in my entire life, I flinched in the face of a kill.

Then I took her.

Then she fought me and tried to run.

And now, there's a devil in me prowling at the bars of his confinement, hungry for another scent of her defiant fire.

I swallow back vodka and the clash of duty versus desire.

There's no place for recklessness like this in my life. There's no place for *her*, or the hunger she apparently brings roaring out in me.

I know what the fix is, of course. It's going back up there to the guest room I've locked her in and finishing what I was supposed to finish back in England at her father's house.

But I know that's not happening. Not now. Not anymore.

Before I can really swallow the full ramifications of my actions, I pull out my phone and dial Jana.

"The police are at the Fairist house, Kristoff," Mikhail's niece and my second least-favorite person sneers into the phone.

"A delivery driver called it in when he found bodies on the front steps."

I wait for what I know is coming.

"Do you know whose body has yet to be discovered, Kristoff?" she rasps. "Who has now been declared *missing* rather than—"

"It's done."

And just like that, there's no going back. Just like that, I've chosen a path paved with a lie, and I don't even fully comprehend why.

I just know I'm not doing this. Not anymore. Not to the girl upstairs.

Jana pauses, and I can almost feel that cunty sneer of hers through the cell phone.

"You were supposed to do it in—"

"Plans change, Jana. It's done."

"Where?"

My eyes narrow.

"It doesn't matter."

"I'll need proof if you want a prayer of getting the information I know you want."

I grit my teeth.

"You'll give me what we agreed on. Not a prayer. Not a hint. And I'll bring you proof."

"I'll come to you. I'd rather see for myself. Where are you?"

"Our exchange is complete. I'll be in touch shortly to tell you how you can deliver me what you *will* deliver to me."

I hang up abruptly, with my only regret being that I'm not in the room with Jana to watch her lose her cool and break something, as I'm sure she's doing right now.

My eyes pierce into the early evening hanging over the lake through the window of my study. The sun leaves a neon bloodstain over the water as I drain the last of my drink and clench my jaw.

What the fuck are you doing?

But I'm already storming out of the study and taking the stairs two at a time. I prowl down the long hallway to the east wing, where the locked guest room is. I half expect to hear her slamming against the door or trying to smash her way through the locked, bullet-proof windows. But instead, there's only silence.

I haven't told her why she's here. Christ, I barely know myself why she's here. But I also haven't trusted myself to even open my mouth around her. Not after she fought me. Not after she squirmed against me.

Not after her scent woke a demon in me I buried years ago.

My pulse running hot in my ears, I deftly unlock the door to the guest room. I step in, frowning as my eyes scan the room.

There's the wooden desk chair she broke against the unbreakable windows. There's the side table she kicked over, and the lamp smashed across the ground.

But that's all I see: her carnage.

Not her.

My eyes narrow as I turn towards the bathroom. And then suddenly, my senses twitch. I whirl back, but by some unbelievable chance, she's actually gotten the drop on me. The second side-table lamp crashes into the back of my head, knocking me off balance. I take a knee, barely bringing my arm up on instinct to stop what might be part of the broken chair from slamming into the side of my head.

What the fuck.

I whirl, just in time to get a foot to the shoulder, knocking me off balance and sending me sprawling. I snarl, lurching up as I see her bolt from the room and dash down the hall towards the stairs.

But it's not fury I feel, watching her run away like that. It's not anger that she tried to hurt me. Not even rage at myself for being careless.

It's fire. It's a savageness I've never felt before.

Not a bloodlust. Not a need to kill or hurt.

But quite simply, a need to chase.

A need to hunt.

A need to catch a little prey who has no idea what's about to come after her.

And we've only just begun.

4

I ALMOST FALL as I dash out of the bedroom door and slip on the long rug that runs the length of the hallway. But I catch myself, my lungs squeezing the air out as terror and adrenaline explode through me.

Run.

I bolt for the stairs, crashing down them to the point just shy of actually falling. I can already hear him behind me. And this time, there's not going to be a mercy if he catches me. Not after I just hit him.

I know I should be paralyzed. I should still be in that room, huddled in a corner sobbing and begging for mercy from the monster who brought me here. And yet somehow, I've discovered a fight in me.

I *will not* die here. And I will not let him lock me in a bedroom to…

No.

Not without a fight.

I dash around a corner, looking madly all over the place for an exit before my eyes land on the front door down another hallway. I hear his grunts behind me, and something like fear mixed with something else surges through my body.

I push myself, running as fast as I've ever run before as I crash through the huge lake house. My hip catches a sidetable near a couch as I sprint past it. I cry out in pain, but I ignore it as I lurch for the door and my only chance at freedom.

I can't hear his footsteps or grunts, but I know he's right behind me. I know it's just my adrenaline dulling my ears, with my only focus on that one chance right in front of me. I hit the door with a painful slam, wincing as I fumble at the lock, twist the knob, and yank the door open as I fling myself outside—

Right into his waiting hands.

I *scream*.

I scream like it's the grim reaper himself who's just grabbed me by the neck and spun me around against his chest. I keep screaming, even with the pressure around my throat and the fear strangling my every thought.

I will not die here. I will not die—

"You're welcome to keep screaming."

The roughness and closeness of his voice against the softness of my ear has me gasping as if I've plunged into ice water. I freeze, tensing against his rock-hard body.

"But all you will accomplish is blowing out your voice. There's no one who will hear you."

My heart pounds against my chest, ringing in my ears as my eyes dart wildly around us. It hurts, and it's so terrifying for a second that I feel as if I'm drowning. But I know he's right.

No one is going to hear me. There's not another house in sight along the shore of the lake. Nor is there a single light on the opposite side.

I'm alone with a monster.

"Please…"

The word breaks through and tumbles from my trembling lips. My body quivers as real terror of what this man might do to me in the darkness and solitude of his lakeside home slams into me.

"Please… please… don't…"

The arm drops from around my neck. I blink, caught off-guard as his body pulls away from mine, releasing me.

I shiver, hugging my arms around the thin t-shirt that covers me as I slowly turn to face my abductor. My captor. My monster.

My pulse skips as I turn to find those piercing icy eyes stabbing into me, sucking the breath from my lungs. He towers over me, his jaw clenched tight, but a calm, almost amused look on his face, not anger.

His chiseled, utterly gorgeous face.

I know in my heart how fucked up it is to call him that. There's just no other way to describe him. But then, Jeffery Dahmer was deceptively handsome. Thousands of evil-hearted men who prey on women every single day, all over the world are deceptively attractive, the way carnivorous plants use bright flowers to lure in their next meal.

My eyes drop to the tattoo ink visible under the now-open collar of his dress shirt. The swirls and designs coming down his forearms, and across the back of one hand. The easy, half-amused smirk on his full lips. The slight cleft in his chin. The glint in those lethally blue eyes.

And yet however handsome it makes him, it's like I'm looking at an artist's rendering of "handsome." It's all *too* perfect.

Unnaturally so. Deceptively so.

It's like I'm looking at a mask. Because through it, along the cracks and deep behind his eyes, there's something else lurking.

Something darker, something unsmiling, and more disturbing, something that ignites a spark deep in my core.

Fear mixed with excitement. Danger mixed with curiosity. Horror mixed with attraction.

The seconds tick by without a word from those lips. Without so much as a gesture from him. Just the two of us, standing on the gravel driveway by the front door to his luxurious lake house.

I shift from foot to foot, still hugging myself and swallowing down the lump in my throat. I try and look away, but it's like I'm unable to pull my gaze from his eyes.

"I…"

I shiver.

"I… um, what—"

"*Run.*"

The single word sends a bolt of fear and adrenaline shooting through my core. I tremble, swallowing again as I stare up into his icy gaze.

"I… I don't understand…"

His eyes narrow slightly, the corners of his lips curling dangerously.

"I would like you to *run*. Away from me, that is."

The hum of blood fills my ears—the faint ringing sound of it lancing into my head.

"I—"

"If you escape," he murmurs quietly, his voice low and heavy. His eyes never once blink; never once look away from deep into mine.

"Then you are free. And if I catch you…"

He shrugs.

"Then I catch you."

I tremble, my skin prickling into goosebumps as something heated throbs in my center.

"Escape where?" I whisper hoarsely.

"The property perimeter is clearly marked. You'll know it. If you can get past it without me catching you, you are free to go."

I stare at him, my chest heaving as I suck in heavy breaths of thick air. My mouth thins, eyes narrowing at him.

"What the hell is this?"

He smirks darkly, predatorily.

"An opportunity."

"For?"

All he does is smile thinly, and I shiver at the glint in his eyes.

I shake my head, my arms hugging myself tighter, wishing I was wearing much, much more clothing than sleep shorts and a baggy t-shirt.

"No."

His brow arches faintly.

"I wasn't asking."

"You *want* me to run?"

"Precisely."

My head shakes.

"I don't want—"

"Of course you do."

My breath sucks in as he steps closer to me. My skin prickles, arms hugging tightly, legs squeezing together.

Nipples puckering against the fabric of my shirt.

I swallow another lump in my throat, my breathing labored as I stare wide-eyed up into his grim, gorgeous, frightening face.

"I'm not even wearing shoes."

"Then next time, be aware of your needs and surroundings before you make an escape."

I stare at him, trying to find the joke; the "gotcha." Literally any indications that this is a really fucked up, demented, unfunny joke or prank.

I don't find it. Because this is not a joke.

"I'm counting to three. And then, you *will* run from me."

My breath comes faster.

"One."

My gaze is still hooked with his as I start to back away, my bare feet crunching over the gravel before they find grass.

"Two."

Something snaps in me. Some deeper, primal force wrests control away from normal me. And before I can process it, suddenly, I'm whirling, and I'm fucking *running*.

I run like I've never run before, my pulse screaming in my ears as I fling myself headlong into the trees surrounding the lodge home. My breath comes ragged, terror and adrenaline ripping at me as I crash recklessly through the trees.

Just like my dream. Only there'll be no waking up to save me from this.

Branches rip at me, cutting my skin. The ground tries to trip me, a low branch slamming into my shin and a twisted root jamming my toe so hard I scream in pain. But I keep going. I keep running, sucking in air and forcing myself not to turn around.

Keep running. Just keep. Fucking. Running.

I don't even know if he's telling the truth. In fact, he's probably not. But I know one thing: not running is giving up. Not running is giving in.

And so, I dive into the darkness of the trees. My every nerve shrieks in my body, every synapse firing at once, and every ounce of adrenaline dumping through my system. I dodge around trees, lurching over roots and brush, my breath ragged in my burning throat and my ears ringing with the pulse of my blood.

Then, I hear it.

I hear *him*.

And he's right behind me.

The sheer terror ignites the last of my reserves. And suddenly, I'm surging into the trees. I can hear the monster chasing me—his even, deep breathes, the crunch of his shoes against the underbrush. The snap of branches, getting closer and closer.

I scream. I scream a ragged, guttural sound as I dodge and weave through the trees. He's drawing closer, though. His footsteps are louder, and so close that I swear I can feel his breath hot against my neck.

I know what I'm feeling is pure terror. But it's not just that. The faster I run, and the longer I keep ahead of him, suddenly, that fear turns into a surging sort of energy.

An excitement.

An exhilaration.

And for the first time in longer than I can remember, I feel absolutely *alive*.

The thrill of not being caught—or maybe it's the thrill of being chased, as fucked up as that sounds—courses through my veins like a drug. I push myself harder, my entire body throbbing and shivering with this newfound power and thrill.

My skin throbs. My pulse invigorates. My nipples harden, and a horrible, betraying wet heat pools between my thighs.

My sprint through the dark woods becomes a sort of dance—dodging left and right, my lips pulling into a grin as the sick, twisted, consuming heat throbs through my core. I can see sunset up ahead—a break in the trees.

"The property perimeter is clearly marked. You'll know it. If you can get past it without me catching you, you are free to go."

I'm almost there. I'm actually almost—

Long, powerful fingers wrap around my throat. The scream gets trapped and choked as he yanks me back against his huge body. Adrenaline detonates like a bomb—like the pure thrill and energy I've just built crashing headlong through the forest explodes out of me all at once.

My eyes bulge, my mouth open and silent as he whirls us like a dark dance and slams me back against the trunk of a tree.

We pause like that—his hand on my throat, his piercing, consuming, lethal blue eyes pinning me to the tree trunk at my back. Both of our chests heave with breath from the run, and I can feel his pulse in his fingertips thudding against mine under the soft skin of my neck.

"*So close, printsessa*," he murmurs darkly.

My ears ring. My core clenches and spasms and twists. My legs shake as my eyes go wide.

"Now wha—"

His answer that cuts me off isn't words.

It's his mouth, slamming to mine—his lips searing to my own to steal the very breath from my lungs and fire from my very soul.

A hard kiss.

A punishing kiss.

A first kiss.

Stolen.

Just like me.

5

It's like fireworks going off behind my eyes and deep in my chest. It's like a million fiery sparks flinging to land across every inch of my skin, engulfing me in flame until the air is sucked from my lungs.

The roughness of him is still there—the grip of his fingers on my throat, the scruff of stubble across his strong jaw. The masculine, woodsy and leather smell of him. The hardness of his body as it pins my much smaller frame to the tree.

But what I feel most through all of it is the searing softness of those lips. The way they sear to mine. The way they demand, unquestioning. How his mouth coaxes mine open. How his lips part mine and his tongue invades.

How at twenty years old, by proxy of all-girls boarding schools and being the daughter of the cold, dangerous Peter Fairist, king of the vicious and old-school Balagula Bratva, this is my first one.

My first kiss.

My first *anything*.

In boarding school, it was a non-issue. Maybe something I was teased about; something some of the more "worldly" girls giggled about behind my back. But in my head, I knew college would be a place for me to explore. A place to start fresh without everyone knowing me as "the daughter of the Russian Mob Boss."

Spoiler: it wasn't.

I landed at Harvard, and it was like the entire greater Boston area knew who I was. Or more specifically, who my father was, and very specifically, what he was capable of. I went through four roommates during the first semester of my freshman year. Each one staying for a week at most before their parents demanded they not be rooming with a mafia princess.

Sophomore year, I roomed with a Korean girl named Ji-woo. That lasted almost the full year, because I think through the language barrier, she thought my father being the head of a Russian mafia family was a joke.

And those were just female roommates. The opposite sex avoided me like the plague.

Not at first. Early on, there were a couple braver types who'd ask me out to coffee or something. Those dates would last until they realized the seven-foot-tall, hulking men in black with obvious firearms under their jackets weren't going anywhere. Or until one of those brave or foolish dates would try to even hold my hand, and one of those menacing bodyguards would grunt and shake their head.

And that's how you reach your twentieth birthday without ever having been even kissed.

Until now.

Until he came, and stole me, and gagged and handcuffed me, and chased me.

And then caught me.

The fiery heat against my lips surges hotter and stronger. The fingers at my throat splay out, sliding over my neck and up to cup my jaw. A low rumbling growl in his chest vibrates through my core, making me quiver as I find myself sinking against him.

Opening my lips wider.

Tasting his tongue with mine.

Wanting this. Needing this. Not running from this.

My hands seem to move by themselves, slowly raising to touch against his chest. But the second they brush his shirt, I jolt as his hands suddenly grab mine and shove them above my head. I gasp as he pins them there with one firm hand, grunting into my lips before his other hand drops back to slide over my jaw.

Heat surges through my core. A horrible, rebellious desire that just seems to grow hotter and hotter. My body trembles against his, my nipples so hard against the cotton of my shirt that I know he can feel them through his as well. My hips lift as if they've been trained to do so. My pulse screams in my ears. And as he keeps kissing me in that slow, fierce, demanding way, my body starts to shake to the point of boiling, like a kettle left too long on the stove.

And then right before the whole thing explodes, he pulls away. It's so fast and unexpected that I stand there like an idiot for another two seconds—eyes still closed and lips still parted—until I realize what's happening.

I blink, stuttering out of the swirling storm of fantasy and crashing back into reality.

Where I've just kissed the man who stole me.

Eagerly.

My lungs ache, and I realize I'm still not breathing. I gasp, filling them with air and trembling as his vicious and hard ice-blue eyes cut into me.

"Caught you."

The growled words are barely audible. And I'm still reeling from that kiss when he suddenly grips me and hauls me off the ground. I choke on the gasp as he throws me across his shoulder and turns to start prowling through the trees.

I want to scream, but I'm still in shock. I want to fight, but I'm frozen. Or scorched to a crisp, more accurately. My face is throbbing with heat as he carries me through the dark trees until he steps out onto the rocky shore. My eyes shift to the left, and my heart sinks.

I was running without direction, heedlessly, to get away from him. And all I managed to do was run in a big U-shape. That "freedom" of the shore through the trees that I saw was merely the same lakefront that the house sits on, just twenty meters down the shore.

The sun has dropped over the opposite shore now, and the woods and the lake grow dark purple with night. The air seems cooler, even with the heat still throbbing beneath my skin.

Wordlessly, my mind still numb from the kiss, we move over the rocks of the shore back to the house. I know I should be fighting, but it's like I'm completely drained and empty—from the morning, from the trip, from being locked in a room in a strange place.

From being chased.

From being caught.

From being kissed by the beautiful, unnamed masked monster who stole my first.

He carries me through the same door I tried to flee from. Up the same stairs I tripped down. Down the hallway I slipped on. And back into the room I escaped from.

This time, I know I won't be getting out as easily.

He sits me on the edge of the bed and stands a foot back from me. I tremble everywhere, my breath heavy and fast and my cheeks flushed. I raise my eyes to his, wondering what comes next.

First, he chased and kissed me, now he's got me on a bed, towering over me…

"Goodnight, Tatiana."

He turns, and without another word, leaving my shocked jaw hanging open, he walks out of the room. The door shuts with a firmness behind him, and the click of a lock drives it home.

Something is very, very wrong.

With all of this, yes. But specifically, with me. Because the second he leaves me locked behind the door, instead of… whatever savagery my rampant imagination came up with a second ago involving force, it's not necessarily relief that I feel.

It's not the opposite, either. I suppose there's some comfort in my own sanity that I'm not *disappointed* he didn't rip my clothes off and take what he wanted from me, heedless of my own opinions on the subject.

But it's somewhere in between.

A gray area.

A place where darkness bleeds into the light and muddies the clarity of right and wrong.

Good and bad.

Fear and excitement. Danger and desire.

Sane and insane.

Less than twelve hours ago, I was clear on which side of all of those scales I was on. But now?

Now, after that kiss, though, I'm not so sure I know a single thing about who I am.

6

The seconds bleed into minutes, and then into hours. At first, I pace the room, treading gently past the two smashed lamps on the floor. I try the door, but just like before, it's thick, and locked tight. The white tile and black iron fixture bathroom has a window, but it's locked the same as the wall of glass across the front of the bedroom facing the lake.

It might be a gorgeous jail cell, but I'm very much a prisoner here. And there's no getting out.

I slink back to the bed, sitting on the edge of it. I hug my knees up to my chest, chewing nervously on my lip as my pulse thuds in my ears.

Now what happens?

What happens next? With him, with me, with any of this. I mean it's not like the man whose name I don't even know kidnapped me out of my life to bring me to his glamorous and yet solitary lakeside house exclusively to chase me around the woods and kiss me.

Unless he did.

I swallow thickly, shivering as I hug my knees tighter. The same swirling gray of dark and light bleed through me. The same juxtaposition of heated desire versus terrifying horror. And all the while, visions of those piercing ice-blue eyes stabbing into me bring a clenching sensation to my core.

The way he chased. The way my blood felt like deliciously explosive fire in my veins as I fled—terrified of being caught and yet anticipating it with bated breath. The way his powerful fingers grabbed my neck and yanked me around like a toy. The way he slammed me to that tree, pinned me to it, and devoured my lips like they were his to enjoy.

Like *I* was his to conquer.

My eyes close as I tense.

Something is wrong with me. Broken. Askew. The "gorgeous man with the beautiful eyes" isn't a boy from class. It's not some guy smiling at me at a coffee shop before realizing that the two giant henchman behind me are glaring at him.

He's a killer. A kidnapper. A deranged psychopath for all I know. And here I am replaying the way he kissed me like it's some sort of sexy romantic thing, not what it really was.

A fucked up game. A lunatic chasing me through the woods after being ripped from my life. And then a kiss I never consented to—taken from me, stolen from my mouth, heedless of my wishes.

I shiver as my eyes harden.

This is wrong. I've been sucked into the lunacy of even being here and acting like this is all some kind of crazy Escape Room experience.

But this is real. I'm *really* a prisoner. He *really* shot the guards and who knows who else back at my father's house and flew me handcuffed and bound on a plane to God knows where. To do God only knows what to me.

I need to get the hell out of here.

I stand and go to the wall of windows. They're enormous panes of glass, but even when I slammed a chair against them before, it was the chair that broke first. There's not even a crack on the one I was trying to smash out.

My eyes trace along the bottom ledges of them. They're the kind of windows that can be swung out, but they're all firmly locked—with actual key locks along the side of the window frame opposite the big black iron hinges that they swing open on.

My brow furrows as I trace my fingers over the hinges. It's like there's a clue here I can vaguely see, but not quite grasp.

A chain is only as strong as its weakest point.

I frown, pausing my finger on one of the hinges. I peer closer, running my fingertip over the way the hinge fits into place, before suddenly, I go still.

The weakest part of this chain is the *hinge*.

The heavy windows are set in a way where the interlocking hinge is two parts: one part connected to the windowpane itself and the other to the window frame in the wall. The window*pane* part of the hinge looks like it's been slid in from the top to lock into the bottom part attached to the wall frame.

As in, that part of the hinge can be lifted back *out*.

I stare at it, wondering first how I just thought of that, and two, if this is really going to be as easy as it suddenly seems like it is.

Only one way to find out.

I drag the desk from the corner over to the closest window set into the wall and set it on its side. The chair I broke earlier is conveniently splinted into leverage pieces now, and I jam one broken leg under the bottom hinge, against the window-pane part of it.

Then, I push down, using the edge of the desk as the fulcrum point. The window is even heavier than it looks, but I grit my teeth. I groan, pushing with every last piece of strength I have, until slowly, I see it happening.

The window begins to lift out of the hinge.

Sweat beads my forehead, and my arms and core ache. But I don't stop. I can't stop. I keep shoving down with everything I have, inching the window millimeter by millimeter up out of the hinges it's set into. I watch all three parts of the heavy iron frame lift free, until suddenly, the entire, huge, heavy windowpane slips free.

The corner of it drops with a thunderous bang, denting the hardwood floor before the whole thing starts to tip. I have just enough strength to catch it and lay it gently across the floor.

My pulse soars. My heart hammers in my chest as I go still, tuning my ears—waiting to hear the sound of him storming to this room to see what the hell that sound was.

Seconds tick by. Then minutes.

He's not coming.

My breathing quickens as I turn to peer out into the darkness of outside. Crickets and nighttime birds fill the woods with background noise, along with the lapping of the moonlit lake against the rocky shore.

My heart thuds. I swallow thickly.

Time to do or do not.

I'm on the second floor, but there's a slight overhang of porch or something under the windows. I step out barefoot, shivering at the cool of night before I bring my other foot out too. Every nerve in my body is jangling as I creep along the edge to a corner of the lodge home.

An overhanging tree looks sturdy enough. Or maybe not. But I don't really have the luxury of a plan B right now. So I count to three.

Then I jump.

I gasp, jolting as my hands grab the overhanging branch in an iron grip. My pulse thuds as I shimmy myself to the trunk itself, grab ahold, and clamor down, scraping up my knees, my thighs, and the insides of my arms in the process. But a second later, my feet touch grass, and I freeze.

I'm free.

The lights are still on in the downstairs, but I don't see a glimpse of him at all. Part of me suddenly wonders if this is just another demented game of his—like he'd somehow know I'd break out through the windows, and now he's just waiting for me.

Lurking in the shadows of the trees, ready to pounce on me. Ready to drag me to the ground like prey and take much more than a stolen kiss this time.

I shiver.

My core throbs.

Fuck you, self.

I back away from the house, and then turn. Then, I bolt into the trees. My breath is gasping and ragged, my eyes wide as I try and pierce through the darkness to focus. The run earlier was terrifying because I was lost and could hear him right behind me.

Somehow, even without being chased this time, it's even more terrifying.

Every branch feels like a grim reaper's hand reaching out to snatch me. Every sound of a bird, owl, or whatever else lives on this lake sounds like footsteps rushing up behind me, or a gun being cocked.

I choke on my fear, whirling, freezing, and then picking a direction blindly. Then I keep running. Branches lash at me, cutting and scraping my skin and snarling in my hair. But then suddenly, I'm crashing out of the tree line.

Right by the water.

I just did it again. I ran another U-shape, *again*. I'm even standing in front of the fucking house again.

I groan, before I realize I'm actually not quiet where I thought I was. And the structure in front of me isn't the house at all, it's a boathouse, sitting out on the water on the very edge of the shore. I frown, turning to my right and seeing just a glimmer of light from the main house down that way.

My pulse still racing from the adrenaline of flight, and from my mad run through the woods. But I set my eyes on the boathouse.

Boathouses tend to have boats. Boats can get me across the lake to the far side, where maybe I can run to get help.

My heartbeat quickens as I get ready to dart from the trees across the open shoreline to the boathouse. When suddenly, there's movement. Alarm bells explode in my head as I duck down, sucking back the gasp as a dark shape suddenly materializes out of the shadows of the trees a little further down towards the main house.

I sink deep into the underbrush, obscured by a bush of some kind as my wide eyes focus on the figure moving slowly and lithely towards me, like a prowling animal sniffing for prey.

I go rigid, shivering as my hands clamp over my chest, as if to silence my thudding heart. Then the clouds part, and the silver glow of moonlight bathes the open strip of land between the tree line and the shore.

The figure isn't him.

It's a young woman.

She's in all black, and it's all combat attire, almost like she's dressed to play a US Navy SEAL from the movies. She's almost invisible, except she's got what might be a black mask or balaclava or something rolled up, exposing the glint of her eyes, her lips, and her black hair.

She moves closer to where I'm lying, her eyes narrowed as they sweep the tree line. My eyes drop to the assault rifle on a strap across her chest, military style.

All I can hear is the thunderous sound of my pulse in my ears. All I can do is stay absolutely still as my body tries to melt into the ground.

Then she stops maybe twenty feet away. Her brow furrows deeply before she pulls something out of one of her pockets, touches something on it, and brings it to the side of her face.

A phone.

"It's me," she murmurs quietly.

"I just did a sweep outside the house. He's here, but it does seem like he's alone."

I blink quickly, my teeth sinking painfully into my lip.

The woman nods.

"Yes. I'll get it done. If she's here and he hasn't buried her, I will."

Holy fucking shit.

I taste blood as my teeth dig into my soft lip. The thudding of my pulse turns into the roaring sound of klaxon alarms, like an air raid siren in my ears.

If she's here and he hasn't buried her, I will.

Every neuron in my brain screams at me to get up and fucking *run*. Run away, hit the water, and swim as long as I have to in order to get away from whatever the hell any of this is. But if I run, she'll hear me. Or he will, if he's noticed I'm gone and is out prowling the woods looking for me.

All I can do is clamp a hand over my mouth and dig the other one into the dirt beneath me. And wait.

The woman stuffs the phone back into a pocket and then hefts the assault rifle in her hands. Her eyes sweep the trees again, right over where I'm lying, but they don't stop. Her gaze narrows, her lips curling before she whirls and jogs lightly to the shore.

The last of my control breaks. I get up, turn, and I fucking *run*.

If my escape was hectic before, it's manic now. I run without a single idea where I'm going, heedless of the branches reaching out to scratch, trip, or jab me. I'm choking on my breath, desperately trying not to scream as I slam through the underbrush.

There are lights up ahead, and I gasp, veering away from the main house and bolting down a new vector. My bare feet ache with a million cuts and slices, but I keep going, swallowing the pain until I see moonlight on the shore again.

I'm about to tumble out of the trees, when my brain screams at me to stop and drop.

I'm right back at the goddamn boathouse. Right where the woman with the gun just was.

I crouch fast, sucking in air as silently as I can. Panic and fear bang in my head as my eyes narrow at the shoreline, trying to find her.

And then I see it: a small, black rubber dingy moving quietly across the lake to the opposite shore, with the woman in black sitting in it.

My breath lets out in a whoosh. I swallow through the lump in my throat, feeling my heart punching against my chest as I finally let myself breathe for one second.

The threat is gone.

My eyes swivel to the boathouse, my skin tingling as I slowly get up. I can poke around in here for a boat—maybe the same one he brought me here in.

I stand up and slowly start to creep across the open ground.

I'll wait another ten or twenty minutes to make sure whoever she was is back to her side of the lake. *Then* I can get the fuck—

A twig snaps behind me. I gasp, jumping out of my skin as I whirl with my heart in my throat.

A squirrel darts out of the trees, chewing on a nut.

I groan, letting out a shaky breath as my body twitches with all the fight or flight endorphins slamming through it.

It's just a fucking squirrel.

I take a slow, deep breath, letting my heart stop racing. Letting my nerve ending stop jangling. Until finally, I'm okay. Then, it's time to get the hell out of here. I whirl—

And then I immediately scream as I slam right into the strong, rock-hard, snarling chest of the very man I've been running from.

One powerful hand grabs my hair at the nape, and the other slams across my mouth before I can scream. He looms down into my face, those icy-blue eyes flaying me open as his lips curl into a dark, very unamused smile.

"Going somewhere, *printsessa?*"

7

I scream into his hand, thrashing and squirming to get away. But there's no getting away from him.

Clearly.

Through my entire fight, he merely stands there, his piercing eyes practically glowing in the moonlight, his muscles tight as he keeps me pinned between the hand over my mouth and one gripping a fistful of my hair.

And then suddenly, he gives a tug on my hair. Not enough to cause pain to my scalp. But enough to yank my attention away from the attempt at flight. Until my full focus is on him. I go still, my heart thudding as the shock of him appearing like that begins to wane.

He's changed. Now he's in black jeans and a white t-shirt pulled tight across his thick chest. And he's barefoot. He keeps his hand over my mouth for another second, his eyes narrowing slightly.

"I'm going to remove my hand. I would very much suggest not screaming."

I swallow, nodding quickly. His jaw grinds for a second before his hand slips from my mouth.

The other one stays very much tangled in my hair.

"I see you've decided to play the game again without telling me—"

"*Someone was here!*"

I blurt it like one large tumbled word. My captor frowns, tensing. The glint in his eyes when he mentioned "playing the game" fades into something far more serious.

"What did you say?"

"Someone was here. A woman."

His eyes narrow.

"Alone?"

I nod. "I think so. She was dressed in military garb, with a gun. And she was on the phone with someone, right here."

I twist slightly, ignoring the way the pull of his fist on my hair sends a bolt of... something, tingling through my core. I point to where the woman was standing, right by where I was hiding.

"Right there. She said over the phone that it looked like you were alone but..."

I trail off, going cold.

"Tell me."

"Then she left, in a rubber dingy, right there." I point to where the woman must have had the little boat waiting. "I saw her go off towards the other shore—"

"Tell me what she said."

I shiver, wanting so badly to look away, but unable to drag my eyes from his.

If she's here and he hasn't buried her, I will.

His gaze hardens, but then grows softer.

"Tell me what she said, Tatiana."

"I don't even know your name."

His brow seems to cock with amusement when I blurt it out.

"What exactly does that have to do with telling me what this woman said?"

"Nothing," I snap. "I would just be nice to know the name of the fucker who abducted me, flew me on a plane to who the hell know where, made me run through the woods like a psychotic game, and then kissed me without my permission—"

It happens again. No warning, no apologies, nothing held back. His lips crush to mine, stealing my breath and demanding entrance. His tongue dives deep, capturing mine and kissing the absolute fuck out of me until my legs shake and my toes curl.

Then he pulls away.

Nothing is said. I can barely even breathe, just standing there stunned and throbbing with heat—my lips swollen and tingling.

"I would get used to that."

I blink, trying to even remember words and how to make them with my mouth.

"I... get used to what?"

"Being kissed. With or without your permission. Now what did she say?"

He segues right from telling me that he's apparently going to be kissing me whenever he pleases right back to the woman with the gun.

I swallow, yanking my subconscious out of the stupor he's just kissed it into. My eyes narrow at his.

"Were you trying to kill me? At my father's house?" I blurt in a choked whisper. "Is that why you took me?"

He frowns.

"It doesn't matter."

I stare at him.

"Uh, *yes*, it does. If someone wants me dead—hey!"

I shriek as he grabs me, lifting me up and tossing me unceremoniously over his shoulder. He storms off down the shore, moving back towards the main house.

I hit and squirm, but honestly, the fire isn't there anymore.

He fucking snuffed it out when he slammed his lips to mine.

Inside, he carries me through the gorgeous house until we get to a library or study of some kind. I gasp when he shrugs me off his shoulder and plops me down on a couch before turning to grab something off of a desk.

"What the *fuck*!" I yell, springing to my feet. "Tell me yes or fucking no, were you at my house to kill—"

He turns back to me, and I choke on a scream as my face goes white.

He's holding a gleaming hunting knife.

He comes at me, and I scream and lurch back, only to trip over my feet and go sprawling back onto the couch.

"No! Please!"

I shriek as he looms over me and grabs a thin strand of my hair. The knife comes up, and the blade neatly slices off a six inch lock of red. Then he pulls back.

I stare at him, blinking rapidly.

"What the *fuck*!"

My hand shoots up to feel the side of my head and the sliced ends where he lopped off a tangle.

He goes back to the desk, dropping the lock of hair and the knife onto it and picking something else up. Then he turns and strides back to me.

This time, he's got a syringe.

"No—!"

"Give me your arm."

My eyes go wide as I whip my head side to side, paling.

"No… please…"

He grabs my wrist, tugging my arm out straight as he brings the needle to the veins near the surface of my inner forearm.

"Please don't—!"

"Stay. *Still*," he growls.

I wince, a sob wrenching from my lips as the needle bites my skin.

"I'm not drugging you. I'm just drawing blood."

I blink, confusion swirling over me as I watch him fill the syringe with my red blood. He pulls it out gently, quickly covering the mark with a cotton ball.

"Keep pressure on that."

I stare at him as he goes back to the desk and empties the syringe into a test tube. Then he takes it and the lock of hair and puts them into a clear baggy before sealing it tight and dropping it on the desk. He turns, folding his arms over his chest as he leans against it, letting those blue eyes pierce into me.

"What sort of *sick*, twisted—"

"You're dead."

I stutter, frowning.

"Excuse me?"

"You said someone wants you dead?" He shrugs. "Now, you *are* dead."

I blink and he sighs deeply.

"I'm going to give you a choice, because I think you deserve that."

His gaze levels at me.

"You can be alive, with a target on your back. Your family name and connection have power, and people will be looking for that, viciously. *Or* you can be dead."

I swallow.

"You mean fake my death."

He nods.

"In a sense, yes. But you can never go back to your life."

I start to open my mouth.

"Ever."

The room goes silent and still.

"What does that mean?" I finally whisper quietly.

"It means no more Harvard. It means you never see your roommate Lyra again."

How the fuck does he know all this?

"No more Instagram, TikTok, Facebook, anything. It means as of right now, Tatiana Fairist is dead and gone. Forever."

I swallow the lump that swells in my throat.

"And what does that mean?"

"It means you stay here."

I shiver.

"Forever?"

"I haven't decided that yet."

My core tightens.

"Come with me."

"*Why*," I spit.

He smiles thinly as he turns back to me.

"Because it seems slightly less dignified to carry you over my shoulder, but I'm happy to do that instead if you prefer."

My face blooms with heat as he turns and strides from the room.

I follow.

When we walk past the living room, I glance to the side, letting my eyes land on the front door.

"I'd wait until I had shoes and maybe something to eat before I'd try it again."

His words startle me, yanking my gaze to where he's simply climbing the stairs again, not even looking at where I'm looking.

"But be my guest."

I grit my teeth, suddenly feeling the pang of hunger in my stomach. I glance down, and I wince when I see the bruises, bloodied, and banged-up state of my bare, filthy feet.

Then, I gingerly follow him up the stairs.

At first, I think we're going back to the same room I was in before. But he moves past that, around the corner of the hallway, to another door. He opens it, pausing at the doorway as if to usher me inside. I pause, but then suddenly, the smell of food hits me. My eyes dart into the room, and my mouth waters.

Inside what appears to be another bedroom, there's a small table with a chair set up. And on it sits a plate with a cheeseburger, a heaping pile of French fries, and a sliced-up avocado.

Oh my fucking God yes.

My weakness. It's my absolute favorite, go-to meal if I'm beyond starving, or if I'm beyond stressed.

I freeze.

He knew my name. Where I go to school, and my roommate's name. Why do I get the nagging feeling that my favorite meal sitting here isn't sheer coincidence.

"I'm aware it's your favorite. I was bringing it to your room earlier while you were destroying my windows."

My face burns hotly.

"Sit. Eat."

It's not an invitation. More like a command. But me and my painfully empty stomach are in no place to throw it back in his face right now. I try not to run as I swallow my pride and shame, power walk over to the table, and sit eagerly in front of the food.

"There are toiletries in the attached bathroom. You'll find ready-made meals in the refrigerator—"

My head whips around, blinking in shock to see the mini fridge he's pointing to near the far wall, with a microwave sitting on top of it.

"And the water from the bathroom sink is perfectly drinkable."

I nod slowly, pulling my gaze back to him.

"Is this my new room?"

He nods. I chew on my lip, my eyes darting to the windows along the wall and instantly realizing with a groan that they're slightly different than the room before.

"While I applaud your ingenuity earlier, I can promise you, you'll have a much harder time with these."

I blush, sucking at my teeth before I turn back to him.

"Am I a prisoner?"

He says nothing.

"The new room," I murmur. "Bathroom, food and water, windows that won't open. A door I'm sure locks from the outside…" I swallow. "So? Does this mean I'm going to be a prisoner in here?"

He shrugs. "Would you run if the door didn't lock? If the windows opened?"

I purse my lips, narrowing my eyes at his smirk.

"Then it would appear you are."

He turns and goes for the door. And as I predicted, he fits a key into a deadbolt lock on the outside of the door.

"Enjoy your food. I'll be back by noon tomorrow."

My jaw drops.

"Hang on, *what*—?!"

"And it's Kristoff."

His lethal blue eyes stab into me, turning me to jelly as my breath sucks in.

"My name. It's Kristoff."

The door shuts. The lock clicks.

8

"So, you want me to watch the *lake*?"

"Yes."

I nod into the phone as I climb into the Range Rover. Nearby, the water laps at the side of the dock on this side of things, gently rocking the boat I've just taken over.

"Like, the whole lake."

"If you're not up to the task, I can call—"

"Fuck you," Marko chuckles darkly. "First, I *know* you know insulting me is a bad idea. And two, like hell you know anyone else up to the task. What the fuck am I looking for, specifically?"

I smile thinly.

"Uninvited guests."

"Headed to your spot, you mean."

I nod as the SUV roars through the Finnish night to the private airfield.

"Yes."

"I assume this is as specific as you're going to get on that front?"

"Bingo."

My old friend sighs.

"Fine, I'm on it. Let me take another stab in the dark and assume you need me there like yesterday, yeah?"

"Expedience would be appreciated."

I hear him grunt, as if standing from an especially comfy couch.

"You know you owe me, right?"

"Put it on my tab."

Marko chuckles. We're always like this, even if we don't talk a whole lot. We're the sort of old friends who can lose track for a year or two and then pick up exactly where we were before.

Soldiers who've been in combat together are like that.

Though, Marko and I were never in uniform. And the combat we saw wasn't war, it was merely dealing death and ruin.

Like me, Marko came up through the Ghost Project under Mikhail's direction. Only unlike me, he had the self-awareness to get the fuck out of there as soon as possible. He ended up triple dosing on acid to purposefully tank his psyche evaluation, prompting an immediate dismissal from the syndicate on mental instability grounds.

Funny thing is, it wouldn't be much of a stretch for him to have failed that psyche eval *without* taking psychedelics. Marko's mad as a fucking hatter. But he's also one of the most solid guys I can imagine having on my six. And he might be the single best sniper in the world. And I don't say that lightly.

Tonight, his mission, though he doesn't know the specifics, is keeping watch over Tatiana. I don't exactly relish the idea of leaving her alone—not ever, but certainly not after she saw who I'm sure is one of Mikhail's people prowling around the shore earlier. But I need to have a sit down with Jana and bury this thing. Which means leaving Tatiana alone, locked in her room until I get back.

"Alright, I'm packing up now, I can be there in about five hours. I'll just set up on the roof."

My face darkens.

"No," I growl. Too forcefully.

Marko snickers.

"Kris, I'm not gonna fuck up the shingles or steal your cable, man."

I shake my head.

"There's an overlook cliff up on the western shore. It's got open views of the whole lake."

I've also turned on infrared sensors and motions detectors all the fuck over my property. But I want a guy like Marko as eyes in the sky, watching for anyone else trying to take a skiff over to the house for another prowl.

This time, they won't touch land before he puts a bullet in them.

"I think I remember that spot, yeah." He sighs. "Alright man, I'm on the way. If I *do* spot anyone headed over... weapons free?"

"Yes."

He's silent a second.

"Is that a problem?"

"You know it's not," he grunts. "I'm just curious what sort of shit you're into. I mean, don't get me wrong, I always appreciate a catch up call, brother. And I'm happy to do this, I mean that. But... what, Boris Tsavakov doesn't have some guys he can spare out of the almost literal army he's got working for him?"

"Oh, but Marko," I sigh. "None of them are as ornery as you."

He chuckles.

"Yeah, fuck you too, pal. Really, though. You good?"

"I'm fine, Marko. Just being safe."

And no, I can't call Boris, my vile piece of shit of a boss, about this. For one, he wouldn't give a shit. For two, he very obviously doesn't know I have any connection at all to Mikhail and the Ghost Syndicate, let alone that I've just pulled two jobs for them.

But I *will* do everything in my power to keep Tatiana safe while I'm gone.

Safe and safely locked away.

I growl deep in my chest, my pulse thudding as my fingers remember the feel of her skin. The spike of her pulse. The panting desperation in her breaths, and the eager, intoxicating pleading for more in her eyes.

The taste of her lips. The whimper of her moans against my mouth.

The shattering of my walls when I feel her squirm against me. When I watch her run from me through the darkness.

I'm not good. I'm not okay. I'm sprinting recklessly over thin ice.

Allowing myself to think these sort of thoughts about her is one thing, and that's bad enough. But defying Mikhail is another thing altogether. I may detest the man, but I wouldn't ever make the mistake of letting my disdain for him cloud my appreciation for his lethality.

Mikhail Arakas is an unemotional, brutally cold sociopath. Crossing him isn't something even I take lightly.

And yet, she's there, clouding my judgment. Making me break my own rules and forget who and what I am. And if she saw that—I mean if she really saw what I *really* am? She'd scream a hell of a lot louder and run a *hell* of a lot faster from me.

"I'm about to get on a plane. But I'll have my people wire you the cash—"

"Eh, like I said, brother," Marko chuckles. "I'll put it on your tab. Catch up soon, yeah?"

"Definitely. And thanks, Marko."

"Anytime, Kris."

An hour after I touch down in Berlin, I'm standing still as a statue in front of a set of double doors. The two guards to either side of it, though Syndicate trained, aren't nearly as still or stoic as I am. I bite back my amusement and keep my face cold and neutral, even when I catch them glancing nervously at me, and then each other.

Reputations can be a useful tool. And these two know *exactly* who I am.

I stand there another minute, allowing Jana one more minute of her petulant power game of making me wait out here. As if she's… what, busy? Taking meetings? It's two in the fucking morning, and *I* set this meet up at her Berlin offices.

After the minute is up, though, I sigh as I move to the doors. Playtime is over.

The two guards make a nervous, half-assed attempt to stop me. But when I level a withering gaze at them both, they back down. One fumbles for his earpiece.

"Uh, Miss Kapinos? The *buka*—"

His face goes white as his eyes snap horrified to mine.

"He's here."

I don't wait for her reply. I just move forward and shove the double doors open before striding through into the office beyond. Jana looks up from a laptop on her desk, smiling thinly at me as she stands.

"Ahh, Kristoff," she gushes in a painfully fake way, blowing me air kisses. As if she's some sort of socialite at a fundraiser.

I shut the doors behind me with a heavy click and then cross the room to where she's standing behind her desk in a dark blue three-quarter-sleeve business dress. Dior, I'm guessing.

The dress is as purposeful as making me wait outside. Power games. The dance. To someone like Jana, every single aspect of life is a game of seduction and attack. Because she was trained that way her entire life.

Besides being his second in command and his niece, Jana was also Mikhail's most prized pupil in the Ghost Syndicate's secondary program: the Swan Project.

Where young boys like me were trained to shed our humanity and immerse ourselves in brutality, the young girls recruited to the Swan Project take a slightly different route. Yes, they're trained to kill. They're trained to be ruthless, and cunning.

But there are many different kinds of weapons when it comes to war.

Some, like Marko and I, are blades that cut from the shadows. Monsters you never see coming. Others, like Jana, are a blade that sinks into your heart—not from the monster you never saw coming, but the one masquerading as a beautiful woman you just invited into your bed.

Mikhail's "swans" are taught cold brutality. But they're also taught lethal seduction. Weaponized sexuality. It's how Jana was able to worm her way into Peter Fairist's bed, probably still warm from his late wife, in order to pull the strings for Mikhail.

Nikita was in the swan program when she died.

"Well?"

Jana lasers her gaze onto me, using what I'm sure is a purposefully selected haughty tone designed to both goad me and maybe even seduce me just a little. Her dress—a mix of fashionable business and a bit of flirtatiousness with the top button undone—her hair, the perfume she's wearing, the way her undeniable beauty seems to radiate across the room...

It's all by design. It's her training. It's all meant to pull at invisible strings, to get me under her spell.

None of it is going to work. Not on me.

I reach into my jacket pocket, and then drop the sealed baggie in front of her.

"It's done."

Jana frowns and then arches a single brow. Her gaze drops to the lock of Tatiana's red hair and the little vial of blood.

"*Kristoff—*"

"It's *done*, Jana. I'll take what I was promised now. Then, we never have to speak again."

She sighs, folding her arms across her chest.

"You call this proof?"

"It's her hair, and the blood will show lethal amounts of ricin."

A toxin I've added after the fact.

"It was necessary to move locations from the house. I injected her in the car."

Jana's eyes narrow just slightly.

"I fail to see how her disappearance will help the narrative that *killing her in her own house* was going to tell."

"I have more blood saved. From before the injection. It will be found by authorities and verified."

She sucks on her teeth, eying the hair and blood on the table.

"I just don't see how this proves—"

"What do you want, her fucking heart?"

Her eyes snap up to mine.

"And if I do?"

"Then I suggest you buy a shovel."

Anger flickers over her face.

"And where should I dig, Kristoff. Specially."

My jaw clenches. She's pushing back hard on this. Not unexpectedly, but still.

"She'll be found. The blood will tip off authorities. They'll do a search, and the body will be recovered."

It obviously won't be. But so long as I have my end of this deal in hand, I could give a fuck about Mikhail and Jana's stupid political games.

"I'll take that information now."

She raises her eyes to mine, her blood-red lips curling slightly.

"Mikhail won't be happy."

"I consider that a bonus. The information. Now."

Her lips purse.

"If this doesn't check out, I know I don't need to remind you—"

"And *I know* I don't do threats, Jana," I hiss coldly, stepping close to the desk and leaning menacingly across it.

She wants to play seduction games? I'll play monster right back.

Jana flinches slightly when I leer close, swallowing thickly.

"Do not. Fucking. Threaten. Me, Jana."

She swallows, regaining her composure as she glares at me.

"I'll need to bring this to Mik first."

"You do that. But our deal is concluded. Do not contact me again, unless it's to give me the information we agreed on."

I turn and march to the door, where I pause and glance back at her.

"Don't make me come looking for that information, either. Neither you nor Mikhail want that."

Another hour later, I'm back on the jet, heading back to the pretty little captive I left in my house.

The forbidden fruit who's clouding my judgment and breaking my rules.

The prey I cannot wait to chase again.

9

AGAIN, it's a pretty cage… but it's still a cage.

Hours after he leaves, I finally admit defeat. There's no getting out of this room. The windows are a slightly different make, with the hinges actually hidden within the frame itself. They're definitely not breakable, either.

I really am trapped in here.

At first, I rage. I scream at the silence, pacing the room furious at my situation. But eventually, total exhaustion begins to win. I've been kidnapped, chased, and kissed. My adrenaline reserves are officially depleted. My mind is numb, and my eyes hurt from lack of sleep.

I don't *want* to… because the idea of actually getting into the bed in this room sends a jolt of fear through my core. And the thought of letting my guard down when he could be back any time is equally terrifying.

But I'm objectively *exhausted*. I need to sleep.

Then next time, be aware of your needs and surroundings before you make an escape.

His own words from before are what eventually convince me to rest. I've already eaten the cheeseburger plate he left out—deciding that if he wanted to kill me, it seems his preferred method would involve hunting me through the woods, not secretly poisoning me.

But I'm also still hungry.

I end up exploring the mini-fridge and finding a selection of ready-to-heat meals: pasta with red sauce, what might be ratatouille, and chili. I heat a container in the microwave, confirming that it *is* in fact ratatouille as I devour it.

While I eat, I let my mind wander to the world outside. The world that may very well think I'm dead at this point, since I'm sure by now the carnage he—Kristoff—left at my father's house has been discovered.

I'm not dead. But someone wanted me to be. And I think that someone sent the very man who has me captive to do it.

I try not to think too hard about the people who'll be heartbroken to know I'm dead. It's a short list of mostly not very close friends. But, Lyra, for one. Senna, my father's housekeeper—at least, provided she isn't dead, too.

I close my eyes, shivering.

Jana, my stepmother, will at least make a show of grieving for me, but she and I have never…

I tense, going still in the chair at the little table.

Jana.

Jana, the mysterious and stunningly beautiful woman who stole my father's cold heart not long after my mother died. The one who was all for sending me away to boarding school —convincing my father that the school was known for its medical staff. Specially, a psychiatrist who could help me with the glitches and memory stuff I still have from the boating accident I was in when I was sixteen.

Jana who wasn't at the house the other day for the violence.

Jana who would become the head of the Balagula Bratva in the event of my death.

I freeze, the bite of food lodging in my throat as I stiffen.

No.

I swallow, shaking my head. Jana might be the epitome of young second trophy wife. She might've always been cold to me, but that was all to do with me being a reminder of her husband's first love.

She's a bitch, but she's not a wicked, evil step-mother type.

I shake my head as I finish my food. After, I absently poke around the room. There's a collection of basic toiletries in the bathroom. Gratefully, I brush my teeth with them.

When I open one of the drawers of a dresser in the main bedroom, I'm surprised to find a clean t-shirt and a pair of grey sweatpants. They're Kristoff's, obviously. And I'm going to be absolutely swimming in them. But I've been wearing the same pajama shorts and t-shirt for more than twenty-four hours, including two chases through the woods.

I need to shower and change.

Back in the bathroom, I crank on the water and strip down before I suddenly have the unnerving question of surveillance.

As in, is he watching me?

I shiver, a flush creeping over my skin as I reach for a towel. But then I pause. If he's going to spy on me, he's going to spy on me. I *still* need a shower and fresh clothes, though.

The happy medium I decide on is to shower in the dark. Yes, night vision exists. But, whatever. This is the best compromise I can come up with.

After my shower, I change into his baggy clothes and slide onto the bed. Actually getting under the covers seems like more of a leap of faith than I'm prepared to make. It seems *too* vulnerable.

Even if the taste of his lips is still tingling on mine. Even though my core quivers at the mere thought of it.

My head hits the pillow, and before I'm even aware of it, I'm asleep.

It's grey dawn outside when I wake up. I frown, blinking away sleep before I realize it's the sound of the front door downstairs that's woken me.

He's back.

I swallow, trembling slightly as I curl into a ball on top of the covers. I could pretend he's just going to go about his day. But when the footsteps draw closer and closer down the hall towards my room, I know that's not true.

The door unlocks and swings open. And there he is—towering in the doorframe in black jeans and a grey henley shirt with the sleeves pushed up.

He looks like a rock god and a Navy SEAL had a baby and raised it to be a male model.

I blush fiercely, mentally chastising myself as I chase that thought away.

His eyes land on me, setting me aflame in ice blue fire.

"Did you sleep?"

It *could* be a kindly, hospitable question. But not the way he says it. He words it like a demand. A warning.

"I…" I swallow. "A little, yeah."

"Good."

He marches over to the bed, making my pulse spike as I sit bolt upright. His muscled arm extends, and I shiver when he grabs my hand in his, tugging me from the bed.

"Wait, where…"

He shoves a pair of women's running shoes—new, and seemingly my size—into my free hand before pulling me with the other.

Wide awake, I tumble after him as he pulls me from the room, down the hall, and then down the stairs. We step out of a side door of the massive, sprawling lodge into the misty stillness of the lake-side morning.

It's there that I finally wrest my arm back from his grip, glaring at him when he turns to peer at me.

"What the fuck are you doing?" I snap. "Why did you bring me out here?"

His eyes shimmer with a darkness that both scares and horribly excites me. The air goes still as he draws in a slow, measured breath, his jaw grinding as he renders me frozen with that cold, beautiful stare.

"I want you to run."

Fuck.

Something hot pulses deep in my core, making me shiver as the tingling heat radiates out. I swallow back the blush, chewing on my bottom lip as I try not to make a sound or quiver under his gaze.

"Excuse me?" I whisper.

"*Run.*"

I tremble, the air growing thicker as I shake my head.

"No."

Kristoff's eyes narrow.

"*No,*" I choke again. "Both of my parents are dead. Someone wants *me* dead. And I'm a captive being held on some abandoned lake against my will by a *psychopath*."

He doesn't seem phased by my calling him a psychopath.

"So?" He growls, shrugging.

"*So?*"

He shrugs again. "So run away—from all of it."

My lips purse.

"Because you'll catch me."

"Then you've already admitted defeat." His lips curl. "How pathetic."

Fury roars inside of me, igniting a fire in my veins.

"*Fuck you*," I snarl.

He smiles. He fucking *smiles*, like a beautiful psycho.

"There it is."

My lips curl into a sneer.

"There's *what*, asshole?"

"Your fuel. Use it."

I tremble at the way his deep, rumbling and ever so slightly gravelly voice teases over my skin and into my ears.

"You're a monster, you fucking—"

I gasp, choking on my words and fumbling back as he looms close to me.

"You have no fucking *idea*," he mutters darkly, still smiling thinly.

He leans even closer, arresting my ability to breathe, or run, or scream. His hand comes up, and his thumb and forefinger touch and lift my chin, making me shiver

"But I'm guessing enough of one to know deep down that when I tell you that you should run…" his eyes simmer. "You should *run*."

My jangling pulse hums in my ear. My skin throbs with a slickness, tingling with heat.

"And?" I whisper hoarsely.

"And the same thing I said yesterday. If you make it past the property line, you're free."

I swallow.

"This is a fucked up game."

He shrugs, spreading his arms.

"It's this or you sit angry and simmering in your room like a jail cell."

"Until?"

He doesn't answer.

I draw in a slow breath.

"And if you catch me?" I croak.

His eyes spark, but he says nothing.

"Three."

My pulse spikes, my heart instantly racing and lurching into my throat. A sick, perverse sort of thrill creeps over me, sliding over my skin as quickly I start to yank the running shoes over my bare feet.

"Two."

I whirl from him, and I start to run.

I crash into the tree line, hurling through the branches that reach out to snag and hold me back. I zig one way, aiming between two trees and darting between them before switching to another vector without warning.

Panic starts to explode through me. But with each step, and with each panted, frantic breath, that panic begins to morph and change.

It begins to bleed into something different. Something... exciting.

I can hear the crash of him pounding after me through the trees—the crunch of his footsteps, the measured rhythm of his breathing. But he's not as close as he was the last time we did this.

I'm getting better.

I might have a chance.

I dart right, digging the heels of my new shoes into the dirt before I take off harder than before. My blood roars like diesel in my ears, churning and burning and flinging me forward. I crash through underbrush and the gray morning mist that weaves through the black trees. I swear I can hear his footsteps trailing farther behind me and knowing I'm winning gives me a second boost of energy.

Grinning wildly, my blood on fire and my skin throbbing with raw, fucked up excitement, I go careening through a patch of tress. I aim for what looks like an opening or a clearing in the trees ahead, surging forward, seconds away from—

I shriek when he explodes out of the forest right next to me —a predator who's chased me to *exactly* where he wanted me to go. The scream shatters from my throat before his hand clamps roughly around it. Hot, wicked excitement ignites in my core as he whirls, yanking me around with a snarl on his lips to pin me roughly against a tree at my back.

I gasp for air, eyes bulging, skin throbbing.

Nipples aching and hard against my shirt. My thighs slick and quivering with horrible, mutinous desire.

I flail at him, but he quickly grabs my wrists and shoves them above my head. One hand keeps them there, the other stays wrapped around my soft, heaving throat as he looms right over me. Those eyes pierce into me, cutting me open, slicing my clothes and barriers away until he can see not just my nakedness, but the dark, filthy secrets in my soul.

He can *see* that this is a thrill to me.

Time stops. Our pulses thud together—his fingers against my throat as the moment is held.

"You call that running away?"

My lips curl, eyes narrowing at the mocking intonation in his voice.

"*Fuck—*"

"I barely broke a sweat. Almost as if you wanted to be caught—"

I have no idea how it happens. But one second, I'm pinned to the tree with his hand tightly holding my wrists and throat. And the next, I'm whirling and twisting free of his grip. I spin, shove his chest back, and then suddenly, my hand slaps *hard* across his face.

Everything goes still. Everything goes cold as my heart drops along with my jaw. My face pales as my eyes widen.

Oh God what did I just—

He surges into me like a force of nature. His hand grips my neck, pushing me back hard until I'm flat to the tree. His eyes flash icy blue fire as he looms over me.

And then suddenly, and yet inevitably, his mouth slams to mine.

Without warning. Without mercy.

And without a doubt, the hottest, most electrifying moment of my life.

10

Lightning explodes through every part of my psyche—electrifying and scorching me. His lips sear to mine, his tongue demanding entrance as it did before.

And just like before, I let him take everything.

I simmer as his tongue dances with mine. His huge, rock-hard body pins me roughly to the tree, and when I feel his thigh open mine, I whimper eagerly into the kiss.

My legs spread.

The fire consumes me as I cling to him, riding a wave of molten desire as he kisses me hard enough to bruise. His thigh grinds against my center, rubbing against my pussy through the baggy, soft sweatpants.

My pulse jumps into outer-space orbit. My entire body ripples with heat. My legs quiver as I moan hungrily and shamelessly into his lips.

Kristoff growls into me as he presses harder, firmer. His hands slide to my waist, lifting the shirt enough to let a bare finger trace across bare hip. My eyes roll back, my breathing gets erratic as one large finger traces the waist of the sweatpants to the front, right below my navel.

The finger slips under the elastic.

I choke into his kiss, gasping for air while feeling like I'm floating. Or maybe drowning. He twists his hand, pushing it deep under the sweats and letting his fingers graze down the over the soft skin of my stomach… down, down, down…

He grunts hungrily into my lips when his fingers push over my pubic mound. My body tightens and squirms, and then suddenly, it's like I'm melting entirely.

His finger has just rolled over my clit.

My whole world goes slack as silken pleasure claims me. I moan into his lips, clinging to his forearm—my muscles seemingly confused if they're meant to push his hand away, or pull it closer.

The second wins, even if I don't think there's a chance in Hell I could push him away from me right now if I wanted to.

And I don't.

His thick middle finger sinks between my lips, opening me as I cry out. My clit rubs against his finger as the tip curls into my entrance.

And I'm *drenched.*

He grunts, dragging his lips from mine and delving his face into my neck. I whimper, shuddering as his teeth rake across the softness of my earlobe.

"Such a messy little pussy for me, my little toy."

Holy. *Fuck.*

Blame the lack of dating life. Blame never having been even kissed. But it's unquestionably the most filthy, erotic, hottest thing I've ever heard. And immediately after he says it, his thick finger sinks to the knuckle deep in my pussy.

I cry out, clinging to him and feeling my legs go slack. It's rough, but I want more, and more. His palm grinds against my clit as he strokes his finger in and out of me, curling it deep against the spot that makes my knees stop working.

I cling to him desperately as his teeth drag over my neck, my legs so wobbly that I'm half sure the only thing keeping me standing upright is his hand cupping my sex, fingering me into oblivion.

"Coat my hand with your greedy little pussy, *printsessa*," he rasps, grinding against my clit.

He moves harder and faster, mercilessly and recklessly dragging the pleasure from my core. I start to cry out again, when his mouth slams roughly to mine. I scream into his lips as his finger pounds into me, his palm rubbing my clit over and over until the world blurs to white.

His other hand snakes up under my shirt, making me surge with pleasure as he cups one of my breasts. His fingers find my nipple and he pinches hard just as he sinks his finger to the hilt.

My mind goes blank. My body clenches to the point of wrenching out of alignment. He pinches again before his hand shoves up through the neck hole of my shirt to grip my throat tight.

His hand squeezes. His finger sinks deep. His palm grinds against my clit, and my mouth falls open.

And suddenly, I'm coming. *Hard*.

He swallows my scream, keeping me pinned roughly to the tree by the neck as he finger-fucks my pussy into a second, and then third climax. My entire body shakes and shivers, quivering against him as he demands the orgasms from me.

When it's over—when I feel his fingers uncurl from my neck and his hand slide from between my thighs, I can barely think. Or move. Or talk. Or stand. I start to fall, before he's suddenly lifting me up and cradling me in his arms.

He turns, and he starts to walk through the woods.

I curl into him, still trying to catch my breath as my entire body quivers and throbs. The swing from the filthy roughness—the dirty talking, the choking, the hard finger-fucking that had me exploding—to the softness of cradling me as he carries me has my head swimming.

But I'm here for it.

Inside, he carries me up to my room and drapes me across the bed. For a second, when he pauses to look down on me with those hard, ice-blue eyes, I think maybe this is about to go further.

He's already stolen me, my first kiss, and my first time doing what we've just done.

Maybe he's about to take the rest...

I stiffen, caught between the ache for more of what I just felt at his hands, and the nauseating fear of him just *taking* me.

"I lied, before," he mutters quietly.

My brow furrows.

"You ran well. You were close."

"You caught me," I whisper.

"Of course I did."

I pulse, shivering as the heat creeps over me.

"Next time, Tatiana," he growls, leaning over me until a fist goes to the pillow beside my face, keeping his a scant few inches above mine.

"Next time, I won't be able to control myself as much."

I bite back the aching groan.

As if *that* was him controlling himself?

"Next time, *printsessa*," he rumbles.

I whimper as he drops his mouth to tease right next to my ear.

"I'll have all of you."

He straightens, letting his eyes sweep over me once again before he turns and strides from the room. The door closes, and locks, behind him.

I lay there shivering in my bed, panting as I stare wide-eyed at the ceiling and try and process what just happened.

My legs squeeze together. My chest rises and falls as my nipples strain against the t-shirt.

My hand drops to my stomach, and before I can even begin to question my sanity or what I'm doing, it's pushing lower. Fingers slip under the waist and delve deep between my legs. I twist my head, face scrunched as I bury the moan in the pillow next to me.

I stroke my finger over my clit, rubbing the aching button in slow circles before I slide lower. I sink one, and then two fingers—because I need the thickness of *his* finger—deep inside. I stroke like he stroked, fingering myself faster and harder. Until I'm rocking my hips up hard against my hand as I pound my fingers deep into my pussy.

I come screaming into the pillow, thinking of nothing but inked fingers and ice-blue eyes.

THE SECOND SHOE doesn't drop until after I've showered. When I'm sitting on the edge of the bed wrapped in a towel, and the gravity and insanity of all of this hits me like a truck.

What is wrong with me?

Why am I like this?

My eyes close as I drop back across the bed and wrap the duvet over me, cocooning myself in darkness.

I want to hate what happened to me in the woods just now. I want to hate *him* for doing it.

But I don't, and I can't.

Because I liked it. A. Fucking. Lot. But that only leaves me with one, gnawing, horrible question burning a hole in my psyche:

What the actual *fuck* is wrong with me?

11

For the rest of the day, I'm alone. The house is silent, to the point where I actually wonder if he's left again, this time without mentioning it.

At some point, still tired from yesterday, and honestly from the morning's chase and... *other* activities, I nap. When I wake up forty minutes later, I startle when I find a tray of food set at the end of the bed; a BLT sandwich, a salad, some roasted veggies, and—oddly adorably given the rough, savage-like man who's got me locked in a room—a chocolate chip cookie.

I end up devouring all of it. But I'm only a single bite into the sandwich before I really comprehend that he brought this while I was sleeping.

Helpless. Unconscious. Vulnerable.

I shiver. But the feeling quickly blooms into something... heated. Something exciting. I quickly shove it away, my face throbbing as I try and comprehend how I never realized how broken I am if something like that actually excites me.

He's also brought clothes, I realize, after I've basically demolished the lunch. They're all obviously his. But any expansion to my current wardrobe choices of two different extra-large t-shirts, a pair of sleep shorts, and some baggy sweatpants is a plus.

This new haul includes... more t-shirts, a hoodie, another pair of sweats, and a men's boxer-brief style swimsuit that quite honestly must look *obscene* on him. On me, they're like big shorts, once I cinch the drawstring as tight as I can.

But after that, there's nothing. No knocks, no movement in the house. I try the door just to try it, but obviously, it's still locked.

Instead, I pace over to bookshelves along the side wall near the bathroom door. Some are in Russian, others in German, and more than a few in what I think might be Finnish, which is interesting. My Russian is *passable* if I'm reading slowly, but I keep looking until I get to a shelf of books in English. From that selection, I find an old worn copy of *The DaVinci Code*.

I curl up on the bed, open to page one, and lose myself in fiction. That is, until I drop into another nap.

I wake up an hour later bewildered and shocked to find yet another tray of food waiting for me. It's dark out, and it looks like dinner sitting on the tray this time.

My brows furrow. His timing on entering only when I'm napping is uncanny. Part of me starts to wonder if maybe he's even like, gassing me or something through the air vents. But then I realize how completely insane that is and let it go.

I eat dinner, I take another shower and wash my hair, and then I climb back into bed with the book. I make it *almost* to the climax before my eyes start to droop.

"Gassing me again?" I blurt out loud, sleepily, to no one. Then, I'm out.

My lungs burn. I drag in a rasping, haggard breath, my shin aching from being smashed off a stump twenty seconds ago. But I push harder, faster. I twist, slamming shoulder-first through a tangle of underbrush and almost crashing into a massive tree on the other side of it. I dodge left, dragging another hot lungful of air before I surge in a new direction.

It's a day after our last chase. Or, *his* last chase. My last flight. This time, I'm already lasting longer than yesterday.

And yet, even still, I apparently have a garbage sense of direction. I keep getting twisted and turned, always ending up further down the shore from the house when I exit the trees instead of finding the way *away* from the lake.

For a second, my mind recalls the brief highlights of some article I once read, or maybe a YouTube video I watches about making your own compass. But, yeah, sure. As if I've got time during these manic, exciting, thrilling, and yet still terrifying runs to consult a fucking handmade compass.

The sound of branches snapping to my left has me gasping as I surge right. I trip, but then catch myself as I run headlong through the trees.

Another round of the sick, twisted game I can't escape from. The one I dream about later at night.

The one that deep down, in a broken, blackened part of my soul, I look forward to.

I dodge again, shifting directions and pounding through the trees. The branches close in, whipping and scratching at me, until suddenly, I feel something go loose around me.

It's the drawstring of the shorts going slack.

My pulse lurches as my hand flies down to stop the shorts from falling down my legs. I only slow momentarily, but it's a pause I don't have time for. I lurch forward, panting, eyes darting wildly as I cling to the waist of the shorts and fling myself through the trees towards the light ahead.

A break in the forest. And this time, it may just be my freedom.

Except those thoughts are dashed away when I crash headlong out of the tree line and come skidding to a halt in front of the boat house.

The fucking *boat house*.

My heart sinks, my eyes wide and hollow as I stare utterly crestfallen at the familiar outbuilding. My sense of direction is *fucked*.

Keep running.

The voice screams in my head, jolting my heart and my muscles back into action. This isn't over. He hasn't caught me yet. I still have a—

The weight slams into me from behind, and a huge hand clamps over my mouth before I can scream. Powerful muscles clench around me, bringing me down to the ground with his body pinning me there.

I scream into the hand, squirming against him. But it's no use. There's no fighting his brute strength and sheer size.

But I fight anyway. I throw an elbow back. But this time, he's ready for it. He deflects with his own arm, and then the other side before he suddenly grabs my wrists and shoves them up above my head to the ground.

His body presses into me, pinning me to the mossy, grassy ground with his muscles clenching against me and his low growl rumbling through his broad chest against my sweat-slicked, heaving back.

And then suddenly, through the squirming and the shifting and the fighting, I feel it. At first, I'm unclear what it is digging into my ass—maybe a gun? But when he shifts, and it throbs and pulses thick against me, my eyes widen.

My pulse thuds, and my skin tingles.

Heat pools between my thighs.

And then suddenly, we both go still.

It's his cock. His very hard, *very* big cock swollen and thick against my ass. And suddenly, I'm aware of one other detail: that in the fall and struggle, I've let go of my shorts, and they're now bunched around my knees.

It's my completely bare ass that the bulge in his jeans is pulsing against.

The world goes still around me. All I can hear is my panting breath against the grass and moss beneath me. I can feel him push his hips slightly, almost imperceptibly grinding that bulge against my ass. I can feel his hands tighten on my wrists, and his muscles flex against my back. I feel his breath tease over the back of my neck.

And I whimper.

God help me, I don't scream, or fight, or swear, or try and shove him off of me. I fucking *whimper*.

I fucking shiver with excitement.

And then I *push back*.

Not to loosen him. Not to get him away. To feel more of him. To relish the feel of his swollen bulge nudged against the cheeks of my ass.

His fingers wrap tighter around my wrists. I feel his breath hotter on my neck and realize he's leaning down. His lips brush the nape, and I whimper again—a soft, reckless, broken whimper.

"*Caught you*," he rasps darkly against my tingly, slick skin.

My core clenches. My nipples are hard as diamonds against the t-shirt and the ground. And I'm literally dripping wet.

I gasp when I feel his teeth rake gently over my neck. My eyes close and roll back. My teeth capture my bottom lip and bite, stifling the moan. He presses his lips to my skin. They part, and I shiver when I feel his tongue drag across my skin, like he's tasting me.

My body melts, throbbing for him.

One of his hands loosens on one of my wrists. The thought of using this moment to escape or throw him off flashes into my mind for a second. But then, his hand is tangling in my hair, pulling just tight enough to make my core clench with desire as he pushes it up away. His mouth descends again, kissing and sucking and biting the skin of my neck.

Oh my fucking God…

His mouth trails slowly and wetly down the side of my hairline, until he captures the lobe of my left ear in his teeth, nipping just enough to make me gasp sharply.

"And when I catch you, *printsessa*," he growls lowly into my ear. "That makes you *mine*. And when you're mine, you're mine to do with as I please."

His teeth nip, and I cry out with the mix of sharp pain and deep, throbbing arousal.

"Mine to toy with."

His mouth lowers down the curve of my neck before suddenly sucking at some sort of magic spot on my skin. My mouth opens involuntarily, the choke of pleasure ripping from my lips as my eyes roll back.

"Mine to play with."

His bulge grinds shamelessly against my bare ass as his mouth returns to the back of my neck. He reaches between us, grabbing a fistful of the hem of my shirt, at the back. He lifts from me, and I choke when he shoves the cotton up over my slick skin, all the way to my shoulder blades.

"Mine to *taste*."

I choke as he moves down, and then I whimper softly when I feel his lips and tongue drag down my now bare and exposed spine. He groans into my skin, moving lower and lower, one notch of my spine at a time. Slowly raising the temperature past boiling, until I'm squirming against him, shamefully lifting my hips, and clinging to the grass with tight fists.

He doesn't have me pinned. But I'm not going anywhere.

His mouth creeps lower, and lower, and I feel my entire body shivering and pulsing with anticipation. The wet sensation of his tongue tasting the sweat from my lower back has me biting back a cry of pleasure.

His hands skim down my sides, over my bare hips before gripping me. He pulls, lifting my ass slightly as his tongue starts to dip between the top cleft of my cheeks. My whole world turns to throbbing heat. My mouth falls open, my face crumpling as he drags lower and lower, down between my ass cheeks as his powerful hands lift my hips.

And then suddenly, for the first time in my life, I feel the sensation of a wet, thick tongue dragging over my slick pussy.

Holy fucking shit.

He groans into me, and suddenly, his tongue is plunging into me. I cry out, whimpering wantonly as he pushes it as deep as he can, sending me in to outer-fucking-space. The rumbling of his grunts ripple through me, and I cling to the ground with clenched fingers as he strokes his tongue in and out of me.

He moves lower, slipping his tongue down between my lips to suddenly circle my clit. And if I thought I'd tasted heaven for a second before, this is something else.

This is nirvana.

I can't even moan. Or breathe. Or do anything but try and process the sheer sensations I'm feeling for the very first time. His rough, strong hands grip my hips and my ass, spreading me lewdly and pulling me back as he tongues my clit.

He wraps his lips around the aching bud, sucking hard enough to make me cry out in shattered pleasure. His tongue dances around it as I moan into the grass and, my nipples dragging over the soft moss beneath me.

Every nerve in my body catches fire. Every muscle twitches and shivers. My mouth goes slack, and my eyes roll back as he sucks and licks and growls against my pussy until I'm trembling from head to toe.

One of his hands drops from my hips to elsewhere. I feel him shift, as if he's about to stand up. But he doesn't. He just keeps devouring my pussy, but I can feel his shoulder moving rhythmically.

Oh holy fuck.

I'm a virgin, but I'm not an idiot.

He's touching himself. He's touching his cock while he licks my pussy. And when that dawns on me, it's quite possibly the single hottest realization I've ever felt.

His tongue keeps swirling my clit before it slowly drags up through my lips. He plunges it into me, fucking me with his tongue as I squeal in pleasure. The wicked thing moves higher, though, and before I can even process it, my whole world melts when I feel his tongue swirl around my asshole.

Even through the pure pleasure, shame suddenly spikes into me. I squirm and shift as if to push him away.

Right. As if that's happening.

He growls, his hand on my hip suddenly gripping me tightly and pinning me to the ground. He tongues my ass harder, dragging and ripping the shameful cry of pleasure from my lips.

"I *caught you*," he rasps between licks. "Which makes you mine. And when you're mine, I will do…"

I choke on a guttural moan as he drags his tongue over my most private place again.

"What I want with you. I will *taste* what I want, touch what I want, and I will have you any way I please, *printsessa*."

I want to scream *yes* as loud as I can. In that moment—pinned to the ground with my shorts tangled at my knees and his tongue dragging wetly over my ass and my pussy—I want to beg him to do whatever he wants.

But I can't even speak. All I can do is nod and whimper pitifully. All I can do is choke on my breath and squirm beneath him as he drags that tongue back to my clit. His thumb delves between my cheeks, rubbing my asshole in slow, deliberate circles as he devours my pussy.

The world goes numb. The light darkens at the corners of my vision. My lungs scream for air as my body coils and twists and shudders. And then suddenly, it all explodes.

I'm coming.

I scream into the grass and moss beneath me, my body clenching and spasming as he drags the orgasm from me. But he keeps me pinned tight, his thumb and his tongue never stopping their slow, torturous motions as I explode for him.

And then suddenly, just as I'm losing myself in the fog of pleasure, he rips my shorts the rest of the way off, grabs my hip and flips me over sprawling onto my back. My eyes go wide, and my face reddens.

Holy shit.

He's knelt between my askew legs. His t-shirt—ripped and dirtied from the chase—is bunched up around his chest, showing his rippling ab muscles clenching.

His eyes pierce mine, his face a mask of pure fury and lust.

But it's what I see lower that steals the breath from me. What ignites a fire in me.

His jeans are open and shoved partly off his muscled hips. And there, with his fist wrapped tightly around it, is his big, swollen, pulsing cock.

And he's *huge*.

His arm muscle bulges and ripples as he strokes himself. His jaw clenches as he reaches for me with one hand. His fingers slide wetly thorough my lips, and I moan as he sinks two of them deep into my pussy. He strokes hard, fingering the spot just inside that quickly has me gasping in pleasure. My eyes lock onto his pumping, swollen cock—slick and glistening at the tip as it bulges obscenely from his fist.

His thumb rubs my clit. His fingers stroke against my g-spot. Suddenly, like pulling a trigger, I'm coming for him again. And just as I shudder, my hips spasming off the ground with my climax, he explodes.

With a deep, rasping grunt, his abs clench and ripple. The grooves on his hips suddenly stand out corded and ripped. And his cock pulses in his fist. My eyes go wide as thick ropes of white cum spurt from his swollen head to hotly across the skin of my stomach and my breasts.

His thumb keeps rolling my clit, pushing me into yet another orgasm as I feel his warm cum drip across my skin, covering me.

Marking me.

Branding me as his.

And even if he hasn't taken me *that* way—at least, not yet—something's still been claimed today.

And something else—something dark and wicked and both terrifying and thrilling—has awoken. Something I've had locked in a cage I never even knew about.

And I'm not so sure that thing, whatever it is, is ever going to be going back behind bars.

12

Twenty-one years ago; age fourteen:

"Oi, you're late."

There's a dark scowl on Jackson's face as he looks up from tuning his guitar—his prized black Gibson Les Paul that I doubt there's anything in the world he loves more than.

But the scowl fades into that roguish grin of his that's already causing trouble with girls when I toss him the pack of smokes I nicked from the corner store.

"This supposed to make me forget how to read a clock, Kris?"

I roll my eyes as I brush past him and pick up my own guitar—a far less expensive, pawn-shop-bought sunburst Fender Telecaster.

And it's a knockoff.

"Nah, it's supposed to give you throat cancer so you stop talking so much shit."

He snorts, sticking one between his lips and lighting it with a flick of a zippo. Jimmy gives me a nod from behind the drum kit. Tyler does the same as he walks his fingers up and down the neck of his bass, filling the grimy practice space with a rhythmic line.

"Oi."

I turn back to Jackson as he stands, carefully setting the Les Paul on its stand. But then he lasers those eyes of his into me as he walks over. We're the same age, and I'm actually slightly bigger and more built than him. But somehow, even at fourteen, Jackson has that sort of magnetic, cocky swagger to him where even grown, tough adults end up deferring to him as if *he's* the authority figure.

And in most situations, he just is. That's just who Jackson Havoc is: the kind of person who was born to walk out onto a stage in front of a million people and have them kiss his fucking feet.

I mean I can *play* the guitar. But I'm not him. Few are him. And we both know I'm mostly here because playing rock-n-roll and punk music is a slightly better outlet for me than getting into street fights. Tyler's decent. Jimmy can keep a solid beat. But Jack's the born star.

And there's no doubt in my mind the world will know it one day.

At the moment though, he's staring me down with a mix of concern and anger.

"What?" I grunt.

He nods his chiseled chin at my face.

"You been fighting again?"

I shrug it off, turning to finish tuning the Telecaster slung over my shoulder.

"Nah."

"Bullshit."

It's only half bullshit. I'm not "fighting again" like he thinks. I've stayed clear of the Boyton gang who hangs out by Winchester Park—even though I usually win when two or three of them jump me. Usually.

And I'm also out of the whole underground circuit I was screwing around with. The cash was good, but you don't need to be a genius to see that bareknuckle fights in abandoned warehouses run by the mafia are a great way to die young.

"Fuck off. I'm serious."

His brow darkens.

"Your mum's guy been using hands on you?"

I tense. He mean's Mikhail, mom's latest boyfriend. This one at least seems serious, even if there's obviously something weird with him. We live in a shit-hole, where we barely make rent even with my grocery delivery and boxing money. And when he comes to stay the night, Mikhail rolls up in one of several peak luxury vehicles—Porches, Mercedes G-Wagons, Range Rovers, Bentleys, you name it.

I *do* get the sense that he actually likes and cares about my mom. But… it just doesn't add up. The expensive fancy clothes, the ridiculous cars, the cash he flaunts around while dating the Russian cleaning lady with the work visa who lives in a slum.

I shake my head and go back to twisting the tuning heads.

THE HUNTER KING

"Nah, mate. Nothin' like that."

Mik *has* hit me. But, not like Jackson's insinuating. He's hit me in a ring, a couple times over the last few months, where he's told me he wanted to "evaluate me" as a fighter.

He also took me to a shooting range after I mentioned how my dad used to take me hunting, years and years ago when we were still in Russia.

Before dad fucked off.

Before men came looking to collect his debts from my mother.

Before we left Russia forever and came here to Liverpool: home of the Beatles, Liverpool FC, Castle Street, and now a Russian kid with third-hand clothes and no heat in the winter, who no one gives a fuck about.

Except for Jackson. And now Mikhail, in a way.

Mik who says I'm a beast in the ring and the most natural born marksmen with a gun he's ever seen. Mik who's been teaching me some basic martial arts across a few different disciplines—Judo, Muay Thai, Jiu-Jitsu, Krav Maga.

Mik who just told me today that he actually runs a school—a training academy, of sorts, where he says he can mold me into the best student he's ever had. An academy, he says, for young people who want to change the world, be the best they can be, and most importantly, make more money than they even know what to do with.

That all sounds fucking *great* to me. I just need to make up my mind. Going to his school means leaving my mum, "for a long time," Mikhail's said. It means being broken down into nothing so that he can build me back into something superior.

It means I'm going to get the shit kicked and ground out of me.

But still, it draws me. It's a pull I can't seem to shake, even if he's warned me it's going to be brutal in ways I can't fathom.

But that's why I'm late to band practice. And that's why my face is all bruised up.

"Mate, you can tell me—"

"Jack, I'm fucking fine."

He holds that stern "disappointed parent" stare at me, the cigarette hanging from his lips as he shoves his fingers through his messy sandy-brown hair. Then he shrugs.

"Alright, bruv. Fuck it." That roguish, troublemaking, heartbreaker grin creeps over his face. "You wanna make some noise?"

"Fuck yeah."

He slings his guitar over his shoulder, cigarette still in his lips as Jimmy counts us off. And then we're right into it, a wall of pure fucking sound, teen angst, and rebellious fury pouring out of two guitars, a bass, a shitty drum kit, and the voice of a rock *god* that has no business coming out of the mouth of a fourteen-year-old little shit like Jackson.

But as we play, and as I watch him, transfixed—because it's impossible to watch Jackson Havoc play rock-n-roll and *not* be transfixed—an epiphany hits me.

This is what draws him. The beautiful chaos of rock-n-roll is what breathes air into his lungs. The same way the urge to fight, and hunt, and carve a piece of this world off for myself is what fills mine.

We're not even through the second song on the practice schedule before I know I've made my decision.

Jackson was born to play.

And I was born to hunt.

Present:

LINES HAVE BEEN CROSSED. Smashed. Swept aside. It started with refusing my orders and tossing out the mission when I made the choice to spare her. It escalated when I took her.

The cracks appeared when I felt the heat of her skin beneath my fingers, catching her after a chase. And the top began to bubble over when I kissed her and tasted those fiery lips.

But it went nuclear today.

It's hours later now. She's back in her room, and the cameras tell me she's back on the bed, reading *The DaVinci Code* again.

She hasn't showered since what happened earlier.

My cum is still dried on her skin.

The thought of that has me gritting my teeth as a surge of something primal and heated swells inside of me. Knowing I've marked her, and that she'd done fuck-all to change or erase that, is… fuck.

An addictive thought. A vicious one. An alluring one.

But it's not purely a lust thing. I mean, yes, the knowledge that she's chosen to leave my cum on her skin makes my cock surge with a hunger I'm pretty sure only she'd be able to quench. But there's another element to it. It's something… possessive.

Savagely territorial. Consumingly protective.

I drum my fingers over the top of my desk. My tongue runs along my bottom lip.

I can still taste her.

My eyes narrow as I reach for my phone, and dial a number I swore I'd never call again. When I took these last two jobs, it was amusing to me that Jana was so adamant that I not "involve" Mik. That this was "her op," and she didn't need me going over her head.

As if I'd ever want to talk to that piece of shit again.

And yet, circumstances have changed. Priorities have shifted. And now here I am, calling him.

For a long time, I thought of this man as my father. My bio dad was long gone, and even when he was around, he was a devil. Mik was never anything close to the warm fuzzy type. Nor was he even much of a role model, or one for dolling out life lessons and platitudes.

But he was *there*.

First, he was the mysterious rich guy who seemed to have a thing for my mom. Then he was the man with the academy who wanted to turn me into his best pupil. Then it was that role *plus* the new one of being my mom's second husband.

Then the father of my half-sister.

So, in a fucked up way, Mik was my dad. Sort of. Though, the fact that he wasn't really has made cutting him out of my life like a cancer a much easier task.

The other end of the line answers with a click, followed by a low sigh.

"Well, this is a surprise."

My eyes narrow as I bring the glass of vodka sitting in front of me to my lips.

"Did you send someone to my house."

There's silence on his end. The seconds tick by. But I know what he's doing. The silence and lack of response is one of his mind games. Like a boardroom power-trip game to see who speaks first, guaranteeing them to be the loser of the negotiation.

Every conversation with this man is a negotiation. He wants me to break the silence first, which gives him power. But I know these games. I've mastered them now. And so, I simply sit there, letting the silence bathe us both as I take another sip.

It's Mik that finally breaks. But I'm not naïve or cocky enough to gloat over it like it's a win. It's just a chess move that Mikhail has chosen to make. A pawn he's elected to give up.

"Why would I do that?"

"I believe that's part of my first question."

He takes his time responding.

"Are you not with Boris?"

Completely dodging my question. Mik and his fucking games.

He means my boss, Boris Tsavakov. Boris is a cretin of a human. A sad sack of shit who rules his heavily Bratva-connected business empire like an unhinged, alcoholic tsar. He's reckless, unreliable, and a buffoon.

Which is precisely why I was placed in his organization by Mikhail himself, years ago. The intent was to plant me there and let me gain Boris's confidence over the years, until I could rise in rank. And then eventually, behead the king, take the reins, and give them to Mikhail.

The years have gone by, but that's not how things have panned out. For one, I left Mik and the Syndicate after what happened to Nikita. But then, I found a reason to stay, and to *not* take over the Tsavakov empire for myself:

Boris Tsavakov's son, Misha.

A boy I see so much of myself in, I basically view him as a little brother. A boy nothing like his shit-stain of a father. A boy of fifteen who already has a worldliness and a weariness of it about him that ages him far beyond that.

A boy whose very existence came from a violence I once helped bury. And for that, I owe him everything, the least of which is the empire he was born to lead one day.

"No," I finally grunt in answer. "I'm taking personal time."

Mikhail chuckles darkly.

"I didn't realize Boris was such a magnanimous boss."

I roll my eyes. He's the opposite. He's a blight on the world. But he at least recognizes when it's best not to rattle things—

things like one of his best captains and advisors telling him he'll be taking some time off.

"I won't ask again, because I'm sure you have no intention of answering. But let me put it this way, Mik. I don't need or want you checking up on me. And if I find one of your people snooping around my house again, I will put them down. Is that clear?"

Silence, of course.

"This is the last time I'm doing this. I hope that's clear."

"Doing what, Kristoff?"

My eyes narrow.

"*Business* for you. These last two hits are *it*. This completes our business. I know you have the proof of death for the first. Jana has the proof for the second. Now, I want you to pay up."

That dark, raspy chuckle fills the phone again.

"A man like you," he sighs. "Do you really need more money—"

"We both know I'm not talking about money, Mikhail. Give me what we agreed on."

"What we agreed on..." he muses, as if he's trying to remember.

"*Tell me where my sister is buried,*" I hiss.

He goes silent again, for a long half minute. But I wait.

"I'll see what I can—"

"You'll see what you *will* do."

Silence again.

"Your tone has grown insolent, Kristoff," Mikhail grunts quietly.

"And yours has grown boring and out of touch. I did my part to put you on the Balagula throne, Mik."

"I'm looking around, and it doesn't seem as though I *am* sitting on the throne, Kristoff."

"That's on you. But I've done my part. I did it in the past, and I did it with these hits. We've had this discussion before. I'm *done* with you and this organization—"

"You'll be done when I say you—"

"Goodbye, Mikhail."

I hang up, tossing the phone onto my desk before leaning back angrily in my chair. I hate being fucked with and dicked around with. Mik isn't usually one to do that, either. But he's testing me right now.

Antagonizing me.

It's not a wise move. It never was before when I was what I was—the *bukavac*. It's equally unwise now, being who I am with the power I wield within the Tsavakov empire.

The anger surges, and I grit my teeth as I shake with rage. But then, slowly, I breathe out. I let my mind go blank. And in that blankness, I see trees. I see a chase.

I see her, fleeing and shrieking before me, willing me to catch her. Urging me on. Provoking me.

The fury begins to dissipate. Slowly, the tension leaves me as my mind wanders back to the chase earlier.

The one she was eager for. The one where she shrieked when I caught her, but not out of fear or anger.

Out of excitement. Out of arousal.

I swallow, my eyes narrowing at the tumbler of vodka on the desk in front of me. Even through the liquor I've drank, I can still taste her. I can still feel her shuddering under me.

This is a dangerous game. And I'm playing it fast and loose, which is not how I operate. But I'll see it to the end.

My eyes drift back to the cameras focused on her, lying on the bed in her room.

These are rough seas.

But we'll both go down together.

13

Days go by, and I fall into a routine.

A boring, and yet somehow also exciting routine.

Boring, because every day is the same. I wake up and immediately go try the door to the room, which is always locked. I either find breakfast waiting for me when I wake, or else it's there in my room when I get out of the bathroom from brushing my teeth. Then I read for most of the morning.

Lunch is either delivered, or twice now, Kristoff has unlocked the door to my glamorous prison to bring me to a gorgeous glass atrium of a room. It's filled with plants and has a view of the lake. Both times, he's sat with me drinking a cup of coffee, asking me random questions about my life.

My life.

Nothing about my father, or the Balagula organization. It's not as if he's fishing for something, which would make sense. But the questions are just things like what my favorite books are. Movies I like. How I like Harvard, and Boston. In fact,

THE HUNTER KING

the only questions that come close to asking about my family's business is how it effected me growing up and then at college.

He nods slowly at my responses, like he's memorizing them. Then, when I'm done with lunch, it's back to my room for more reading. There's also a TV attached to a Netflix account now, so, there's that, too.

Then it's dinner—mostly in my room, but once I ate in the atrium with him for more casual conversation with my kidnapper.

After that, I shower, I read, and I sleep.

But when I'm with him, I sit there talking on the outside, but wondering on the inside—wondering if he's thinking about what happened in the woods as much as I am.

Wondering if he's been replying the vivid, lurid, core-clenching details of the way he shoved me to the ground, ripped my shorts down, and devoured me in a way no one ever has before. Like I am.

But then, to him, maybe this is just how he spends his time. Maybe this is life for him: kidnapping girls, chasing them through the woods and using some kind of fucked up voodoo or mind games to trick them into thinking it's sexually exciting for them.

There's probably no way that's true. And if it is, it's probably a sign of mental illness on my part that the idea of him chasing another girl, or doing to her what he did to me makes me...

Jealous.

Angry.

Stabby.

Jesus Christ, what the hell is wrong with me?

In any case, what's happened here with him is *not* normal for me. Not the kidnapping, obviously. But not any of it.

Not the kissing.

Not the touching.

Not drowning in heated gasps as his lips and tongue dance over my pussy. Not crying out as his fingers make me come again as his cum splatters my throbbing, electrified skin.

Not normal in the life of Tatiana Fairist. Not even a rarity.

Unprecedented.

As in, it's *never* happened to me before. None of it. Because at twenty years and, what, five days, old?

I've never done any of it. Because of who I am, and who my family is, I've done *none* of the sexual exploration basically every other twenty-year-old at college does.

Until him.

And now I can't stop thinking about it. It's almost *all* I can think about, actually. And I've got a lot of time to be thinking about things right now. I replay the feel of his stubble against my thighs. His tongue swirling around my clit as his groans hummed through me. The way he both pinned me to the ground and pulled me against his mouth.

That feeling of twisting heat and forbidden desire when he pulled his thick, *large* cock from his black jeans, wrapping his fist around it. The way I came just as his own release fell hot across my skin.

It has me on edge. It has me twisting under the covers at night. It has me wanting… more. More of that, and more "new."

And that's how I know I really am truly messed up in the head. A man stole me, took me to his forested, lake-side house, chases me through the woods, and goes down on me for the first time. And all I can think about is doing it to *him*.

A lot.

I wonder if there's any therapy textbooks on the bookshelf alongside the genre fiction.

But when I'm not thinking about all of that, I'm left wondering why I'm even here at all. Part of me wants to ask, but I'm also afraid of the answer. I'm afraid being here might even be a temporary thing. Again, maybe next week, he's got a different girl to kidnap and chase around.

So I just don't ask. And he doesn't mention it either.

That last time in the woods where he pinned me down and made me come on his tongue was the last time he's chased me. In fact, I'm beginning to wonder if it'll even happen again.

It being the chasing.

It also being "the illicit orgasming."

That's the exciting part—the counterpart to the boring aspects of my days. It's the constantly wondering if and when he'll do it again. Part of me even questions if this routine and asking me questions about my life is all part of a game—all a ruse to get me complacent, so that the next chase takes me by surprise and makes it more thrilling for him.

For me.

On the fifth morning after the last chase, the routine starts all over again. I wake up, I rub the sleep from my eyes as I slip from the covers, and glance over to see that breakfast is already waiting on the table for me. Then I walk over to the door.

It's obviously locked as always, but it's like this tick I can't get rid of. Like I *have* to check it every morning. I'm still half asleep when I pad over, absently reach for the knob, and give it a shake, as always.

I stiffen.

The knob turns, and the door pops open.

I stare at it, shivering, my pulse beginning to quicken. My fingers curl around the door, and I pull it open more, peeking out into the empty hallway as my mouth goes dry.

Is this a trick? Or did he really forget to lock up after dropping off breakfast? I open the door wider, poking my head out and glancing up and down the hallway.

My pulse quickens, and I swallow thickly.

Then next time, be aware of your needs and surroundings before you make an escape.

My heart thuds in my chest as I gently close the door and bolt back into the room. I wolf down breakfast quickly, and then change into the baggy shorts, a hoodie sweatshirt, and the running shoes. Then, I slip back to the door and open it again.

The coast is still clear.

I'm really doing this.

When I step into the hallway, my brain already starts to formulate a plan as I speed walk as quietly as I can to the staircase. If he's not downstairs waiting for me, I'll slip out the first side door I can find, and make for the woods. My track record of always circling back to the water in my other forays has been colored by the fact that I've had him chasing me those other times.

This time, I can pick a direction and move in a straight line. Then, I'll be free. And if somehow, I get all turned around again? Then fuck it. I'll steal his boat to get to the far side of the water. And if that doesn't or can't work? I'm a decently strong swimmer, and it's not *that* big of a lake.

Whatever I have to do, I can make it.

I tread lightly down the stairs, barely daring to breathe. I glance around, but there doesn't seem to be a sign of him. And when I check at the back door, there's a dirty spot on the side mat where his shoes usually are.

My heart races.

It's time.

I open the back door and slip out, glancing around nervously before I make a break for the trees. I half expect him to be waiting for me, ready to spring this trap he's set. But when I get into the shade of the forest, I'm alone.

Holy shit, I might actually do this.

For a second, the fear of what might happen to me if he realizes I'm gone and comes after me snags ahold of me. The last few days, and even before that, he's been gruff and maybe rough at times. But not angry or cruel.

He's chased me, but we both know damn well I've been thrilled by those chases.

And yet, this is different. This isn't one of our games. This is me sneaking out, defying what is clearly a set "rule" in his world, and trying to run away.

Things might get darker and deadlier very quickly if he chases after me this time.

I shiver violently before I glance around and take a deep breath.

Fuck it. I'm doing this.

Without the immediate threat of someone chasing hot on my heels, I take a second to get my bearings. I look up at the morning sun low past the trees, and I make that my point. I set off for it, jogging lightly through the forest.

My eyes dart side to side, and I flinch at every bird call and snapped twig. But it's both a fear and a thrill. And yet, that's all there is: just regular noises. Not the sound of footsteps hunting me. Not the rhythmic, dark sound of his breath as he chases. Not the tingling sensation that comes right before his hand wraps around my throat from behind.

I pick up my pace as the trees begin to thin, and then suddenly, I burst out of the forest.

Right in front of the lake.

My jaw drops as my heart sinks.

"Are you fucking kidding me?" I hiss to no one.

My pulse beating quickly, I turn just over ninety degrees away from the lake, in a direction that will guarantee not actually hitting the water again, and I take off. This time, I run faster, legs pumping as I barrel through the forest. Except five minutes later, I'm bursting out of the trees again.

Right in front of the lake.

What. The. Fuck.

I try again, turning once more in a random direction and bolting in a straight line. Except once again, there's nothing waiting for me after a few minutes of running except more lake.

And then suddenly, something occurs to me.

Something both obvious and horrifying.

I don't turn back to the trees this time. I turn left, and I start running on the shore. I want to be wrong. I want so badly to realize my theory can't be true. But five minutes later, I round a bend of the shore, and stop short, jumping behind a fallen tree.

Up ahead is the main house. And a little way past it down the shore, the boat house. There's still no sign of him, though.

I turn, and I start sprinting back the way I came. I vault over the rocky shore, a sheen of sweat clinging to my back as the sun rises higher. The boulder-strewn coast drags on, twisting and turning around random tiny inlets and miniature-sized harbors, always in the shadow of the trees.

Minutes tick by. Then more, and more, until I'm panting heavily as I push myself to keep running. Until suddenly, the cold truth peels around the bend ahead, stopping me frozen in my path.

It's the boathouse.

I've just run *away* from the boathouse and main house, only to come back around to it from the other side.

Because I'm not on the far shore of the lake.

I'm on a fucking *island*.

I'm standing there, staring at the boathouse as I process this information. When suddenly, a stick snaps behind me. I whirl with the gasp lodged in my throat, only to find myself frozen to the spot, lost in the icy-blue lethality of his piercing gaze.

His lips are thinned, and I realize the snapping twig sound came from the broken one he's holding in his hands.

I tense.

The snap was purposeful. He *wanted* me to know he was there. It wasn't to scare me.

It was to give me a head start.

14

I'M BARELY through the tree line when I hear him crashing after me.

So much for that head start.

My heart thunders, having just gone from zero to one thousand in the snap of a branch. My pulse roars through my veins, my feet pounding the underbrush as I hurl myself through the trees.

The fear is there, like it always is. But it's colored by something else—something I'm still desperately trying to pretend isn't excitement.

Giddiness. Anticipation of being caught, and what comes after that.

But there's still enough of a primal fight or flight reaction in me to run like my life depends on it. There's still enough of a fear factor that I push myself, slamming through the branches with my heart rate whining in my ears like an air-raid siren.

Until the hand grabs my hair. Until I shriek, gasping with the powerfully intoxicating swirl of fear and arousal.

He yanks me back into him, spinning me around as a hand wraps around my throat. My eyes go wide, my pulse jangling as he backs me hard into the trunk of a tree. I shiver as he slams into me, pinning me to the bark at my back as his mouth suddenly bruises to mine.

My legs go weak. My brain short-circuits, twisted in knots by the combination of the one firm hand tugging my hair with the other on my neck, and the lips igniting me with fire.

His hand slips from my hair, his fingers tracing around the hollow of my neck to the front, until they slip to my collarbone. I tremble as I feel him grip the zipper of my hoodie and yank it down, letting the two halves fall apart to reveal my breasts.

And then suddenly, just as his hand slips down, something clicks in me. Something snaps. And before I'm even aware of thinking through the action, it's happening, as if someone else is controlling my body.

My arm whips up, breaking his hold on my neck. As if in slow motion, I watch his brow furrow in surprise as my palms shove against his chest, knocking him back. In one fluid motion, I drop to a squat, throw a leg out, and spin—sweeping his legs and sending him crashing to the ground.

For a second, it all goes still. I just stare at him in shock, unclear on how exactly I even knew *how* to do that, let alone actually do it. And from the confused, scowling, and maybe slightly amused look on his face, I can see I'm not the only one.

But I don't stop to discuss it. I turn, and I *run*.

I make it all of twenty paces before I scream at the feel of his body slamming into mine. Powerful arms circle me, twisting me and shoving me back until he pins me hard to another tree. His eyes pierce into me, making me tremble.

"Where the hell did you learn to—"

My arm flings up and to the side again, as if to break his hold on me once again. But this time, he grabs my wrist and shoves it above my head as his mouth descends. I whimper as he kisses me fiercely—a possessive, triumphant kiss that has me trembling between his rock-hard body and the tree at my back. A kiss that has every nerve ending in my body humming, and my skin throbbing with heat.

"*Caught you*," he rasps quietly against my lips.

I shiver as he sucks the bottom one between his teeth, nibbling just hard enough to make my core tighten and quiver. I feel his other hand slide over my waist, fingers dragging up over the soft, exposed skin of my stomach. He traces higher, deftly pushing the two open halves of the front of my hoodie to the sides. I whimper when I feel the cotton tease across my nipples as the hoodie falls away from my breasts.

An electric jolt I've never felt before electrifies me when I feel his thumb and finger suddenly pinch one of my nipples. I gasp, blushing as it quickly turns into a shameful moan. He twists his finger and thumb, sending heat and pain and pleasure erupting through my core.

Until suddenly, it happens again. The gut-reaction.

I drop down, my body already coiling to sweep his legs again.

I don't. Because he's ready for it this time.

His shin shoves to the side, knocking *my* legs out from under me. I gasp as I sprawl to my knees, and then whimper tightly as he grabs a fistful of hair at the back and tugs, hard. My body ripples with heat as I fall to my knees, breasts exposed, head tilted back, pulse racing, and my eyes utterly captivated by his icy blues.

The entire forest seems to go still.

It feels like I can taste the very scent of the woods on my tongue and smell the soft dirt and pine needles under my bare knees.

I can feel how fucking wet I am.

My pulse roars like liquid fire, humming loudly and overpoweringly in my ears. My skin throbs, and I swallow thickly as I lose myself in his fierce gaze—for seconds, or minutes, or it could even be hours.

But then, I break that gaze.

My eyes drop down over the t-shirt pulled tight across his broad, muscled chest. My gaze traces lower, to where his shirt is bunched and pulled up from his waist, showcasing a glimpse of chiseled abs, grooved hips, tattoo ink, and a dark trail of hair slipping from his tight navel down into his jeans.

And when my gaze lowers even more, something throbbing grips me, melting into my core.

He's *hard*.

He's so fucking hard it's bulging the front of his jeans obscenely. And for the life of me, I can't look away. I just stare at his throbbing erection, feeling my skin pulse and a forbidden desire pool between my thighs.

Slowly, my eyes drag back to his. The look on his face has changed. In the still, pulsing heat of the moment, his gaze hardens, sparking into something fiery.

I bring my hand up tentatively, feeling a shiver ripple down my back. And before I can stop myself, or ask myself what made me this way, or wonder how I lived twenty years without someone realizing just how fucked up and insane I am…

I reach for him.

His hand tightens in my hair, making me whimper just before my hand rests over the obscene bulge in his pants.

I shiver from head to toe, almost unable to breathe as the rush of danger and excitement chokes me. I swallow thickly as I drag my eyes up to his, my hand resting on the thickness in his jeans.

"I…"

"Open them."

The words are growled thickly. A demand. A command. A dark dare.

I pull at the button of his jeans, flinching slightly as it pops open. I can feel his cock pulse against the denim between us, as if reaching for me.

Heat pools thick between my thighs.

I pinch the zipper and tug, feeling the metallic teeth click open one by one. Until suddenly, as I peel his pants away from him, his cock slips free.

My eyes bulge, and my jaw drops.

Oh *fuck* me.

He's freaking *huge*. I saw him before, when he crouched between my legs the other day. But I was distracted by the screaming orgasm wrought by his fingers deep inside of me. He was half covered by his powerful fist.

This time, he's right there, right in front of me, hanging heavy, thick, and swollen. Veined. Throbbing. Wet at the tip.

"I'll take my prize now for catching you."

I gasp as his hand tugs at my hair—not enough to hurt me, but enough to make my nerve endings scream with a thrill. Enough to send my pulse roaring in my ears as he tugs my head back, dragging my gaze to his.

"Open your mouth."

The words purr and growl animal-like from his lips—a deep, rasping, heavy voice that makes my core quiver and my blood run hotter.

My eyes drop to his cock again—so hard, so thick, and *so* big. Fucking hell, will that even *fit* in my mouth?

Shaking a little with both fear and a thrilling lust, I raise my hand to reach for him.

His pushes mine away with a shake of his head. When I look up, his jaw clenches into a thin, wicked line, his eyes piercing as he wags a finger.

"Uh-uh, *printsessa*. You don't get to use your hands."

Something primal and raw swells hot inside of me.

"Now open your *fucking* mouth."

And I do.

It's not the fear that he'll hurt me, or some sort of threat of retribution. Though I have no doubt this man could physically pin me to the ground and do anything he damn well pleased to me. With his hand in my hair, he could *make me* take him into my mouth.

But I open my mouth because I want to.

Because he does something to me. He flips a switch. He breaks down a door that should've maybe stayed locked.

But there's no putting whatever dark perversions that've been freed inside of me back behind locked doors.

My mouth opens as I half move towards him on my volition, and half let him guide me by the hair. I shiver when his swollen cock head slides across my bottom lip, gasping slightly at the salty sweet taste of the slickness on his crown.

But he doesn't shove inside. He guides my mouth down the side, groaning through clenched teeth as my wet lips slide down the veined length of him.

"*Lick*," he purrs thickly.

I tremble with heat, letting my tongue dart out to drag over his hot, silky skin. He guides my mouth back up, across the head again, and then down the other side. His hips rock, a grunt on his lips as he thrusts, pushing his cock wetly over my lips and cheek.

I. Am. *Soaked*.

My body quivers, my thighs aching to squeeze together to relieve some of the aching pressure between them. I lick and hum and whimper against his fat cock as he rocks it back and forth across my open mouth, before suddenly pulling back.

He guides the head between my lips, and the heat coursing through me surges. My lips are already swollen, and wet with my spit and his precum. And I whimper as he pushes into my mouth until his swollen head hits the back of my throat.

I choke, and he pulls back. But then he's thrusting back in, making my body shiver with heat and a thrill as he claims my mouth again. I choke again, and he pulls all the way out. Spit obscenely stretches between his cock and my bottom lip, turning me to liquid fucking fire at how perverse and filthy this is.

But this time, I move before he can guide me by the hair. I lean forward, opening my lips and eagerly sucking him into my mouth. He hisses in pleasure, and the sound seems to spur me on, igniting something in me. I moan, wanting to take more of him—to swallow all of him.

To please him.

Because maybe I'm broken. Maybe I've slipped into some kind of Stockholm syndrome thing.

Or maybe, this fucked up blackness has always been inside of me, waiting to be broken out.

I swallow him deep again, taking him to the back of my throat. I whimper, feeling wetness dripping from my lips wantonly. I look up, and I tremble when I see the sheer intensity and desire in his eyes.

"Touch yourself," he murmurs darkly. "I want to watch you feel how wet being a good girl for my cock has made you."

Oh my fucking God.

I should be ashamed to. I should feel nauseated by the thought of doing something so personally intimate in front of someone—let alone this man. My captor. My dark desire.

But maybe it's because of that, not in spite of it, that I let my hand drop and slide into my baggy shorts. I've been without underwear for days, and my hand slides unhindered over my pubic mound until I feel the slick, soft, wet heat of my lips. My finger pad rubs over my clit, and I whimper around the thick cock in my mouth.

"Good girl."

My core throbs, wetness dripping down my fingers at his words. I moan, sucking wetly, heedless of the mess I'm making of my lips and chin. I swallow him deeper and then try for even *deeper*. He groans, his hand grabbing a fist of my hair and pulling me closer as two of my fingers curl deep inside of me.

My clit grinds against my palm as I stroke my fingers against my g-spot. Kristoff's hips buck, fucking my mouth like it's his to use.

It's the single hottest thing I've ever experienced.

My whole body melts to liquid fire. My eyes roll back, and I hum deeply around him. My pussy clenches around my fingers, my clit throbbing, before suddenly, I'm exploding.

I cry a muffled cry, whimpering a filthy, perverse, pornographic sound around his bulging, spit-soaked cock as I come hard. My body spasms and jolts, lost in the forbidden depravity of all of it.

Kristoff groans, and suddenly, his muscled hips push forward, plunging his swollen cock into my mouth. I feel him swell as his balls tighten. And then suddenly, I can taste him as he roars into the trees.

His hot cum spills over my tongue, shocking me; the taste taking me by surprise though it's not unpleasant. More and more empties between my lips, filling my mouth as I wonder if I should—

"Hold it there."

My eyes slip up to lock with his, my body shivering.

"Keep it there on your tongue."

His jaw ripples with a sort of pleasure as he slips his still rock-hard, swollen cock from my lips. I keep them shut, pulsing with a filthy desire as I feel his hot cum on my tongue.

"Now you may swallow."

And I do. Without thinking. Without hesitation. For the first time. On my knees in the woods, hand in my shorts stroking my pussy. With him towering over me, all with my eyes locked with his.

"Show me."

My face burns hotly, throbbing as I open my mouth and stick out my tongue.

"Good girl."

The door's been smashed open. The perverse depravity that it was holding back is now roaming free, sinking its black claws into every part of me.

And I don't think it'll ever be letting go.

15

My pulse is still throbbing when I sit down into the Adirondack style chair on the deck overlooking the water. My hands are still twitching from the hunt—the chase.

The catching her.

Something dark and hungry prowls beneath the surface of my skin. Needing more. Wanting it again. Hungry for her.

It's been like this for a week, since the morning she realized I'd left the door to her room open. The day I needed the chase so badly to be real, I made it real. I made it a real flight for her—an escape.

And it did what it was intended to do. She ran faster. She fought me stronger. She moaned deeper and squirmed more delectably. She whimpered more eagerly.

She came harder.

And that's what every day since has turned into. We're in a new depraved routine, where she wakes, finds her door "mysteriously" unlocked, and bolts.

And I chase.

I catch.

I slake my thirst for her with my mouth on her sweet little pussy or my cock spilling my cum down her throat. Or on her skin as she writhes in pleasure.

After, we return to the house. I make a show of bringing her to her room.

But the door stays unlocked, and she knows it. Just like she knows at this point that there's no accident or oversight involved with it being unlocked in the mornings. Or how she knows she's allowed to basically walk around the house as she pleases.

It's a game we both play. A dark, mercurial, viscously raw and most certainly fucked up game we play.

But we're both in it. We're both hooked like junkies on the thrill and the rush of it, and we both know it, though we never talk openly about it.

It's her own additions to it that get my blood burning like jet fuel. Her own twists that keeps the hunt thrilling.

Some days, it's the morning when she "escapes." Other times, it's at night, or midday. Two days ago, after a morning chase that ended with her on all fours with my mouth on her pussy, I led her back to her room.

Ten minutes later, she was bolting again. That one ended with her tongue on my balls before my cum spilled all over her tits.

And so, it goes, day after day. And where this ends?

I have no fucking idea.

All I know is, my days are filled with chasing something I never expected to find: a prey who makes me want to hunt. A prey who craves it as much as I do. But there's no master plan here. No end goal. There's just this: keeping her here.

Keeping her mine.

I sigh as I sink back in the chair, gazing out at the water surrounding my island home. This place—the land, at least—once belonged to my family. My Finnish grandfather owned this place and had a modest house on the shore not far from where the current lodge home stands.

The Nazi's took it from him during World War Two. After the war, when Russia was turning into the Soviet Union, and Finland was trying to figure out what the hell to do about that, this whole area—the lake, the surrounding hills, and the island—became up for grabs, and was "reclaimed" by the retiring CEO of a mining company.

I was prepared to give him whatever he wanted for it. Until I did the homework and put together the pieces. Before I realized "Erno Korhonen" had once been "Karl Schmidt," a senior officer in the SS.

After that, I gave him the same deal the pieces of shit he worked for gave my grandfather: I stuck a gun in his face, told him the island was now mine, and offered him the opportunity to "swim for it."

My grandfather was a much better swimmer than Karl.

I had more money than I knew what to do with when I was working for Mikhail. But when I was inserted into Boris's organization, I was supposed to be an up-and-coming, hungry young soldier. To Boris, the island was just something that'd been in my family. When I left Mik behind and threw myself into the Tsavakov empire and making even more money, I used the opportunity to build the house and boathouse.

Now, it's my refuge. It's my solitude. And hardly anyone has ever been here before.

Never a woman.

I exhale again, gazing out over the stillness of the lake. But my thoughts are clouded. Not just by Tatiana. But by the voicemail I got hours ago from Boris that he needed to speak with me.

So much for refuge and solitude. So much for my hidden island outside the turning of the rest of the world, where Tatiana and I can just play these fucked up games.

I unlock my phone and call Boris's office line at his main house. Besides being incompetent, Boris is comically paranoid of "the government" or his "enemies" spying on him. The irony is, he *was* once being spied on—by me, for Mikhail. But I know his systems and his organization now inside out.

No one's bugging Boris's phones.

Now, the Tsavakov empire most certainly does have enemies. But Boris likes to fancy himself a top-dog in the Bratva world, despite *not* being Bratva. Sure, he's got his fingers in illegal pies all over the place. But that's business in Russia. Boris's criminality lies in bribing local officials for building permits for his construction empire. Maybe paying off a few site examiners and coding officers.

And yet, he walks around like he's fucking Scarface.

That alone would be amusing enough. But he's dragged his son, Misha, into it all as sort of a prop. And that enrages me.

Misha's a good kid. Even with the brutalist, hard-love way his shithead father has raised him. Even at fourteen, Misha's a big kid. He's built and muscled. But he's been hardened by Boris from a very young age, so that he can show off his son like a prop—like some sort of token tough guy and ladies' man.

A toughness Boris himself doesn't have in the slightest.

Luckily, he's out of his father's house now, finally away at boarding school at the illustrious Oxford Hills Academy as a first year.

The phone picks up with a click, and then silence.

"Tsavokov empire. You may kiss the ring, or ass."

I grin widely when I hear Misha's voice answer his father's phone.

"Aren't you supposed to be at school?"

"You realize with the amount of money my father is dumping into that place, I could literally just walk around campus naked all day skipping class and getting stoned, and I'd probably still graduate with honors, right?"

I sigh, rolling my eyes.

"You're welcome to try it. But I'd take a second stab at that theory."

Oxford Hills Academy, set in the bucolic English countryside, might be the top private preparatory school in the world. And Boris might have some serious cash to throw around—as do the very much Bratva connected parental figures of Misha's two best friends, Ilya Volkov and Lukas Komarov, who are both also first years at OHA.

But even with Bratva blood money thrown around like rain, you have to be *smart* to get into OHA. Not just rich. Not just connected. Yes, the other students there are the sons and daughters of world leaders, literal royalty, and titans of the corporate and banking world. But they're also *very* intelligent. And if Misha thinks he can coast through because of his dad's money, it's going to be my job to burst that bubble.

Immediately.

"Look, Misha, OHA is an opportunity you can't even begin to fathom—"

He starts to laugh. I scowl.

"Kristoff, *chill*, man. I'm fucking with you. I'm psyched to be there, and I get it. Believe me, I'm gonna dominate that place."

I chuckle.

"No slacking off?"

"Nah."

"No walking around in the buff, either."

"Jury's still out on that one."

I grin before my brow furrows.

"I am curious though what you're doing at your father's house a month into classes."

"Eh, dad wanted me to come along to this board meeting with him. You know, the whole training me to be king one day thing."

More like making sure all of his cronies see what a great, strong, handsome son he has. A son at OHA. A son who's already notching up his bedposts with girls.

Because *Boris* forced him to see a prostitute on his fourteen birthday. Because he's a fucking psychopath.

I grit my teeth, pushing that fury away for another day.

"Right. King training. Always important."

"Eh, it's alright. I think I prefer it when you're training me."

I chuckle. "You prefer it because my lessons are in hand-to-hand combat and shooting things."

"Well, *yeah*, no shit. Which is why I miss it when you're not the one training me."

I grin. "Me too, Misha."

"Oh, shit, I don't think I told you yet. That house that Ilya's uncle hooked us up with on campus?"

I shake my head, smiling. As if it wasn't already going to disrupt the fuck out of the old-money, old-guard establishment of OHA to have three conniving little heirs of Bratva Kings and Oligarchs prowling the halls. Ilya's uncle and guardian, Yuri Volkov, head of the Volkov Bratva, worked out some sort of backroom deal to let Misha, Ilya, and Lukas live in what was formerly the school president's mansion, rather than the regular student housing.

Which sort of feels like handing a bazooka to a toddler. But, what the fuck do I know.

"I heard it's pretty nice."

"Dude, it's *sick*. The parties are going to be out of fucking control, Kris."

"Misha—"

"You'll have to come visit! We can throw a real banger!"

I roll my eyes, smiling.

"Yes, drinking games with high school first years. That's definitely on my to-do list."

"Buzzkill."

"Someone has to be the adult."

"Not it."

I grin. It's a miracle that Misha's turned out how he has, given his failure of a father and the horrors of his beginnings in this world. Someday, I'll have to reckon for the ways I buried those violent beginnings of his at Boris's orders.

Some day.

"Hey, my dad's here, by the way. You want to talk to him?"

Not at all.

"And here I thought you were in charge now."

He chuckles.

"One day, Kristoff."

I smile.

"Hey, Kris, play your cards right and maybe I'll keep you on when I am."

I laugh loudly.

"Punk."

"Catch you later, Kristoff."

"Hey, Misha."

"Yeah?"

"Keep your fucking pants on, yeah?"

"Dude, no promises. Later."

I smile to myself as the phone goes silent. The smile fades when Boris's raspy, cigar and vodka-soaked voice grunts into my ear.

"I hear a rumor, Kristoff," he rasps.

I prepare myself for some snippet of outdated intel on some rival company, or something about one of the Bratva families he fancies himself as "bad" as.

"Oh yeah, boss?"

"*Da*. The you were working for some old friends."

My eyes narrow, and I stiffen.

Shit.

"Whatever you've heard, it's only rumors—"

"Kristoff, do not insult me. I know you've been working for Mikhail."

Mikhail who Boris knows socially. Boris is fully aware that Mikhail runs his training academy. He's just too thick to see the connection of my having done work for the Syndicate before magically working my way into *his* organization.

But that was always part of Mik's plan. I gain confidence from the inside. He becomes friends with Boris on the outside, off-putting any suspicions Boris might have had.

I sigh.

"Boris, any work I did or did not do was a favor. Nothing more."

He grunts. "I'm not looking for a cut of your blood money, Kristoff. But I hear another rumor."

I'm silent.

"I hear that Mikhail and that bitch of his have been making a play for the Balagula Bratva, now that Peter Fairist is dead."

My jaw sets.

"They tried to kill the Fairist girl, you know."

My teeth grind.

"I heard the same rumors. But I believe they *did* kill her, Boris."

"*Nyet*. Not what I hear. The rumors I hear are that they failed to remove her from succession."

Something digs at my senses, scratching at my mind. I don't like that this is a rumor at all.

"She's dead, Boris," I mutter flatly. "I believe Jana is already being made head of the Balagula."

It's never been spelled out to me, but Jana is careless and easy to read. I know the plan was that with Peter dead, killing Tatiana would make *Jana* the new crown of the family—what with her having married in, and with no heir alive to claim it.

Once she was seated on the throne, she'd bring in Mikhail somehow—pretend to marry him or something, probably. Once they were both "inside," I'm sure the plan was to cleanse the council of anyone but loyalists. Which is what I would do, at least. And then finally, Mik would have his fucking Bratva, like he's been gunning for for decades.

"No no, Kristoff. I have sources close to the council that has been running the Balagula. There are dissenting voices that think she is not—"

"The girl is *dead*, Boris."

Shit.

The words bark out *far* too fast. Too quickly. Too obviously. I've let my walls down, and even an imbecile like Boris can see it. He pauses for a few seconds, but I know the damage is done.

"By your hand" he prods quietly.

"No. Of course not."

"Then I think maybe these rumors might be true. In which case, she holds the keys to the kingdom, Kristoff. You know the ways of the Balagula. She's the female heir, which means she needs to marry to ascend the throne."

My eyes narrow.

"Think of it, Kristoff. A man could find her, tame her, marry her, and be very *very* powerful and rich."

"Boris, I'm sure she's already dead—"

"*Find her,*" he snaps suddenly, making me frown. "For me, Kristoff."

My eyes narrow to slits, seeing red.

Boris chuckles, oblivious to the fury he's set off in me.

"I mean Christ, even without the assets, I would do *unspeakable* things to that girl—"

I almost break the phone in my bare hand I grip it so hard. But I take a breath, calming myself. I control myself, because I always do.

"Kristoff."

I swallow thickly, glaring at the lake.

"Yes, boss."

"If she's alive, I want her."

"I'm confident they're just rumors, Boris."

He's silent for a moment.

"Don't forget where your loyalties lie, Kristoff."

My eyes narrow.

"I never have."

"Good. Keep it that way."

We hang up, and I grind my teeth as I glare at the still water.

Shit.

16

I JOLT when I feel a presence in the doorway to the library.

At this point, though he's never explicitly said it, it seems I'm allowed to go where I please in the house. The door to what I'm fairly sure is his office is locked. As is the whole third floor, where I imagine his bedroom is.

But beyond that, we're both quite clear that the door to my bedroom prison isn't ever locked. Which means the room really isn't a prison at all anymore.

And yet, still, when he looms in the doorway of the huge, light-filled library, I startle as if I've been caught doing something wrong.

I blush.

It wasn't *wrong*, but… I also wasn't only reading in here. I was glancing out the window towards the shore of the lake, where he was just sprawled in a chair talking on the phone. The first part of it, he was smiling. He looked happy, even, and not the cold, calculating man I've been living with.

Then, that part of him came back, as if flipping a switch halfway through the phone call.

My brows knit as I look up at him in the doorway.

"What—"

My words choke when he reaches behind his back and suddenly pulls it back out.

Holding a gun.

My face pales before I realize he's holding it by the barrel.

"Come with me."

I stiffen, swallowing as I arch a brow dubiously.

"And where am I going?"

"With me."

He leaves the room. I chew on my lip for a second before I put the book down, stand, and follow his footsteps through the gorgeous house to the side door. Outside I catch up to him, hiding a smile when he glances to his right to find me suddenly in step with him.

We head into the woods, following a small trail until we get to a clearing I've only caught glimpses of.

While being chased.

Heat floods my core.

We come to a stop next to a pile of corded wood a chopping block marred with ax marks. Across the medium sized clearing sits a wall of stacked wood, and hanging from it, facing us, are targets. Kristoff turns to me, and I shiver when he holds up the gun again.

"You need to know how to use this."

I frown.

"Why?"

"Because the world is a dangerous place."

My lips twist into a half sneer. "Well, aren't I just a captive here forever? Just playing these sick games with you?"

He smiles thinly.

"Ahh yes. Those sick games that make you wet enough to drip down your pretty thighs."

Desire stabs into me as my face burns hotly.

"Do you mean those games, *printsessa*?"

I simmer under his smirk, blushing.

"The woman who was here that you saw that night. Next time…"

He raises his hand, and my eyes widen when I realize he's handing me the gun, stock first. I hesitate, but he nods. And slowly, I reach out and wrap my finger around the heavy metal.

I know I've shot before. Or, I think I have, when I was a kid and my grandfather Casmir would let me come hunting with him. But that was ages ago.

I take the gun from him, lifting and hefting the weight as his hand drops away. And then suddenly, it's like we're both aware of the power shift.

I'm the one holding a gun.

If I wanted to, *this* would be and could be my exit. My escape. I could keep him at bay while I got the boat from the boathouse and crossed the lake.

I could shoot him.

The seconds tick by, the air around us as still and heavy as the gun in my hand.

Kristoff clears his throat, eying me.

"The target is there."

I shiver, the spell breaking. I turn, shaking the remnants of it away as I face the targets across the clearing.

"Hold it in both—like that."

My second hand has come up to help heft the weight, steadying the gun.

"You want your arms firm, but not locked. There isn't a lot, but this *will* have recoil, and you need to be ready for it. Now, stand… exactly."

My feet shift into a widened, uneven stance just before he tells me to.

"Good," he growls quietly. "Very good. You've shot before?"

I shake my head.

"Not really. Just a few times with my grandfather when I was a kid."

He nods slowly, his eyes tracing my stance.

"Look through the target. Past it. Center the sights on where you want to shoot. Like this."

I shiver with heat as he moves behind me, pressing his body to mine. His hands skims down my arms, clicking the safety off and hefting the gun along with me; bringing it in line with my eyes.

God, do I like how he smells. How he feels.

When he pulls away, I scowl at the absence that comes with it.

"Now, we'll try a few shots."

He slips a pair of heavy noise-cancelation headphones onto my head. I breathe out, looking through the sights, past the target.

"Don't worry about accuracy. I just want you to be able to point at something and do some damage if you need—"

I squeeze. The gun explodes in my hand; once, twice, and then a third time in close succession.

The woods are suddenly silent after the thunder of sound. I lower the gun, my thumb absently clicking the safety on before I blink, as if suddenly aware of what I've just done. I whirl to see Kristoff a few feet away, his brow furrowed and his hands over his ears.

I wince as I pull the headgear off.

"*Shit*, sorry, I didn't mean to—"

I frown. He's not looking at me. He's looking past me. My brow furrows as I turn to follow his gaze and then stiffen.

For a second, I assume I've obviously missed the target entirely, sending bullets hailing into the trees behind it. Until I focus, eyes narrowing and my heart skipping.

What. The. Fuck.

The entire yellow center of the target is blown out. The tiny, maybe two-inch-wide bullseye is completely missing.

My mouth falls open as my brows shoot up.

"Holy *shit*!" I squeal, whirling to him with a huge grin. "That was awesome!"

Kristoff stares at me, brow furrowed.

"Are you fucking with me?"

I frown. "What? No?"

"Do that again, here."

He pulls me by the elbow over two feet, so that I'm now facing the target hung on the pile of wood next to the first one. I wait, then glance back as if ready for him to position me again. He just shakes his head.

"You do it."

I shrug. Okay, guess we're learning today as a lightning round. I square up, slip on the headgear, shift my feet, raise the gun, and click the safety off. I look down the gun, past the target. And I squeeze, just once.

The shot thunders through the forest, echoing and sending birds scattering again. This time, when I safety the gun and pull the headgear off, my jaw is dropped again.

There's a hole right through the yellow.

"Where did you learn to shoot like that?"

I turn, staring at him, perplexed.

"I… didn't?"

"Yes, you did."

I frown.

"No, I didn't. I think I'd remember that. Beginners' luck?"

He reaches out and plucks the gun from my hand.

"There's beginners' luck, and then there's defying a billion to one probability. One bullseye would be luck. Four is improbable."

"Yeah, well…" I gesture towards the targets and shrug again. "I don't really know what to tell you."

"How about the truth."

I scowl at him.

"That *is* the truth. I've shot a gun like four times before."

"So you're a prodigy. That's it?"

I roll my eyes and then glare at him.

"Okay, screw you."

"Tell me."

"I *don't fucking know*, okay?! But if you're all bent out of shape because you wanted to impress me or something, and it turns out I'm a better shot than—"

I scream, flinching and covering my ears as he raises the gun to his side, staring right at me as he blasts off three shots.

All three targets drop to the ground.

He's just shot the tiny wires holding them up to the wood pile.

Without looking.

I shiver, staring at him. And he stares right back as he removes the clip, slams in another one, cocks the gun, and hands it to me.

"Again."

17

Thirteen years ago; age twenty-two:

"Can't believe you're missing fight night, mate."

I grin. "Aww, now look on the bright side, Prince. You might actually have a shot this week without me there."

Oliver chuckles.

"My master plan is always to have you face Ransom first so you can take him down a peg."

"I'm not sure I have any interest in fighting your battles."

He laughs. I grin.

It's a decently smart move on his part. Besides the fact that Oliver Prince and Noel Ransom seem to perpetually have it out for each other in a very "frenemies" kind of way—over grades, girls, cars, or literally anything you can fight over—Noel's father was the late and great *Colin* Ransom, champion UK boxer.

In their perpetual fighting, there are ways Oliver can take down Noel.

Boxing is not one of them.

"Sorry to miss it, though," I sigh, my mind flickering to the regular Friday nights the eight of us have, and the traditions that entails.

"Just had to deal with a work thing."

Oliver goes silent. It's his way of disproving of my line of work: as in, doing dirty jobs for Boris Tsavakov, the Bratva-connected oligarch I've been working for the last couple of years. But if Oliver disproves of *that*, I can only imagine if he knew the real me.

The killer.

The nightmare.

The *bukavac*.

But he lets it go. That's a bit of the beauty of the eight of us somehow becoming friends. Though we come from varied walks of life, somehow—even Noel and Oliver—we're all friends.

The truth is, the lynchpin of the whole thing is our friend Thomas. He's the one that seemed to pull us all together our first year at Lords College of Business, even if by any standards, the eight of us mostly have no business being friends.

There're men like Oliver, who come from upper society, privilege, and wealth. Thomas is of that world, too, and Braddock McCreed. So is Lars Ulstäd, coming from royalty. But from there, things become grayer.

There's Noel, who grew up blue collar, and yet also part of the same world as Thomas. His father, Colin, was the Ashford family personal trainer, which meant Noel grew up in that world alongside Thomas, almost like a brother. In fact, it's Thomas's father Geoffrey Ashford's generosity and love for Noel that got him into the prestigious—and expensive—Lords College.

Then things go from gray to black when we get to men like *me*. My friends don't even know the half of my background. But they do know that I'm here at Lord's College bankrolled by Boris Tsavakov, who decided it would behoof him to have a top captain with a Masters from one of the best business schools in the world.

Along with me in the shadows, there's men like Adrian Cross, the newly crowned head of the Cross Family mafia. And of course, Maddox Rook, who is a dark, shadowy mystery to basically all of us.

And yet, we're all friends. And on Friday nights, we get together for dinner and a few pints before heading into a secret back room of our favorite pub to have fight night—which is basically us pairing up and boxing until a single winner remains.

It's Noel almost eighty percent of the time. But truth be told, it'd be more like fifty percent of the time if I wasn't holding back.

Thomas has always liked to say that in all of us, each of us, there is both king and villain. Hence, our name: the Kings and Villains.

It's not a club. There're no fucking membership cards or any shit like that. It's just a collective of men who will one day rule the world, either from boardrooms or the shadows.

"Well," Oliver clears his throat. "You'll be missed."

"Maybe you can trip Ransom coming down the stairs and clear him from the docket for the night. Then you won't miss me as much."

He chuckles. "Stay safe, mate."

"You too. Mind that famous Ransom right hook."

I hang up smiling. This friendship and camaraderie isn't something I expected much in life. It was there a bit when I was a punk kid playing bad rock-n-roll with Jackson Havoc —the same Jackson whose new band, Velvet Guillotine, just went fucking *platinum* in both the US and UK.

But it's been gone for years. There was no camaraderie in Mikhail's nightmare academy. You didn't make friends there. You made rivals. You fought to the death, literally, to rise to the top.

And you don't make many lasting friendships being the most feared killer for hire on earth.

I slip my phone back into my pocket, and then look up at dark, dismal gray tenement building. My smile fades.

It's not good to be home.

This isn't me "taking my mask off." I'm merely switching to a different one—removing the façade I put up around my Kings and Villains friends and donning the other one I wear.

Both to hide the demon beneath.

Frowning, I head into the foyer of the building through a doorframe that I believe once used to have a glass door in it.

In *this* neighborhood.

THE HUNTER KING

Past graffiti-marred walls, I skip the long-dead elevator and take the stairs up to the fourth floor. At the door to my mother's apartment, I take a final sigh and then knock.

"Kristoff!"

The scowl instantly evaporates at the sound of my six-year-old sister's voice. I grin as the locks draw back, and then suddenly, the door is flinging open, and there she is.

"Hey, Nik-nack."

She giggles, lunging into my arms and hugging me tightly.

"You're here! Mum said you weren't coming until tomorrow!"

I wink, giving her a kiss on the cheek.

"Well, surprise!"

She grins, jumping around from foot to foot as she pulls me through the doorway into the apartment. I shut the door, locking all four locks and making a note to myself to see about hiring someone to keep watch over them. This neighborhood was always rough, but it's looking vicious these days.

"Mum! Kris is here!"

My mother turns from the smell of onions over the stove to smile at me. It's a nice enough smile, though it's nothing like the welcome I've just gotten from Nikita. I cross the kitchen and give her a light hug before she pulls away brusquely, going back to her onions.

We've never been that close.

I used to wonder if it was because she saw my father in me. I'd wonder if she'd look in my eyes and see the same blues that used to make her bleed and cry. Or else, maybe I was just that constant reminder of the choices she'd been forced to make in life.

We were never rich by any stretch of the imagination in Russia. But when she was forced to run with me, seeking a work visa to the UK where she had some distance cousins, we left it all. And here, she was *this*: a cleaning lady living in a slum, cooking onions over a dinged-up stove.

Maybe I used to be mad that when she'd look at me, she'd get that anger and fear in her eyes, because of who and what I represented to her. But then, I grew up.

I grew colder, and more walled off.

Then, I just let it go.

Nikita is something else, though. Even though she's Mik's daughter, with *my* mother. Even though Mik is long gone and my mother refuses to sign any divorce papers.

She's the most loving thing I know. And she's my family.

When she looks at me, she sees Kris, her fourteen-years-older big brother, who lives in glamorous London and attends a ritzy business school.

She doesn't see a monster.

A killer.

A trained gun.

The *bukavac* that lives under her bed when a nightmare grips her.

Just Kris.

THE HUNTER KING

"What'd you bring me!"

"*Nikita!*" My mother scolds, shaking a cooking spoon at my half-sister.

I just grin.

"I brought something for each of you."

My mother's eyes harden a little when they swivel to watch me pull a thick envelope out of my jacket pocket.

Giving my mother money has become an exact science for me. I'd give her a million pounds, and move them out of this shit hole *tonight*. But her pride won't let her do that. The same pride that won't allow her to sign the divorce Mikhail has been hounding her for for six years.

But on the other hand, she's a survivor. She'll take the money, so long as it doesn't cross an imaginary "pride" line of hers—and that line fluctuates like a tide. So it means me guessing, and trying to get as close to that absolute top figure as I can get without going over, or she'll refuse the envelope.

Today, I've guessed twenty-two thousand pounds; cash.

She eyes the envelope as I hand it to her. There's a beat—her customary show of weighing it out. But then, she takes it, hefting it slightly before opening it up. Her thumb flicks over the ends of the bundles of fifty-pound notes, and her brow cocks.

She folds the top of the envelope back down and slips it into her apron pocket.

I resist the urge to visibly take that win.

"And for *you*, my Nik-nack..."

JAGGER COLE

I whirl and pull a little jewelry case out of my other inner jacket pocket. Nikita's eyes light up. My mother's narrow skeptically.

"If it's flashy, you know she cannot wear it outside. It'll draw—"

"It's not flashy, mom."

I turn to my sister and extend my hand holding the box.

"But it is special."

I watch, smiling, as she tears it open and gasps at the little ring with the puzzle piece adorning it.

"*Wow!* Mum, look!"

My mother seems to nod an approval of its lack of flashiness.

"It's very nice, *rypka*."

I nod, turning back to drink in the happiness on my sister's face as she slips the ring on.

"Kris, I love it!"

"*Good*," I beam as she hugs me fiercely.

"*Rypka*, why don't you go watch TV for a minute. I need to speak with your brother."

Nikita gives me another big hug, grinning from ear-to-ear before she runs off into the living room.

"Mom, it's not—"

"It's very nice, Kristoff," my mother smiles a weak but genuine smile. "Maybe she can wear it on chain, *da*? Under her shirt."

I nod, turning and opening the fridge but not finding much.

"There is vodka in the freezer."

I nod, reaching in and pulling out the chilled, cheap bottle.

"Am I pouring one or two?"

She shakes her head. "Not for me."

I pour a splash into a glass, sipping slowly and grimacing as she cooks.

"You guys are doing okay?"

She nods silently.

"You know it's no trouble for me. Say the goddamn word, and I'll—"

"*Bogokhul'stvo*, Kristoff!"

Blasphemy.

I sigh.

"Say the word, and I'll move you both wherever you want."

"We are fine here."

"The hell you are. The neighborhood is looking rough out there."

"We're fine, Kristoff."

"*Mom*, I'm telling you, point to a place on the map, and it'll happen. Tonight. You can live *anywhere*. You wouldn't have to work, Nikita wouldn't have to stay inside when it gets dark—"

"Mikhail wants her to go to the academy."

The words hit me like a slap. I blink, short-circuiting at so many parts of it—that she's talking to that shit-bag, for one. But the biggest part rears its head like a dragon.

"*What*," I snarl.

"Mikhail—"

"Like fucking hell she is," I snap.

She whirls, glaring at me.

"Her father thinks it will be—"

"Her *father* is a sociopathic, manipulative, evil piece of—"

This time, what feels like a slap is *actually* a slap. I stand there stunned, my face stinging from my mother's palm. She glares at me furiously.

"You will *not* speak of your father—"

"Oh *fuck off*, Yulia."

She looks horrified at my swearing, but she grits her teeth.

"Mikhail is *not* my fucking father," I spit.

"Well he's Nikita's! And he's my husband—"

"Whose been pounding down your door for a fucking divorce for six years! He's gone, mom! Mik is fucking *gone*."

The kitchen goes silent. The sound of the My Little Pony theme song drifts in from the living room as mom and I glare at each other.

And then finally, she huffs loudly. She shakes her head and then grabs the vodka out of my hand.

"Give to me."

She takes a heavy sip, exhaling before looking up at me again.

"He wants her to go."

"That isn't happening."

"It's not your decision—"

"That lunacy of Mikhail's isn't a school," I growl. "It's cruel and it's brutal, and—"

"I know what that school is," she says quietly, coldly. "But look where it took you."

I shake my head.

"It's cruel, brutal, and merciless, and that's for the *boys* who are recruited. The girls—"

My jaw grinds, vivid fury surging inside of me as I replay things I wish I couldn't. Things I saw and heard in Mikhail's nightmare academy.

Like the Swan program; where young girls were trained to be both killers and seductresses.

My hand grips the countertop so hard it almost breaks.

"She is *not* going to that place."

"Kristoff, it is not your—"

"Nikita!" I roar, whirling towards the hallway to the living room.

"It's not what you think!" My mother screams, jumping in front of me, shaking her head.

"You think I don't know what happens at that place? You think I would send my daughter to *that*?" She chokes.

I grind my jaw.

"She will not be doing what I know you're thinking. Mikhail says—"

"Mikhail speaks purely in lies."

"She's his *daughter*, Kristoff," she snaps. "I know you don't like him very much—"

"That's one way of putting—"

"But you cannot think he would put his daughter into a program like that."

I glare at her.

"She will be schooled, and yes, taught some of the things you were taught," mom sighs. "But after a few years, Mikhail wants to put her into an accelerated learning program and fast track her to university. Maybe even Lord's College, he says."

I look away.

"*Please*, Kristoff."

Her hand touches my cheek again—softly this time.

"*Please*. Listen to what I'm saying, and trust me, *da?*"

"Kris?"

I blink, turning to see Nikita standing in the doorway to the kitchen, twirling her new ring around her finger.

"Is everything okay?"

I smile broadly, squatting down to hug her tightly.

"Everything is fine, Nik-nack. We're all fine."

"*Da*," my mother says, clasping her hand and putting on a smile. "We eat now, yes?"

It's all going to be fine.

Except it isn't. Because a year later, my mother is dead, and Mikhail and the Ghost Syndicate swallows my little sister *whole*.

18

TATIANA

A HYDRAULIC WHOOSHING sound clunks from the machine without warning. And then suddenly, a skeet disc soars into the sky over the lake.

But I'm ready this time.

Standing on the edge of the dock by the boathouse, I swivel, training my eyes and the barrel of the rifle across the sky.

Shoot.

My finger pulls back on the trigger, and the gun recoils against my shoulder. The clay skeet shatters to dust and bits that scatter to the wind and the lake.

I'm about to smugly glance back at him, when I hear the machine clunk again… and then a second time right after.

Shit.

I suck in a breath, whirling again to follow the first disc I track. My finger pulls, it vaporizes, but I'm already swinging around to track the second. It's going, going…

about to drop away and get lost in the gray tones of the water.

The trigger pulls.

Disc number two shatters to dust across the still surface of the lake.

This time, I do allow myself that smug grin.

"That was impressive."

I'm still grinning as I turn to see him leaning against one of the dock pylons next to the clay skeet machine. He's in jeans and a t-shirt, his tattoo ink rippling on his arms crossed over his chest.

"Yeah?"

He nods.

"Well, stick around, and maybe I'll teach you some moves."

Kristoff smirks.

"Don't get cocky."

But it's hard not to. In the week of shooting practice since that first time in the clearing, I'm getting good. Really, really good, actually. Spookily so.

I'm getting better at a lot of things, actually. At running from him. At dodging when he surprises me out of the trees. At switching things up to keep it interesting when I "escape" from the house.

At kissing him.

At coming for him.

At making *him* come.

My face burns hotly as I turn away to safety the rifle. I still don't quite know or understand what it is about these games, or this entire new reality of mine, that makes my heart pump and my skin tingle.

But I'm willing to keep going, to find out.

The afternoon is fading into evening. Kristoff takes the rifle, slips it into a carrying case, and shoulders it. He lifts the bag of extra discs as we turn and walk down the dock back towards shore.

Halfway up from the shore to the house, the bag slips in his hands, and three of the clay discs tumble out.

"I've got it."

I scoot over, bending low to scoop them up. When I stand, I shiver, my face heating when I realize he's staring right at me.

At my chest.

I swallow, glancing down to see that my ring necklace has fallen out of my shirt. Early on when I first came here, I took it off and put in one of the bedside table drawers in my room. I was worried about losing it when he chased me, or getting it caught in a branch and strangling myself. But recently, I've been wearing it again, under my shirt.

It's not that I'm "missing my old life" or anything like that. But with my wardrobe basically consisting of his hand-me-downs, with no makeup and essentially an elastic or two for my hair, I felt like "dressing up," even if it was just a little bit with the necklace.

The same one Kristoff is currently staring at, with hardened eyes, the same way he did the day he took me.

I swallow, chewing on my lip.

"What?"

His icy eyes drag up to mine.

"Where did you get that ring?

"Why?"

"Because it looks like one someone I once knew wore."

My brows knit.

"I'm sorry, are you accusing me of stealing it?"

He smiles wryly, taking the clay discs from my hand.

"No, I'm merely curious."

I purse my lips.

"I got it when I was sixteen, right after an accident I had at summer camp."

His eyes sink into me, piercing me curiously, making me shiver a little.

"Interesting," he muses. "Summer camp."

"Uh, yeah?"

"What kind of summer camp?"

I frown. "I… don't know? Regular summer camp? I don't really remember it much because of the accident."

"What was the accident?"

The cold feeling that always creeps up my spine whenever I try and replay that day comes tingling back. I shrug.

"I don't really remember it. But I've been told it was a boating thing. I fell into the water and got held under by something, and I almost drowned."

He nods slowly, slipping the gun carrier off his shoulder and setting it and the bag of discs on the ground before he turns back to me.

"That the same summer camp where you learned to shoot and break a choke hold?"

My brow furrows.

"Wha—"

Without warning, he suddenly surges right into me, his fist flying viciously towards my face.

It happens on autopilot. I dodge left, twisting and grabbing his wrist and yanking, pulling him through his own punch as my thigh juts out to trip him. Kristoff grunts, taking the hit but then rolling into it. He tumbles onto the ground before popping back up and whirling on me.

"What the *fuck*!?" I scream, backing away from him. My face pales, and my nerves scream in fear at the sudden burst of violence.

But he doesn't advance on me. He just looks at me curiously, folding his arms over his chest.

"Are you fucking *deranged*?!"

He fucking smirks.

"And they taught you jiu-jitsu at rich girl summer camp?"

I scowl at him.

"*No?*"

His smirk fades.

"Then how the fuck do you know how to fight."

I glare back at him.

"I wasn't *fighting*. You tried to hit me, and I didn't want to get hit."

"And that move just... *came* to you."

I swallow, shaking my head. "I... I don't know."

"Do it again."

"What? No, I'm not—"

I shriek as he lunges at me, fists up. This time, I fling a forearm forward, blocking his down-swing before my leg kicks out like I'm the karate kid or something. He blocks that, but I'm already lunging forward, knees and elbows flying as I crash into him.

We both topple to the ground; me on top, his brow cocked curiously. I gasp when he shifts his weight, flipping us and suddenly pinning me to the ground with his body as I squirm and flail. My legs lock around him, my body screaming with the mix of adrenaline, fear, confusion, and forbidden heat at the way we're grinding together.

Kristoff smirks and loosens his hold on me. He starts to get off of me, when I suddenly counter. My knee slams into his mid-section, making him grunt as I shove him away, lunge back into a backwards somersault, and spring up to my feet.

The air is still as we eye each other, a few paces apart; that same swirling, fiery mix of aggression and lust igniting inside of me.

"Again."

This time, we rush at each other at the same time. I bend sharply to the side, dodging a serious punch before my knee slams into his solar plexus. He hisses in pain, but my win is shattered when his forearm slams into me, knocking me backwards. I whirl, dodging his next hit before throwing my fist forward with a fury and precision that scares the shit out of me.

It connects, and Kristoff grunts as he whirls away, backing off. I dance back from him, panting, feeling my pulse roar in my ears and the sweat sheening across my back.

He glances at me, and I gasp sharply when I see the blood trickling from the corner of his mouth. I tremble, fear surging in me.

"Oh my God, I'm so sorry," I choke breathlessly. "I didn't mean to—"

"Yes, you did."

He reaches down, and I blush as he peels his t-shirt off, revealing his ridiculously chiseled, sharp, gorgeous body—all muscles, grooves, and tattoo ink. I swallow thickly as he tosses it aside and looks back into my eyes. He shifts his feet into a sort of fighter's stance and raises his fists like we're in a kung-fu movie.

"Wait, what—"

"*Again.*"

He comes at me, and this time, it's like another version of me takes over. I dodge, blocking his first attack with one of my own. My forearm knocks one of his punches aside, but then I'm gasping as his leg sweeps mine out from under me.

I sprawl to the grass, the neck of my shirt catching on his grappling hand or something and ripping loudly as I fall. He lunges, but I roll out of the way at the last second and pop up to my feet with a dexterity that surprises me.

I glance down, blushing when I realize my t-shirt is half torn off—ripped clean down the front between my breast almost to my navel. But there's no time to give a shit about that.

He comes at me again, and we slam together, grappling before my legs sweep his. We crash to the ground, panting, bodies writhing against each other as we scuffle.

And grind.

And tangle in each other.

Until suddenly, we both stop moving. We're panting, his mouth inches away from mine as he pins me to the grass. I hiss, arching my body as if to throw him off, but he doesn't budge. He just presses into me harder, igniting a flame inside of me as his hips grind to mine.

My thighs spread and lock around his muscled waist. I flail with my hands, but he grits his teeth and slams them back down, pinning my wrists to either side as he looms above me.

My pulse thunders in my ears. My whole body is quivering, shaking, and tingling with heat, lust, and energy. And I quiver when his eyes lock with mine, cutting into me.

And then suddenly, he's kissing me.

It's a punishing, brutal kiss. A kiss that sears into my soul and bruises my lips. A kiss that engulfs me in a fire storm that threatens to drown me in flame.

He keeps me pinned hard to the ground as his lips demand mine open. His tongue plunges in, captivating mine as I writhe against him and whimper into his lips. The heat of his bare skin and rippling muscles sears against mine with the shirt ripped to the sides. And I can feel my nipples aching and hard as they drag electrically against his chest.

He pulls away, and we both freeze. Both of us throbbing with heat and need. Both of us pinned tight together. Both of us aware that we're at a crossroads at this very moment.

He's made me come dozens of times, and vice versa. But it hasn't gone past that. In all of our depraved chases, and all of our twisted, fucked up games where he catches me and pins me to the ground to take what we both want him to take, he hasn't fucked me.

No one has.

I tremble as I feel the throbbing, thick, huge bulge of his cock straining at his jeans; pulsing against my core through my loose shorts. And then suddenly, he's crushing his mouth to mine again, and it feels like the walls have finally crumbled.

The crossroads have been swept aside.

There's no going back.

I gasp, choking on my moans as his mouth drags down my chin and my jaw. His lips and teeth feast on my neck, making me cry out as he bites, leaving marks as he drags lower. His big hands keep mine pinned to the sides as he brings the wet heat of his mouth lower, down over my breast. He groans as he takes a nipple into his mouth, biting enough to make me squeal as my back arches eagerly.

Then he moves lower: unstopping. Unyielding. Unshaken from his hunt to have me.

His fingers slip into my shorts and yank them down my legs. I tremble, whimpering as he shoves them off of my feet and then grabs the backs of my thighs. Heat flushes my face as he shoves my knees back, spreading me lewdly open for his fierce, hungry gaze before he suddenly dives between my thighs.

Oh my fucking God...

His mouth is heaven on my slit. He groans into me, plunging his tongue deep between my lips as I squeal in pleasure. My hands, now free, drop to tangle in his hair—clinging to him desperately as he tongues my pussy.

He drags the tip up to my clit, sucking the aching bud between his lips as his tongue swirls over it. I cry out, my back arching and my body shuddering as he rips the pleasure from me. He reaches up, making me gasp as he grabs the tattered remains of my shirt and rips it away. It falls away from my body as his hand roams higher to cup and squeeze my tits.

Two of his fingers plunge into me, making me moan and writhe as they curl against that spot inside. His mouth hums on my clit—sucking, licking, teasing—as he strokes his finger in and out.

My mouth falls open, my eyes rolling back as my back arches off the grass. And suddenly, I'm exploding against his tongue.

Instantly, he's surging up my body between my legs.

His jeans are already gone. His bare skin slides against mine, and I choke on a whimper when I feel the underside of his bare, thick, rock-hard cock grind against my slick pussy. His mouth sears to mine, capturing it as his tongue duels with mine.

And I let go of whatever has ever held me back.

My legs wrap around his grooved, muscled hips. I feel his swollen cock-head slip over my electrified clit to push between my lips.

And then suddenly, he's ramming inside of me.

Every nerve in my body explodes. Every inch of my skin shivers and throbs. There's a wince of pain as his enormous size plunges into me, and I cry out as my nails dig into his back. I bury my face against his shoulder, biting down hard enough to make him grunt as his thick cock flexes inside of me.

"Is this what you've been waiting for, *printsessa*," he snarls darkly into my ear.

He draws his hips back, and my brow caves in pleasure as the pinch turns into ecstasy.

"To be chased, and caught, and pinned down. To be *fucked*."

He slams into me, hard. The rush of pain and pleasure intoxicates me, surging inside of me as I moan eagerly. His cock slides out again, only to plunge back in to the thick hilt. His hands slide up my body, toying roughly with my nipples and sending bolts of pleasure rippling through me. His strong fingers slide up higher to wrap around my throat, and my core clenches with need.

For more.

For him to do exactly this—to pin me down, dominate me, and *fuck me*.

He rams into me again, his hand closing tighter around my throat. My nails rake down his back, my heels digging into his ass as he sinks that cock deep inside.

"Beg me to fuck you," he rasps darkly into my ear. *"Beg* for my cock."

"Please…" I whimper.

"You can do better than that."

"Please!" I scream, the sweet agony of ecstasy swirling through me like a drug. "Please fuck me!"

"More."

"Please! Please I want your cock—!"

I squeal as he thrusts into me, grinding against my clit before pulling out, only to do it again. And then again. His teeth clamp down on my earlobe as his free hand pinches my nipple, sparking something dark and twisted inside of me.

Something that devours this mix of pain, pleasure, submission, and power.

His mouth drags to my neck, nipping at the skin where his hand isn't gripping me. His cock rams into me, fucking me hard and deep as my body quivers and ripples around him. I can feel my wetness coating him and dripping down my thighs as his mouth drags up to finally claim my mouth.

I cling to him, lost in all of this and drowning in ecstasy. My back arches from the ground, my hips urging him on as he drives his cock into me over and over. His hand grips my throat, the other slips beneath me to grab my ass possessively, pulling me against him as we grind together.

The world starts to blur, and I start to crash.

"Beg me to let you come," he growls deeply against my ear. "Beg for me to give you what you need."

I cry out as my body begins to writhe and clench.

"Please let me come!" I choke, gasping as he rocks into me. His hand grips my hip, his thumb stretching across to roll over my clit. The grip on my throat tightens, and suddenly, all I know is white heat and blinding light.

I cry out loudly, my entire body spasming and surging off the ground as the orgasm explodes deep in my core. My nails dig deep into his skin, his muscles clenching and rippling against me as he grinds his cock as deep as he can get. He groans, his cock swells even harder, and then suddenly, I can feel it.

I can feel him coming with me.

His cum spills into me as I cling to him, lost and floating through space as the climax teases through every single part of my body. His mouth sears to mine as I hold on tight.

I'm adrift.

And I'm not sure I ever want to be found.

19

Someone is screaming.

I flinch, whirling to try and see. But something stops me. Something pins me, pushing me down, until my hands touch water. I shudder, trying to pull them back, but the force presses down on me, sinking my hands deeper and deeper.

The icy chill of the water needles at my skin, sending tendrils of tremors creeping up to my shoulders. I resist, trying to pull back over and over. But it won't let me.

The weight. The force. Something cold and uncaring; immovable and unflinching.

The water thrashes violently around me, churning into a vortex. I choke on the spray and waves as they rear up to crash over me, suddenly sucking me deeper down, until my face is hovering an inch from the choppy surface.

And then, I go under.

I scream soundlessly, the air expelling from my lungs to ripple in bubbles past my wide, terrified eyes. The fear spills down my throat, filling my lungs.

I don't want this. Please. I don't want this.

But the force doesn't listen. Or doesn't care. The force just pushes me harder, forcing me down. Forcing me under.

My hands touch cold, clammy skin. I scream into the dark cold water as my fingers wrap around a throat vibrating with a haggard, pleading, silent cry for help.

The light fades. The malevolent force demands. The water clears, until suddenly, there are cold, horrified eyes staring back at me.

My eyes, begging me not to drown. Pleading with me to let go.

But I can't. The dark weight won't let me.

My eyes bulge in front of me, my own face twisting and screaming in agony, before suddenly, it stops.

I go still.

The light goes out of my eyes.

And I'm *screaming*.

I CHOKE ON THE GASP, lurching out of the bed and falling onto the floor. I scrabble, swallowing a scream as I blink out of sleep into cold reality.

A tremor rips through me, turning my skin to goosebumps as I hug myself tightly.

I *hate* these dreams.

I used to have them all the time, after the accident—these vivid, horrible visuals of me drowning myself and pushing another me deep into the abyss. A therapist my parents took me to brushed it off as night terrors that could be attributed to my "traumatic experience" and the hypoxic shock I suffered when I almost drowned.

Yeah, no shit.

I've been told a million times what happened: that at this summer camp I went to, I was out on a boat about to push off from a dock, when I slipped and fell into the water. The waves slammed the boat hull against my head, and then against the dock, keeping me pinned under it until someone jumped in to drag me out.

I remember none of that. I don't even remember the summer camp at all. Like literally almost none of it aside from flashed images here and there. Apparently, that can happen—the brain erasing everything surrounding a trauma, especially when that brain itself has been impacted.

But everything I've read on that phenomenon mentions the memory self-erasing a day, or *maybe* a few days.

I have zero memory of *a month* of summer camp. Even the few months before I went are blurry now.

I know I could be worse. I could be dead. But, even as much as I've tried to just move past it and "get over" what happened, it's still tough to ignore. And they're rarer now, but I still get the dreams of me drowning myself.

I suck in a breath, shuddering on the floor of the bedroom in the dark. A sheen of sweat glistens over my skin, my pulse still racing. Inhale, exhale. Inhale, exhale.

Slowly, my pulse slows. My lungs unclench. The dream fades, as it does. But as the nightmare slips away and reality comes back, the *reality* of that reality hits me like a heated flush. I simmer, sucking my lip between my teeth as the replay of earlier this evening floods back into focus.

The fight. The grappling with him. Tumbling to the ground as he pinned me to it, and then the dam breaking.

Kissing him. Begging him. Coming for him.

Aching for him to take me like I've never been before. And then the screaming ecstasy of being filled with him.

My body throbs with heat as it remembers the way he gripped me and took me. The way he thrust hard, fucking me into the ground and oblivion with his hand around my throat.

That was not a "tender first time."

That was being *fucked*.

And I wanted every second of it.

In the darkness, I let that reality seep into my skin. I lost my virginity today to the man who kidnapped me from my home and locked me in a room on an island. A man who chases me through the woods only so that he can catch me, pin me down, and tear my clothes off.

A man who doesn't ask before he makes me come with his fingers or his mouth. A man who roughly takes my mouth with his cock until he spills his cum over my tongue.

A man who roughly fucks me for the first time as I half-fight him. Who pins my wrist to the grass as he buries his cock in me.

But the worst part is, I don't hate every second and every part of all of that.

I fucking crave it. And in the darkness of my room, I start to wonder what the hell that makes me.

Broken. Wired wrong. Perverse.

Depraved.

I breathe deeply, still shaking as I get to my feet and then sit on the edge of the bed. I turn, looking through the windows to the low moon glittering over the lake.

The bedroom door opens with a small creak behind me. I stiffen, whirling and waiting for him to step inside. But he doesn't. The door just stays like that, half open, beckoning. Waiting.

Heat pools in my core, mixing with fear and a twinge of anxiousness. I swallow, rising from the bed and slowly padding barefoot in a pair of sweatpants and a baggy t-shirt to the door.

"Kristoff?"

There's no answer. I shiver as I reach for the door, pushing it open a little further. I poke my head, my eyes trying desperately to adjust to the hallway, which is *much* darker than my room.

"Kristoff?"

Only silence replies.

Shivering, I step out into the pitch-black hallway. My room sits at the corner of a right-angle hallway. In front of me stretches the length of hallway that leads to a couple more guest rooms and the stairs that lead downstairs. A single window at the end of it floods it with dim, gray-white moonlight.

To my right, though, the hall disappears into utter darkness. That way leads to a few more bedrooms, another study room, and the stairs to the locked third floor.

My heart pounds as I tip-toe out into the darkness.

"*Kristoff?*" I whisper in a choked tone.

A creak in the darkness has my heart leaping into my throat as I whirl. My eyes go wide, face white as I desperately try and pierce the pitch blackness down the hall.

"*Kris—*"

"*Run.*"

The voice is something from a nightmare. A rasped, heavy, leaden voice. A growled demand. And the effect it has on me is both horrify and electrifying.

My body shivers, heat pooling between my legs as my nipples stiffen to points against my t-shirt. My skin flushes, capillaries opening with the fight-or-flight anticipation of fleeing.

But I'm frozen. I stand there, desperately trying to suck in a breath of air through my clenched throat as I stare hauntingly into the blackness.

I know I could slip back into my room. I don't have to play this game.

But I want to.

A low, rumbling growl creeps out of the darkness, making my pulse skip.

"Run!"

I fucking run.

Without another second of hesitation, I turn and I bolt down the hall towards the stairs. And I can already hear him pounding behind me.

Adrenaline and primal fear explodes in my senses, deafening me with the thudding of my heartbeat. My skin feels electrified, my muscles screaming as I half-fall down the stairs, hearing him charging after me.

I know he won't hurt me. I *know* it's Kristoff, and not a fucking serial killer, or a stranger whose broken in.

But the fight or flight reaction is real. The body can't just let go of millions of years of evolution.

The scream of danger erupts through me, sending me reeling and crashing through the big, dark house. I race through a living room, running towards a doorway that I know leads to the foyer, but then doubling back and vaulting the couch. Through my peripherals, I get a glimpse of a man in all black, and my core clenches tight as the chemicals in my brain go apeshit.

Holy fuck.

He snarls as he lunges for me. I scream, switching directions and crashing around a corner into the kitchen. My hip slams against the doorframe as I do, making me cry out in pain. But I push forward, hurdling through the darkness away from the man in black hunting me like prey.

I skid through the kitchen, hearing the rough drag of his breath so close behind me. My brain screams, my lungs burning as I surge down a hallway towards the library. From there, I can get to the living room through the second doorway in the library. And from there, I'll get to the front door.

I crash headlong into the library, slamming the door shut behind me to slow him. I bolt for the other doorway—

Until he steps out of it.

The scream rips from my throat, strangling me in real, actual fear and shock as he storms towards me. I stagger back, tripping and choking as I go falling back onto the shaggy faux-fur carpet. I kick away from him as he storms over to me, ripping his shirt off as he advances on me on the floor.

"Please!"

Somehow, I lapse into the fantasy. I let myself sink into the depraved role-play.

Scurrying back from him, I jolt when my shoulder hits the front of the couch. Pinned, I whimper when he storms over to me, reaching down, and grabs a fistful of my hair at the back of my head. My eyes go wide as he yanks his sweatpants down, his thick, swollen cock springing out to bob heavily in the air in front of me.

"Open your fucking mouth."

I *melt*. I mean I turn into pure liquid fire at his crude, vicious words. My lips part, and I moan when his swollen cock head pushes past them, sliding deep into the back of my mouth. He groans, throwing his head back in pleasure. Both of his hands thread into my hair, tangling in my red locks as he pushes his hips forward.

I'm so wet it's literally dripping down my thighs.

My hands drop between my legs, shoving eagerly into my sweats. I whimper around him when I start to rub my clit, shivering in heat.

"Such a dirty little girl," he growls thickly. "My pretty little fuck-toy, playing with your greedy pussy while I fuck this mouth."

My eyes roll back. My body trembles and quivers, my fingers rubbing faster as his cock pounds in and out of my mouth. His precum leaks all over my tongue, my spit dripping from the corners of my mouth down his shaft as he swells so fucking hard.

And then suddenly, he's pulling away. Then he yanks my hands out of my sweats, making me whimper as he chuckles darkly.

"You have to fucking *earn* the right to play with that pussy," he rasps darkly, leaning down as he tugs my head back by the hair.

"Because that pussy belongs to *me*, now."

My brain screams as he suddenly spins me around and pushes me roughly down across the carpet. He grabs my hips, lifting my ass up so that I'm on my knees with my face to the soft fur of the rug. I whimper when he grabs the back of my sweats and rips them down to mid-thigh.

My pulse thuds, my breath panting and ragged as he moves behind me and presses his huge cock to my swollen, slick pussy.

"Now be a good girl and *moan* for me."

He drives in hard, plunging every inch of his cock deep into me. A cry of pleasure wrenches from my mouth against the carpet, my face caving with ecstasy. I'm still sore from earlier today. But even still, I crave this.

I need this.

It's like there's this constant white noise humming in the background, and it only finally disappears when he takes me.

Kristoff's muscled hips pound against my ass as he fucks me hard and deep. All I can do is cling to the carpet, moaning over and over as the pleasure drags me under.

One of his hands stays gripping my hip possessively. The other slides up my spine, shoving my shirt up with it. He slips his hand under me, cupping my breasts and twisting one of my nipples, sending me into fucking orbit. His hand slides away, moving to grab a fistful of my hair as he drives his thickness into my eager pussy.

"Reach back," he growls thickly, grinding himself deep. "I want you to reach back and spread those pretty holes for me."

Holy. Fucking. Shit.

I've never even fantasized about someone talking to me like this. I've never watched rough, Dom-sub porn or anything.

But the way he talks to me in that filthy, depraved, perverse way has my body shuddering and aching to explode. It has me dripping wet around him, struggling to even process how fucking hot it is.

"Fucking *now, printsessa*," he rasps darkly as he brings a palm down hard across my ass.

I yelp, whimpering in pleasure and nodding eagerly without words. I reach back, panting into the rug as I grab my ass and do as he says. I spread myself, the lewdness of it bringing heat to my face and a throb to my core.

"Good girl."

His cock drives in deeper, making my eyes roll back as the aching throb inside of me surges. His hips pound against my ass, his hand pulling my hair. He bends over me, thrusting hard as his other hand wraps around my throat.

Sweet fucking God yes.

The walls cave in. The world erupts. His big, gorgeous cock rams into me hitting every single right place. His thickness fills me to my limit with each thrust, forcing me forward so that my nipples rub over the rug.

It's the sheer power of him. The dominance he holds over me. The submission I willingly, eagerly give.

The way he demands I just let go.

And I do.

I don't realize the sound I'm hearing vibrating in my ears is my own screaming orgasm until it's already pulling me into the depths. My fingers dig into my ass, my face crumpling against the rug as my body convulses and clenches. The orgasm erupts through me, wrenching me and sucking the air from my lungs.

I feel him groan as he pulls out of me. I gasp when I feel the hot spray of his cum splatter across my ass and my pussy, dripping down my lips before he centers his head and pushes in again.

His hand slips from my throat. He grinds himself into me once more before he pulls out again. I'm shuddering on the ground—not because I'm hurt, though I'm sore as shit. But because I can barely breathe or think.

He's just fucked the senses right out of me.

I'm dimly aware of him pulling me up and then into his arms. He lifts me, and I murmur, turning into him as he cradles me in his arms. His mouth descends, kissing me slowly and deeply, letting me breathe out the manic-ness of our depraved roleplay.

He turns, carrying me gently through the dark house, climbing the stairs until we get to my room. He moves directly to the bathroom and sits on the edge of the bathtub with me in his arms.

I stiffen.

"I—I don't do baths—"

"Trust me."

I swallow, clinging to him as the tub fills with hot water and bubbles. And he just holds me.

A possessive and yet soft embrace.

He shuts off the water and then steps in, still cradling me. I flinch at the hot water against my sore, sensitive sex. But slowly, it melts away. Slowly I sink against him, resting my face against his firm chest as his arms and the steamy hot water surround me.

There's no malevolent force. No dark weight. I'm not drowning—at least, not the way I was before.

This time, I'm just drowning in him.

20

"THESE THINGS TAKE *TIME*, KRISTOFF."

My eyes narrow. I've had my chain jerked around before. Private clients in my days as a monster, for instance. Clients who thought, for some bewildering reason, that it would be fine if they simply did not pay the very demon they'd hired to destroy their enemies.

And this smells like bullshit.

"You've had weeks, Jana," I hiss, a dangerous tone slipping into my voice. "You have your proof. Give me my fucking information."

She sighs heavily, flippantly. It's not stupidity that has her ignoring that warning edge to my tone—she's not an idiot. Which means it's hubris, which is equally as dangerous.

"Kristoff, I've told you, I'm working on it. You'll have the location of Nikita's remains soon, I promise."

"Your promises mean fuck-all to me."

My hand clenches the phone tightly.

"Don't make me go over your head and go to Mik on this."

I can hear the sharp intake of her breath. She doesn't need to know I've technically *already* gone over her head. But I like that this seems to be her pressure point.

"Give me two weeks."

"The fuck would you need two—"

"Because *I* don't have it, okay?"

Threatening her with Mikhail has thrown her off her little high horse. In a way, I get it. I used to understand that power he has over people. I may hate him, and he may be a sociopathic sadist. But he knows how to use people. It's been his life's career to use and mold people to his needs and aims, and he's fucking good at it.

Jana's his own niece, for Christ's sake, not to mention his number two. And even she's terrified of his retribution.

"Mikhail?"

She's silent for a moment.

"So help me God, Jana, I *will* go to him—"

"*Please*," she mutters darkly. "Please, just let me handle this, Kristoff. I'll get you what you want, okay?"

"You have two weeks until I'm done playing games."

I hang up with a scowl, glaring out over the slowly setting sun across the water. Slowly, a smile creeps over my face as I watch a solitary figure swim languidly back and forth, parallel to the shore, about ten meters out.

Tatiana.

Who I happen to know is swimming naked.

I'd like to take credit for her going from being averse to baths or swimming to suddenly *loving* the lake. But, who knows.

For about the hundredth time this week, I make a note that it might be a good thing to actually get her some clothes if she's going to be staying here… indefinitely, I suppose.

It's a thought that's immediately followed by a second one—also for the hundredth time this week: why the fuck would I get more things used to cover her up from my eyes?

I simmer in the chair on the shore, gritting my teeth and feeling my pulse hum as I watch her.

I've known addicts. In my youth, where and when I grew up? *Everyone* knew a junkie. Hell, most people had one in their family back then when heroin ravaged the slums of Liverpool.

Through my years, I've seen people do terrible, debased things for their fix. For that hit they crave. For one more drink.

I am officially one of them. And my drug of choice is Tatiana.

The scent of her skin. The way her muscles move, rolling under my fingers. The fiery red of her hair that matches that defiant flame surging in her heart and soul. The greenish-brown of her eyes, flecked with gold.

The way she moans. The way she screams. The way she keeps me on my toes.

The taste of her cunt. Fucking *Christ*, the taste of her. I could live off of it. I could just stay right there between her thighs, running my tongue over her for days, weeks; forever.

This was never part of the plan.

Obviously not the plan involving Jana, Mikhail, and all of their schemes with the Balagula Bratva family. But I also mean not the plan I had for my life. And now, I'm not sure I know what this means.

At a certain point, I'll need to step back into my reality. At a certain point, Boris's need for me working for him will outweigh his under-the-surface fear of telling me to come back to work.

At a certain point, I'll need to step out of the fantasy we've created here.

But that point is not today.

I stand, dropping my phone, and then my shirt, followed by my jeans onto the lawn chair. Then I turn, and I sprint to the shore and stealthily dive into the water.

She doesn't know I'm there until I grab her from behind. Her scream sends a rush through my veins. Her body squirming against mine, and the whimpered gasp when she realizes it's me has my cock rock-hard in seconds.

Her moans as I slip her legs around my waist and drive into her are all I need to hear.

21

Twelve and a half years ago; age twenty-two:

THE MAN SLAMS his head up out of my grip around his neck, and I grunt when it connects hard with my nose. Blinding pain erupts across my face and behind my eyes, and blood pours down over my mouth.

Coppery slickness chokes me, but I shake off the pain and the dizzying confusion of the hit. I whirl, snarling as I slam my forearm hard against his throat as he charges. But the man is a fucking monster—easily seven feet tall and built like two of me.

I hear the gurgle of my arm slamming into his throat, but it barely stops him. He still hits me like a runaway train, driving me back hard. My back slams into the already broken sink, smashing it off the tiled wall and sending a spray of water gushing to the ceiling and across us both.

I snarl, driving my elbow down into the back of his neck and his shoulder-blades again and again, until his grip on me loosens just a little.

There's no hesitation in me.

My knees slam up, smashing into his face and snapping his teeth. He roars, and I wince as one of his massive fists pummels my side. He hits again, and I see stars when I hear the cracking sound of a rib.

This is not how this was supposed to go. And this is *not* how I operate.

The first fuck-up was that I don't do jobs in London. This is my home turf, where I go to school as a respected, if not Oligarch-affiliated, business student at Lords College. Not where I assassinate people as Mikhail's demonic *bukavac*.

This is where I wear suits and tuxedos and attend lavish parties and charity fundraisers attended by the city's top financial tycoons.

Charity fundraisers like the one I'm at right now. Tuxedos like the soaked, torn, and bloodied one I'm currently wearing.

Yet Mikhail insisted. This was "a one-time ask." A "special favor" to a close associate of his. The target, Salvatore Rosso, is a big player in Italy's mafioso Calabrian 'Ndrangheta—a man in charge of sourcing ways to funnel money in an out of the UK.

Hence why he's here rubbing shoulders with greedy hedge fund managers and buyable politicians.

Location aside, though, I also don't do jobs at the drop of a hat. Bad, quick, or sloppy intel is how you die in this line of work. I take my goddamn time. I know every single dark secret a target has before I end them.

Mikhail put me on Sal *two hours* ago.

That's fuck-up number two. Number three was not realizing I was hunting fucking Bigfoot.

I knew he was big, from the quick Google search I did in lieu of *actual* intel on the way here to the Mandarine Oriental Hotel in Hyde Park. I didn't realize how big, big was until I followed him out of the ballroom, down the stairs to the closed lower-level, and into the men's room.

Fuck up number four can be tied to fuck-up number two's lack of intel. That would be shooting him in the back as he stepped up to a urinal to take a piss, not realizing the motherfucker would be wearing goddamn body armor under his tux.

And now, here we are.

I swallow the pain of the rib, summoning my strength and shoving Sal away from me. But he charges back like a bull, knocking the wind out of me as he slams me into cracked bathroom tiles, my back shattering the gilded mirror above where the sink once was.

I shove him back again, and this time, I have the split second to dive out of the way before he crushes into me again. I dive away, lunging for my gun lying on the floor. But Sal's fast. He stomps on my heel, sending pain exploding through me before he grabs my foot and yanks back.

The hulking motherfucker lunges over me, but I catch his foot, tripping him to the ground with me as he goes for the gun. I grab a fist of his trousers, yanking him back, my teeth gritting as I pit my strength against his.

But my grip is slipping, and his fingers are almost touching the suppressor on my gun.

Fuck this.

In one motion, I let go, whirl, and rip the pocket off my bloodstained shirt. I wrap it around my hand as I snatch a jagged piece of broken mirror off the floor. I turn on him in a blur, hurdling into him just as he turns to fire at me.

He goes toppling backwards, crashing into a urinal and smashing it off the wall in another spray of water. The gun slips from his wet fingers, and he whirls, scrabbling across the slippery wet floor for it.

He doesn't make it.

I lunge onto his back, grab a fistful of his hair, and yank his head back. My shirt-wrapped hand holding the ragged piece of glass slices down hard, slitting his throat at the jugular.

He gurgles, bucking like a stuck pig. But he's not going anywhere. Neither am I. I hold him firm, lifting his head and letting him bleed the fuck out until he goes limp.

And so do I.

Mother. Fuck.

I groan, feeling the cracked rib, the bashed nose, the swollen ankle, and every other hit suddenly surging into my consciousness. I hate how fucking sloppy this one was at a core level. Because this is *not* how I operate.

I toss the piece of glass aside and reach for the gun. I check the round as I stand.

The bathroom door opens behind me.

"Oh Christ—"

I spin, jaw tight as I level the gun… at *Oliver fucking Prince's* face.

The air goes still. I stare at him in utter disbelief. He stares back at me in abject horror.

"What the fuck did you do?" My friend croaks in a choked, heavy voice.

His eyes drop to the body sitting in the enormous pool of blood and pink water. His face goes white, and he blinks as his eyes slide back to me.

"Kristoff—"

"Goddamnit, Prince."

My teeth grit, my hand tightening around the gun I've got leveled at his face.

Why is he here? Why the fuck is he here?

"I—there was a line at the men's room upstairs," he breathes hoarsely.

His eyes drop back to the body, then drag back to mine.

"Fucking hell, Zima…"

I close my eyes. My lips thin as my arm twitches. I know the cold, calculating way this gets dealt with. The way I was trained. The way that was drilled into me day and fucking night at the age of four-fucking-teen.

The training that broke something in me and turned me into the devil that other devils fear.

But right there, standing in a puddle of blood with a gun leveled at one of the best friends I've ever had, something clicks in me.

JAGGER COLE

I reject that training.

My hand holding the gun lowers. Even with my eyes closed, I hear Oliver exhale slowly. I tuck the gun into the back of my trousers, under the hem of my jacket. And then slowly, my eyes open. The two of us stare at each other, until finally, Oliver nods and looks away.

"I've got a change of clothes in my car. I'll have my driver pull into the alley out back. There's a service entrance down the hall a bit here."

His tone is cool and even. I know he's still trying to process what the actual fuck he just walked in on. But this is a trait of his that'll make him a god-king of business one day: his ability to accept a reality, recalibrate, and move forward.

In another life, Oliver may have made a hell of a fucking *bukavac*.

"Prince—"

He holds a finger up as his cell goes to his ear. He mutters something, nodding and then hanging up.

"He'll be around back in three minutes."

My jaw sets as I look at him coolly.

"I wish you hadn't seen this. I didn't know you'd—"

"Moorebrook and Westerly always sends someone lower down the totem pole to charity things like this."

The hedge fund he's a senior trader at.

He clears his throat, keeping his cool, but avoiding looking at the man face down in the blood at my feet.

"Tsavakov business?"

The calm, cavalierness to his voice is admiral.

Even though he's wrong, I nod.

"Yes."

Better that than dragging my friend down the rabbit hole of what work I'm *actually* doing. He nods, clearing his throat again before his gaze swivels back to me, his mouth thin.

"You okay?"

I snort, raising a brow as I glance down at the state of myself.

"Peachy."

Oliver's lips curl slightly before he glances at his phone.

"He's here. Come on, let's go."

He holds the door open for me as I stagger out into the hallway, and then frown.

"Shit, I can't yet."

Oliver frowns. "Kris, we need to get you *out* of—"

"I need to find the main server room and delete the security feeds." My lips thin as I glance at him. "There'll be footage of me following him in there, then you coming in, then both of us leaving."

Oliver's eye twitches. But he grinds his jaw and pulls his phone out. He turns away, muttering something into his cell before he turns back as he slides it into his pocket.

"I have someone on it."

I smile wryly, eying my friend in a newer light.

"Thank you, Oliv—"

"Let's do us both a favor, Kris, and never, *ever* speak of any of this again. Yeah?"

"Haven't the slightest idea what you're talking about."

He smirks, a little of the color coming back into his face.

"C'mon. Let's get you to a doctor."

22

"It's all there."

I heft the two enormous black suitcases from Marko's grip, turning to march over to the open trunk of my Range Rover.

"You got it all?"

He snickers.

"Down to the specifics."

"Thank you."

Marko sighs. "Look, brother, you gonna loop me in on what's going on here or not?"

"Not."

I close the trunk with a click, turning to shrug.

This meet has been a week in the making. And now, while Tatiana is lost in a book back at the house, I've taken the boat over to shore, and driven to meet Marko for the merchandise.

Clothes shopping is *slightly* beneath his skill set. But I needed someone I could trust. It's not like I could ask one of my underlings within the Tsavakov structure to go purchase a wardrobe full of women's clothes for me without raising several questions.

He eyes me, shaking his head.

"Got it. So, you're just really into exploring your feminine side now. That it?"

"I really appreciate you doing this, my friend."

There's a lot I can share with Marko. This is not one of them. It's not that I don't trust him—I do, implicitly. It's just that there's too much that can go wrong.

The outside world *cannot* know that Tatiana Fairist is alive and living with me at my island house.

Living with.

Sleeping with.

Tangling with.

"Alright, brother. Well, enjoy your crossdressing."

I roll my eyes, smirking as I turn to hop back into my car.

"I mean, unless it's for that girl you've got staying at your house."

I go still.

"Kris, you had me scoping out the whole lake for intruders from a cliff with a zoom scope."

I eye him coolly.

"What exactly did you see?"

He sighs. "I saw the chick you've got living there, or, whatever she's doing there. Whoever she is."

I suck on my teeth.

"She's no one."

"Keeping it casual?" He grins.

"It's not like that."

He arches a brow, nodding like he doesn't believe me in the slightest.

"Got it, got it."

I start to turn away again.

"So you don't mind that I kept watching when she was changing."

Red clouds my vision.

"And I mean, damn, brother. Those are some *great* tits—"

A surge of primal fury explodes deep in me as I whirl on him. I snarl, grabbing his collar and shoving him back against the side of the SUV.

Marko grins.

"I was kidding, by the way."

"Which fucking part."

He sighs. "*Relax*, Kris. I didn't see your girl naked."

"She's not—"

"Right, right. A no one, yeah?" He shrugs. "The kind of no one that makes you want to bash one of your oldest, best friend's face in when he mentions her tits?"

The fury fades. But my hands stay gripping his collar.

"It would be best if you…"

"Already forgot what she even looks like." He eyes me. "Not my first rodeo, Kris."

My hands drop from his collar.

"Sorry," I mutter under my breath.

"Don't need to apologize for shit, man."

He grins as I step away.

"Well, I'll let you get back to no one. You know, the no one you just dropped twenty thousand on lingerie for. Unless that really is for you."

I roll my eyes as I turn and open the door to the SUV.

"I'll be in touch soon. And thanks, Marko. I owe you."

"I'm adding it to your tab."

Perched on the couch opposite the one I'm sitting on, Tatiana arches a curious brow. It's evening now, after dinner, and we're in my study. I bite back the smirk as I slide a large black shopping bag across the coffee table towards her.

The vast majority of what I had Marko buy for her is already up in her room—a stealth move on my part while she was making some tea. But the bag has a… choice selection in it.

She smiles curiously as she pulls the bag towards herself and then peeks inside. Her eyes go wide.

"Oh my *God*!"

She gasps as she shoves her hands inside, pulling out Versace dresses, Chanel skirts, Louis Vuitton tops, and Louboutin shoes. There's also comfort clothes in there—designer jeans in her size, a few Burberry zip-up hoodies, and a smattering of comfy t-shirts. In *her* size.

"You—"

Her eyes snap up to mine, her face flushed.

"This is for me?"

"This and the ten other bags worth already up in your room."

Her mouth falls open.

"I…" she shakes her head. "I don't know what to say?"

I shrug, smirking.

"They're clothes, *printsessa*. Sort of seems like a basic I've overlooked for too long."

Mostly because I very much enjoy chasing her in next to nothing. Or else in nothing at all. But she *does* need clothes. Especially if she's going to be saying here for…

My pulse thuds.

Well, for who knows how long.

A while.

I watch, smiling quietly to myself as she pulls clothes out of the bag. Until suddenly, her eyes widen and her face flushes pink.

I put what she's just found at the bottom of the bag for a reason.

She shivers as she reaches in, her face throbbing with heat as she bashfully pulls out the matching lace, silk, and pearl-adorned thong and demi-bra.

Marko wasn't exaggerating. There's literally another twenty-thousand pounds worth of lingerie just like this or far sexier, naughtier, and skimpier upstairs. But this will be her first taste.

And mine.

As much as I've enjoyed chasing her in baggy shorts and a t-shirt, bra-less and panty-less through the woods, the idea of doing so with her clad in see-through lace has my demon roaring inside of me.

The idea of hunting her through the midnight shadows of this house, and catching her, and ripping a tiny little thong from her cunt with my teeth is… an intoxicating one.

Her eyes raise, meeting mine as her cheeks simmer beneath them.

"I…"

"I want you to try them on."

She swallows, turning to glance at the pile of clothes.

"Which—"

"What you're holding will work just fine."

She shivers, biting her lip.

"Now would be best," I growl softly.

I watch the flush creep down over her chest. She's not mortified by this. Not put off, or nervous.

She's turned on.

"Take off your clothes and try them on, Tatiana."

She sucks her lip, swallowing thickly before she stands.

"Can you... I mean—"

"It's nothing I haven't seen before." My brows arch. "Several, several times."

She bites her lip a little harder, pulsing with the heat on her face as her eyes hook with mine. Slowly, she reaches down and peels her t-shirt off her bare, gorgeous tits. She drops her sweatpants, and my gaze lazily slides down from her nipples, over her stomach, down to her little pussy nestled between her thighs.

I can tell she's wet even from here.

She blushes fiercely as she steps into the tiny lacy white thong, with the string of pearls that sits against the gusset. The bra is on next, if you can even call it that. It doesn't even cover her nipples, instead just cupping the undersides of her breasts as if offering them up to me.

I gave some specifics. But Marko has good taste.

When she's done, she blushes, giggling a little as she gives a twirl.

My cock is steel between my legs.

I wanted to chase her and shred those new panties from her body as I plunged into her. I wanted them ripped and tangled at her knees as she begged for me to fuck her harder from behind, my hand around her throat.

But at this moment, seeing her like this, I know one thing without a single doubt: I do *not* have the self-control to wait for a chase right now.

I growl deeply as I stand and step around the coffee table. She whimpers as I lean down, fisting a handful of her long red hair and tugging her head back. My mouth descends, claiming hers roughly as she moans into my lips.

My other hand slides to her tits, teasing her nipples with my thumb and forefinger, making her groan eagerly against me. I push my tongue deep, tasting and exploring every part of her mouth as she squirms for me.

I need more.

I pull away, and Tatiana whimpers in anticipation as I drop to my knees and reach for her panties.

"Another day, and *soon*," I rasp. "I want you screaming as you run from me, wearing only these. And then, I will tear them from your body with my cock already buried deep in this pretty little pussy."

She chokes on a moan, nodding as her hooded eyes lock with mine.

"But right now, what I need the most is to fucking *devour* you."

I yank the panties down, tossing them aside. Then I shove her legs apart roughly before I dive between them.

"Oh my God, Kristoff..."

She coos, squirming and moaning as my tongue delves into her folds. I drag my tongue up her slit, tasting her eager slickness before it swirls slowly over her clit. My pulse roars, thudding in my ears like a helicopter—

Motherfucker.

That's not my pulse. That's a real goddamn helicopter, hovering over the flat pad of grass designed to be landed on to one side of the house.

And I *know* I haven't invited anyone here.

I pull away from her, looking up as our eyes lock. Fear grips her as her face pales.

"Who— "

"I don't know."

I lunge to my feet, reaching down to pull her up as well. I groan as my hand threads into her hair, tugging her close as I crush my lips to hers.

"But I'm going to find out. While I'm doing that, though…"

"Upstairs?" she squeaks.

I nod grimly. "This way."

I shove the haul of clothes into the shopping bag and grab her hand. We bolt through the house, up the stairs, down the hall, and then up the stairs to my quarters.

She's never been up here.

I take a single second to appreciate the way her eyes widen as she drinks in the huge master suite. Then, I pull her to my walk-in closet. At the back, I open a drawer full of watches, remove a Cartier watch, and tap in a code on the keypad beneath it. The back wall slides open, revealing a comfortable and well stocked panic room.

Tatiana shivers.

"I—"

"I'm going to take care of this," I grunt coldly.

Turning, I open another drawer and pull out a Glock, checking it before I hand it to her.

"If anyone tries to get in here who isn't me, kill them."

Our eyes lock. I can see the fear in hers, but past it, I see the determination I love seeing in those greenish-brown, gold flecked eyes of hers.

I see the fire, and the grit.

My mouth slams to hers, hard. Then, I'm ushering her into the panic room, stepping out, and closing the door.

Then, I grab a gun, grit my jaw, and whirl to go see who the fuck just invaded my escape.

23

"I COULD HAVE FUCKING KILLED you, Prince."

Oliver grins, shrugging as we step through the front door back into the house.

"I thought I'd surprise you."

Mission accomplished. Christ.

"You should have called."

"That wouldn't have been a surprise then, now would it?"

I roll my eyes as we walk through the house into my study. Ten minutes ago, I was languidly running my tongue over Tatiana's sweet little cunt. Now, I'm a minute past almost blowing my friend's head off when he decided to land his own helicopter on my island and jump out of it like a fucking idiot.

Oliver isn't a threat, obviously. But even he can't know she's here. There're too many ripples that could spread from that.

Too many people who'd be far too keen to learn that Tatiana is alive.

It's not that I'm not glad to see my old friend. But now is hardly an ideal time for a visit.

In my office, I turn and lean against my desk, eying him.

"How did you know I was here?"

Oliver sighs, shoving his hand through his styled blond hair. As much as I'm annoyed with him right now, I make a note to figure out later where he got the impeccable midnight-blue suit he's wearing.

"You didn't remember, did you?"

I frown. "Remember what?"

"The date, Kristoff."

My brow furrows deeper as I think. And then, it hits me, and I wince, realizing I did in fact forget.

It's the fifth anniversary of our good friend Thomas—leader of Lords College Kings and Villains—passing away.

"*Fuck.*"

"Shall I pour the drinks, or you?"

I nod, turning without answering and walking over the bar cart. I pour us each a heavy glass of scotch—Thomas's favorite brand, which I still keep around the house, all these years later. Oliver takes his from my hand, and we solemnly clink them together.

"To Thomas," he grunts quietly. "The best of us."

"No argument here."

We drink quietly, but swiftly. When the glasses are empty, I pour us another before we retreat back to the couches and sit across from one another.

"Finally got your pilots license I see."

"I got tired of the ones I was hiring going so slow."

I grin, shaking my head.

"Didn't want to raise a glass to Thomas back in London with Noel?"

Oliver's face darkens. I know I've touched a nerve there, but he can take it. When we were all younger, back at Lords College, I always acted as the barrier between the two perma-rivals.

I won't deny that I half enjoy stirring shit up when I'm with one of them these days.

"Very funny," Oliver grunts. "And no, Kristoff. I have no intention of ever raising a glass with that prick."

I sigh. They both like to act like this whole Cold War of theirs is one-sided.

"You stole his wife, Oliver."

"I stole his *ex*-wife."

"Yes, except you're the one who turned her *into* his ex-wife."

He smirks quietly. I roll my eyes.

"Well, I'm honored that you flew all the way out here to have a drink with me."

Oliver chuckles. "Not to take the wind out of those narcissistic sails of yours, but I was already in Stockholm on business."

He sips at his scotch, leaning back on the couch as he eyes me.

"For fuck's sake, out with it, Prince. I can see those gears cranking from here."

"Something is afoot."

I resist the urge to laugh. We're both rich, powerful men in our own rights and ways these days. But the stark difference in where we came from shows nakedly sometime. Like when Prince says shit like "something is afoot," like he's Winston Churchill, or Sherlock fucking Holmes.

"What precisely is 'afoot,' my friend."

His eyes narrow.

"I was hoping you might tell me."

The room stills a little. I sip my scotch, eyeing him coolly.

"Why don't we cut to the part where we're not beating around the bush, Oliver."

He sighs. "If you insist. What I mean is, men like us don't change, Kristoff."

My eyes narrow.

"I have."

"In part, yes. But, have you?"

"I thought we weren't going to beat around the bush," I grunt quietly.

He looks away.

"That one time, at the Mandarin Oriental, when I—"

"I was under the impression we were never going to speak of that again."

He turns back to level his gaze at me.

"Kristoff, once upon a time, I may have been naïve and young enough to believe that had anything to do with your work for Boris Tsavakov."

I arch a brow.

"And now?"

"And now, I'm quite sure there was a lot more to it than that."

"I think we should go back to drinking to Thomas, Oliver," I say quietly.

"I'm aware of the Ghost Syndicate, Kris."

Something ticks in my head, but I show nothing—no outward sign of even acknowledging what that is.

"What are you getting at, Oliver?"

He takes a heavy sip of his drink and sighs deeply.

"Tatiana Fairist, heiress to the Balagula Bratva family, went missing a few weeks ago." He shrugs. "Missing and presumed dead, in the same coup that killed her father."

"I've heard the rumors."

But that's me, and this is the dark, shadowy world I exist in. I'm more than curious where the fuck *Oliver*, from the world of high finance and mostly playing by the rules, did.

"Well, there are other rumors, apparently. Like that she isn't dead at all."

I hold his gaze casually.

JAGGER COLE

"Keeping up with the inter-politics of Bratva families seems a bit outside of the job description for stock trading and acquisitions, Oliver."

He glances around at the opulent house. Then he turns and holds my gaze without flinching.

"I think we're both more than aware of how much finance work there is within organizations like yours, Kristoff. Or the even more criminal that men like Boris associate with."

He's found a thread. I don't know how, but he has. And now he's pulling at it in that very Oliver Prince way.

He needs to stop pulling.

"What exactly does this have to do with me?"

"Look, Kris, you know I make trades based on publicly accessible information from organizations like the Volkov and Kashenko Bratvas. And you know I've done some business with Boris in the past."

"That who told you I was here?"

His lip curls in the corner.

"You can learn a lot from Boris if you get him drunk, you know."

My eyes narrow.

"You have no right to pry into my—"

"You're my *friend*, Kristoff. You understand what that means, yes?"

I set my glass down and steeple my fingers.

"Why don't you just say what you came here to say, Oliver."

He shakes his head.

"A little personal vacation right after Peter Fairist's daughter disappears out of her house, presumed dead?"

Careful, old friend.

"There are seven point six billion people on the planet, Oliver."

"Yes, and only one of them is *you*." His eyes narrow. "And like I said, men like us don't change."

Our gazes lock, dangerously.

"You're one of my closest friends, Oliver."

"Yes, but we both know the secrets you—"

"And for that reason," I growl in a measured tone. "I'm asking you one last time to *cease* this line of thought. Now."

He holds my gaze unblinking for another few seconds. Then, he sighs, sitting back into the couch and raising his glass.

"My apologies. I just worry about you getting into things above your head."

"You of all people should know you don't need to worry about that with me, Prince."

He smiles wryly, taking a sip.

"Look, things I've done in the past are in the past, Oliver. As are the things you've done, like stealing Ransom's wife."

I sigh.

"But the fact that you saw… what you saw that night, years ago, does not mean I'm part of some secret plan to abduct the heiress to the Balagula throne and keep her at my goddamn house."

He shrugs, nodding.

"No, you're right. That's very true, Kristoff."

He sighs.

"I suppose it doesn't."

"Thank you."

"However, the lacy white silk and pearl thong under your couch begs more than a few questions on the subject."

Fuck.

"Unless of course you've developed some interesting new hobbies?"

He smiles a shit-eating grin at me. As if this is a big "gotcha" and I'm just going to roll over and spill everything to him.

I'm not.

"I'm allowed to have company, Oliver," I say thinly.

He sighs, shaking his head as he realizes I'm not going to give him what he wants.

"Indeed. Indeed, you are."

He drains the last of his scotch and then raises his eyes to me.

"Is she currently here?"

"Are we talking about my guest or Tatiana Fairist?"

He smiles wryly.

"Either."

My eyes narrow.

"*My guest* is indeed still here."

"Then I believe I'll take my exit."

I say nothing, knocking back the rest of my scotch as I stand with him. Outside, halfway between the house and his helicopter, we pause as he turns to me, his brow furrowed.

"It really is just that I worry about you, Kris."

I clap a hand on his shoulder.

"I'm *fine*, Oliver."

"I had some people look into the man who runs that Ghost Syndicate you hear whisper about. And he's not a—"

"Do me a favor," I say thinly. "And *stop* having people do that."

He nods, giving me the same look he once gave me years ago in the trashed downstairs men's room at the Hyde Park Mandarin Oriental.

"I'm not you, Kris," he growls. "But I have resources. If you ever need anything, or help—"

"I appreciate it."

He nods, sighing as he looks up at the night sky.

"I still miss him."

My gaze rises, following his to the stars.

"I do too."

"We're young, Kristoff."

He turns to me, putting a hand on my shoulder.

"I'd rather not lose another good friend so early."

"Well, not stealing their wives anymore might be a good place to start, Prince."

He laughs. So do I.

It feels good.

I shake my old friend's hand and then wait until his helicopter disappears into the night sky.

I ignore the tingling sensation in the back of my skull. It's the one that's been buzzing ever since I was made aware that even someone like *Oliver*, who beyond market investments, has absolutely nothing to do with the world of the Bratva, and Mikhail, and the Ghost Syndicate, and monsters like me, was aware of the situation with the Balagula and Tatiana.

I glance back up at the sky. It's clear, but I know there's a storm coming.

A war.

A reckoning.

I know I won't be able to hold onto this little depraved fantasy escape of ours for forever. There are questions that are going to continue to be asked. There are people who won't stop turning over rocks, and won't stop hunting.

But there are hunters, and then there's *me*.

If they want a reckoning, and answers to those questions?

They can come and find them, waiting for them at the bottom of the same hole I'll put them in.

I turn, and I go back to the house.

Back to her.

Back to all I really actually want now.

24

My skin tingles as I slide my hand lazily over his abs, my cheek resting against his chest. We're both still dewy with sweat and panting slightly from the chase.

And the *very* rough sex that came after, when he finally caught me.

Kristoff's hand slides down to cup my bare ass, pulling me tighter against him as we sit against the inside wall of the boathouse. We watch the water lap at the boat moored to the inner dock. The sun sets slowly through the open door of the boathouse, bathing us in an orange glow.

Fuck, that was hot. A little painful—okay a *lot* painful—but so, so good. And it's never a bad pain. It's more like the sour that makes the sweet all the sweeter. It's all part of the fucked up games we just *keep* playing.

In this case, it was me making a break for it right before dinner. I knew he was in the kitchen, and I skipped out the front door, this time, with a goal of "making it" to the boathouse—all part of our depraved role-playing, as if my plan was to steal the boat and make it to shore.

I did not.

I got close, but then his panted breaths and pounding footsteps caught up with me. I shiver, remembering his powerful hand grabbing a handful of my dress and yanking me roughly back to the ground, ripping the dress almost all the way off my body in the process.

I replay how he grabbed me up and yanked me into the boathouse and over to the very wall that we're sitting against right now. How he spun me to face it and bound my wrists with heavy maritime rope to a hook high on the wall.

How he ripped more of my dress away and then used a knife to slice my panties off. How he spanked my ass red, telling me what a bad girl I was for trying to escape. Then he roughly knocked my legs apart and buried his cock to the hilt in me.

And that was only the beginning.

This is how it is now, here in this bizarre world we've cocooned ourselves in. We're both aware that I'm not *actually* going to run. I know there's a danger out there, and that it's safer if I'm "dead," staying here with him.

How long that will go on, though, I have no idea. Years? Forever?

I shiver, but then I pull closer to him.

It's not actually a terrible thought to spend forever here, as insane as that sounds. For one, I want for nothing. I have free range of the island, the house, whatever I want to eat or drink. And now even clothes, and makeup, and hair products, and basically every other comfort I ever had in my old life.

But *without* that old life, and all the baggage, politics, control, and danger that came with it.

Now, life just feels more freeing.

When it comes to Kristoff and I's "depravity," it's never *just* sex. Sometimes, it's obfuscated by the chase. Other times, by "training." We spar, we dodge, he chases. It always ends with me screaming his name with his thick cock pounding me senseless. And he makes my body twist with a dark need, snarling the most fucked up, filthy things into my ears while he does so.

I like the thrill of escaping someone as good a hunter as him. But I *love* the even bigger thrill of losing.

My hand slips over his thigh to tangle my fingers with his. I chew on my words, but then they finally come out.

"What stopped you from killing me?"

Kristoff goes still.

"Was it because you wanted to… you know."

"Tatiana—"

"Chase me? Fuck me?"

"I stopped because I just couldn't."

"But you had orders to."

He's silent.

"From my stepmother."

Kristoff stills, and I swivel my head to look up into his piercing, narrowed blue eyes.

"*Printsessa—*"

"I overheard you and your friend talking on the phone a few weeks ago..." I frown. "You called him Boris?"

He sighs, pulling me closer against him.

"You said something about how Jana *was* the Balagula Bratva now."

He shakes his head, jaw tensed.

"Tatiana, that doesn't mean that she—"

"I'm not an idiot."

"I know that."

I look away, knowing it's true even if he's clearly trying to protect me by not confirming it.

"She can have it," I spit bitterly. "Honestly. I never wanted that life."

"I worry at times that I didn't give you a choice to decide if you wanted it or not, the day I took you."

I shake my head, smiling wryly.

"You made the choice for me that I couldn't make myself."

"If I hadn't come that day, you would have found your own way out."

I chew on my lip.

"I know you, Tatiana. I've seen the fight and the fire in you. You'd have found a way out."

I smile wryly as I drag my eyes back up to his.

"Did she pay you?"

His chiseled, gorgeous face darkens.

"I don't exactly need money."

"So, you go around contract killing girls for favors? For fun?"

Kristoff's eyes narrow, his lip curling before he looks away. I wince, realizing how cold that just came across.

"Shit, I'm sorry. I didn't mean for that to sound so—"

"No, I don't," he rumbles quietly. His arm tightens around me. "It's a complicated part of my past, and who I used to be. When it came to you, and that day…"

He shakes his head. My heart tenses.

"I don't need sugarcoating. I know what my father was and what my family is, Kristoff."

"Then you know what *you* are."

"And what am I?"

He turns to me, arching a brow.

"The next in line for the Balagula throne."

I shiver.

"No." My head shakes firmly and quickly. "No, I don't want that."

"Well, you're dead."

I smile a small smile, my lips twisting as I peer into his face.

"You're an assassin, then?"

He frowns.

"I was. Now I work for a Russian businessman—an Oligarch with some Bratva connections. But it's an organization that has nothing to do with this thing with your stepmother trying to wrest power and have you killed."

I shiver, and then suddenly, a horrifying thought creeps up my neck into the base of my skull, chilling me. Kristoff frowns as the color drains from my face

"What—"

"Did you…" I choke, tensing horribly. "My… my father—"

"*No,*" he scowls deeply, shaking his head. "No, *printsessa*. That's business I don't have anything to do with. But I…"

He looks away. My hand squeezes his tightly.

"*Please,*" I whisper.

Kristoff draws in a slow, heavy breath.

"I don't think your father's death was an accident."

The words hit like a slap, and yet, it's also like looking at the truth I've always known. Somehow, the shock of the statement is that *someone else* also thinks it, not that it's something I'm hearing for the first time.

"They said it was a car crash," I say thinly, my voice feeling far outside my own body.

"I heard."

I look down, my heart thudding.

"It was Jana, wasn't it?"

Kristoff breathes heavily, his thumb of his huge hand stroking the back of my so much smaller one.

"Jana works for and with a man named Mikhail Arakas. He runs an organization called the Ghost Syndicate, and he…" his face darkens.

"He's had his eyes on your family's empire for quite some time. If I were to guess—"

"The timing of the head of the family being in an accident a handful of weeks before a contract killer is sent to kill his only heir, leaving his second wife with now complete control over the whole empire…" I shake my head, my mouth small.

"You think things through to the end," Kristoff says quietly in that deep voice of his. "Even if it hurts you."

He brings my hand to his lips, brushing the back of it in a small kiss. And yet, it sends something powerful and warm through me, giving me a strength.

"This Ghost Syndicate and that Mikhail guy…" I frown. "Are they Bratva?"

"He wishes," Kristoff grunts. "It's why Mik's been after your family for so long. It's why he had Jana move in and ensnare your father to begin with."

I blanch, turning pale as my heart drops.

"Is that true?"

"Yes."

The answer comes so fast. I shiver, whipping around with a cold dread clutching at my core as my eyes lock with his.

"*You—*"

"I was." His lips thin as his jaw tenses. "I *was* part of that organization. They're who trained me to be what I am. But not anymore, and I was *not* involved with your father's death, Tatiana."

I pull close to him, leaning up to kiss his mouth softly. I sink into him, and it's like another part of my past lets go, letting me be more here.

With him. In this twisted and yet perfect fantasy world we've created.

I pull away gently, dropping my cheek against his firm, strong chest again.

"Why do you like to chase me?"

I can feel the rumble of his low chuckle through his muscles.

"Why do you like to run?"

I grin, my lips twisting in my teeth.

"I think because it makes me feel like I'm remembering things." I shrug. "That boating accident I told you about? When I was at camp?"

He nods.

"I sort of got this amnesia around it. Like my brain short-circuited and erased the events of me falling in and getting pinned under the boat, so I don't have to relive it through memories."

"The brain works in interesting ways. That happens a lot with trauma, actually."

"Yeah," I shrug. "But mine erased the whole time I was at camp, and other times, too."

He goes silent. When I glance up, his brow is furrowed.

"You don't remember going to the camp at all?"

I shake my head.

"How long were you there before the accident?"

"Five weeks, I think?"

His brows arch. I smile wryly as I shrug.

"*Yeah*, pretty fucked up, right?"

"It's unusual, I'll say that." His brow furrows again. "You said it erased other times as well?"

I nod.

"That's what it is about the chase that I love, I think. I don't really know why, but running away like that, and trying to escape when you chase… it's like it's pulling at the buried threads of all these pieces of my later childhood and early teens that got deleted when I almost drowned."

He brings a hand up, cupping my cheek with a gentleness you wouldn't expect from a man like him. A man hardened and cold. A man with piercing, icy-blue eyes.

A killer.

A kidnapper.

"I wish for those memories to come back to you."

I grin. "Me too. Maybe someday. The…" I blush. "The *games* we play… they help."

He frowns, nodding.

"You know if they ever *don't* help, or if they're no longer a game you wish to play—"

"That isn't going to happen."

His eyes spark with something wicked that sends a heated thrill through me. I chew on my bottom lip.

"If I did really ask you to stop the chases… would you?"

"*No.*"

Desire pools in my core.

It's the best answer I could have asked for.

25

"We're leaving."

I blink, surprised by his voice from the doorway to the library as I look up from the book I've been reading.

My brows knit.

"What?"

"You've been here for almost three months." He arches a brow. "You need to get off the island."

I startle, trying to process what he's just said. *Three months?* I've seriously been here for that long? It's bizarre to hear out loud. And yet, it's not shocking in any sort of bad way.

Being here has changed me.

It's like life is resetting and has new meaning. I can breathe like I never breathed before, with the weight of what my family was always pressing me down. It's the lake, and the island air, and the woods… but also, him.

He's changed me. He broke his way into the me deep inside that was locked behind bars and rules and a life already planned for her, and he ripped that true version of me free. He's ignited something in me. And maybe that something is dark. Maybe it's perverse, and a little depraved.

But it's *me*.

Unashamed. Unafraid. Unchained.

"Where are we going?"

"A ball."

My brows arch as a grin pulls at the corners of my lips.

"You go to balls?"

Kristoff smirks, leaning against the doorframe.

"I'm somewhat of a sophisticated man when I want to be."

"When you're not chasing girls throughs the woods, you mean."

His eyes glint.

"I can readily do both."

I flush.

"What about…" I clear my throat. "I mean, I'm dead, remember?"

He pushes off the doorframe, standing tall again.

"It's a masked ball. And we leave in three hours."

He turns to leave as my jaw hits the floor.

"Wait, *what*?"

He turns back to me, and then takes my breath away as he crosses the room in two strides. He bends down, my skin tingling as he cups my jaw in his firm hand.

"You've been on this island for almost three months. So we're going to a gala ball, so that you can view, and be in, and remember what society is. Because I'm worried."

My brow furrows.

"About?"

"About you growing a beard and turning into a fucking hermit if you stay here any longer."

I giggle before his mouth slams hard to mine, kissing the very air from my lungs and turning me to jelly.

"I've laid one of your gowns out on your bed upstairs."

He pulls back, clearing his throat.

"There's also a hair dying kit in your bathroom."

My mouth falls open.

"Wait, *what?*"

I make a face. I *love* my hair. Like, *love it*. And I've never once had any inclination to dye it.

"It's a simple wash-out type. One shower, and it's gone. But I've RSVPed to this event as myself. And I believe it might beg some questions if I show up with a red-haired young woman matching the description of a missing Bratva princess on my arm, don't you?"

I groan. "*Fine*. What color?"

"Neon green."

My gaze yanks back to his in horror, only to see him smirking, clearly yanking my chain.

"Jerk."

"I believe it's called 'autumn chestnut.'"

I nod, and he turns to leave.

"Three hours, *printsessa*. And then we'll see how you like being a ghost amongst the living."

A BOAT, a car, and then a private jet ride later, Kristoff is leading me carefully down the stairway from the plane to a waiting car. I wobble slightly, because apparently putting heels on after three months of bare feet or sneakers is *not* like riding a bike.

But he's there, holding my hand and jutting an arm out to circle my waist before I actually fall. And he looks *amazing*.

The Kristoff I know from the island wears dark jeans and white t-shirts. He goes barefoot a lot. Shirtless often. The man escorting me down the stairs, though?

He looks like he just stepped out of a Dior ad.

The tuxedo fits him exquisitely. His hair is slicked; pushed back and parted smartly, giving him this ultra-sophisticated, old-money look. Kristoff was right: he readily *can* do both.

The savage hunting me through the woods, and the dapper, smartly-dressed, devastating handsome tuxedoed gentleman escorting me to a gala ball in—well, wherever we are, because he hasn't actually told me where we're going.

"*Guten Abend, mein Herr. Frau. Wie war Ihr Flug?*"

My brow arches as the man at the bottom of the staircase, standing beside a Rolls Royce town car, greets us in German. I glance at Kristoff.

"We're in Germany?"

"Austria," he smiles at the man, nodding. "And our chauffeur for the evening was asking how your flight was."

"Oh! Uh…" I turn to flash a flustered, surprised smile at the man. "Good, thanks?"

"*Gut, danke*," Kristoff nods to him.

We slide into the back, the car slides into the night, and then we're off to the ball.

THREE MONTHS IS a long time to be away from society. And on top of that, I'm supposed to be dead. I've been trying to keep the anxiety at bay about leaving the island refuge I've turned into my whole world, and being thrust back into the world at large. But the minute we left the plane, it started to flare up. When we pull up in front of the stunning old pre-war building in old Vienna, and I see all the people milling around outside, the siren blaring in my ears becomes deafening.

But then Kristoff is slipping the sequined black and red mask that matches the stunning gown of the same colors that I'm wearing onto my face. Then he's helping me out of the car and sliding a firm hand over my hip as his arm circles my waist.

The siren blaring in my head goes away.

"Tonight," he growls into my ear, tucking a lock of my now chestnut-colored hair—which I don't actually hate—behind my ear. "You are not Tatiana Fairist."

"Then who am I?"

His eyes glint behind his own mask as he arches a brow.

"Who would you like to be?"

I grin, thinking.

"Sophie Neveu," I finally answer.

Kristoff chuckles, and I blush.

"Too obvious?"

"I've never even read it, and *I* know that's the female lead in *The Da Vinci Code*."

I sigh. "Okay, okay, how about…"

"Serena Kingsly."

I snort, but he's not done.

"*Lady* Serena Kingsly, of the Derbyshire Kingslys."

I bite back a laugh.

"That's sounds ridiculous."

"Too bad, that's your name for the night."

I'm about to protest, when a smiling man in a dark suit with a tablet approaches us.

"Guten Abend, mein Herr. Ihre Namen?"

"Yes, it's under Zima."

The man with the tablet smiles.

"Ah, yes, of course, Herr Zima. And your lovely date for the evening?"

"Lady Serena Kingsly, of the Derbyshire Kingslys."

I groan, wincing as the heat flushes my face. But the man greeting us only smiles as he taps something on his tablet and nods.

"*Danke*. Enjoy your evening."

Kristoff's arm circles my waist again in a thrillingly possessive way as the front doors open, and we step inside.

In my "old life," which now seems like a lifetime and not just three months ago, I went to a hundred of these. Huge, ritzy, lavish galas full of glamorous, moneyed people. My mum would take me, because my father was hardly ever seen in public. But mum and I would go, with a heavy escort, of course. We'd dance together, and even though it was obvious neither of us actually wanted to be there, though it was "expected" of us, we were determined to have fun.

Stepping into this one, though, feels… different.

For one, because there's no objective here. At least, not one I have to play a role in. There're no government officials that my mother and I have to smile and pose for pictures with, or ones who all but fall over to kiss our feet, because of who my family is.

It's just a lavish party, and I even get to wear a mask. Plus, the man whose arm I'm on seems to be sucking every single drop of the lingering anxiety I've been feeling about coming here away from me.

This feels different, because I don't feel the need to be "determined to have fun."

I'm pretty sure simply being here with him means I will.

A waiter waltzes past us with a tray of champagne flutes, and Kristoff grabs one for each of us.

"What exactly is this gala for?"

"The Children of Conflict Refugee Foundation."

"*Wow*, well that sounds like an amazing—"

"It's entirely a front operation to move money between various criminal and government parties."

I make a face as I turn to him.

"Well, that's depressing."

He chuckles, shrugging.

"It is what it is. Hence the masks, and very much why you're no longer a redhead tonight."

I shiver.

"Because people in this line of work could recognize me."

I can feel the siren in my head begin to wail again. A cold feeling clenches me to my core as I start to pale. But then instantly, there's a firm hand on the small of my back, and a familiar scent engulfing me as he pulls me close to him and leans into my ear.

"That is *not* going to happen."

The tension floods back out of me. I swallow, feeling the roaring sound dissipate in my head once again. I quickly take a sip of champagne.

"I, on the other hand," he grunts, his face souring. "Have to go glad-hand some people, if you'd like to join in my misery."

I grin. "Keep the champagne coming and I'm all yours."

"But, *printsessa*…"

I shiver as his hand grips my hip hard and possessively as his mouth brushes my ear tantalizingly.

"You're already all mine."

His teeth bite the soft lobe of my ear, just enough to make me gasp loudly as a shiver of heat teases down my spine. His arm stays wrapped around my waist as he turns and begins to guide us through the lavish ballroom.

"Kristoff?"

Kristoff tenses instantly, and when I glance up at his face, I can see the way he's gritting his jaw at the man's deep voice behind us.

"*Shit*," he hisses under his breath. But then he's straightening and putting on a smile as he turns us.

I blink when we come face to face with a tall, handsome, dark-haired man, silvering at the temples, with deep blue eyes behind his mask. His arm is around the waist of a gorgeous younger woman with strawberry blonde hair and a familiarness about her green eyes, even with the mask on.

"Mr. Volkov."

I turn to ice as Kristoff extends a hand to firmly shake the other man's.

Volkov, as in *Yuri* Volkov, head of the Volkov Bratva empire. A man who absolutely knew my parents and my grandfather, and *absolutely* knows who I am, because he's literally been to our home for dinner before, years ago, when I was a kid.

"Good to see you, Zima," Yuri rumbles in a deep, accented baritone. "I wasn't aware Boris was attending."

"He's not."

"Ahh," the older man grins, rolling his eyes. "Lucky you, since these things are oh so much fun," he drawls in a sarcastic tone, before smiling and turning to the woman on his arm.

"You remember my wife, River, don't you?"

It's almost a laughably rhetorical question. Yuri Volkov's wife, River Finn, was, and still is one of the most stunning and well-known models in the world.

But Kristoff just smiles casually as he takes her hand.

"Of course. Good to see you again, River."

Yuri's deep blue eyes swivel to me, and I tense as they frown with a flicker of recognition. Or maybe I'm just making that up because I'm suddenly freaking out just a little bit.

"And your date…"

Get it together.

"Serena," I blurt. I take a breath, centering myself and letting the fear melt away from me. "Serena Kingsly."

Yuri takes my hand firmly, shaking it slowly as his eyes pierce into mine inquisitively.

"I see," he finally says with a small smile. "Of course. Well, pleasure to meet you, Ms. Kingsly."

"River, hi," his wife says easily, grinning as she takes my hand. She's world famous for her looks. But it's also rumored that she's extremely down-to-earth and genuinely a nice, ego-free person. And in the ten seconds since I've met her, I'm pretty sure those rumors are true.

"Hey, Serena."

"I absolutely *love* your dress, by the way," she gushes earnestly, her eyes dropping down over my red and black gown.

"Oh, thanks!"

Kristoff clears his throat. "How're things, Yuri?"

The older man shrugs. "Oh, fine. Business is steady and low-drama these days, which is always a plus. How's Boris these days?"

"He remains… Boris," Kristoff says in a very diplomatic tone.

Yuri chuckles.

"One day, you'll take me up on that offer to come work with me."

Kristoff grins, but he shakes his head. "I'm fine where I am, but thank you, as always."

"Eh, I know you wouldn't leave Misha."

I raise a brow as Kristoff turns to me.

"My boss's son," he explains.

"Who talks about this man as if he's his favorite uncle or older brother," Yuri adds.

"Speaking of Misha…"

Kristoff's hand lazily circles my waist, teasing my skin through the light silk as he turns back to Yuri.

"I heard the house you had set up for the boys at Oxford Hills Academy is fairly impressive."

River rolls her eyes.

"It's *ridiculous*. They're already going to stand out at that place as Bratva heirs amongst snooty old-money types. And you've gone and put them up on a pedestal in that over-the-top mansion on campus."

Yuri grins, shrugging.

"They were going to stand out anyway. Might as well make them stand out with the biggest, coolest housing on campus."

Kristoff chuckles. "Okay that's actually a fair point."

River sighs as she turns to me, rolling her eyes again.

"I swear, everything with men like them is a dick-measuring contest."

Yuri sighs dramatically as he reaches for his belt. "Well, if you insist, dear—"

"Oh *behave*!" She giggles, swatting his hand before he pulls her close and kisses her softly.

"We should make the rounds," Yuri grunts when he pulls away from his wife.

"Same, actually. It was good to see you both, though."

"Likewise, and lovely to meet you… *Serena*," Yuri adds with a lingering look over me.

"Are you guys staying in Vienna tonight?" River turns to me, smiling. "We could all go get drinks or something after this snooze-fest."

"Oh, I…"

"Unfortunately, I need to get this one back to England before she turns into a pumpkin."

River smiles at me. "Well, someday, then?"

"I'd love that."

She gives me a quick hug as Yuri and Kristoff shake hands. Then they're off into the crowd, and so are we.

"Before I turn into a pumpkin, hmm?"

"Wouldn't want you dropping any glass slippers."

I grin as his hand goes back to the small of my back. We meander through the gala, occasionally stopping for him to shake someone's hand or talk for a moment before we're off again. Until suddenly, a figure moves in front of us.

"I *knew* that was you, Kris."

Her voice purrs like silk from perfect, exquisitely done lips. She's tall, slender, very blonde, about my age, and even with a mask on, absolutely stunningly gorgeous.

And when she sets her bedroom eyes on the man at my side, something in me goes *livid*.

Kristoff frowns slightly, his hand firmly on the small of my back.

"Anastasia," he growls thinly. "I didn't expect to see you here."

"Ahh, now what did we learn last time about you underestimating me?"

Her tone is flirty as fuck. And she's staring at him and batting her eyes at him in this hideously intimate way. And it's making me absolutely seethe with jealousy and fury.

Kristoff clears his throat.

"Anastasia Javanović, this is Serena Kingsly—"

"*Charmed*," she snips quickly, giving me the quickest little biting look in the world before completely ignoring me.

"Kris, it's been way too long."

"Well, let's agree to disagree."

She laughs lightly.

"God, you're such a dick."

I feel pure, venomous fury inside. I want to hit her. I want to break something. Something like her.

"Kris, it's really been forever. You know you never responded to my offer before."

I'm at the breaking point. I've never once felt anything remotely close to this level of pure green jealousy. But I'm there. And I'm right at the edge of dropping all niceties with this bitch.

"I'm fairly certain that should give you my answer. Now if you'll excuse us, we—"

"Listen, I'm having a little get-together at my place in Paris, tomorrow night. You should come."

"I'm sorry, we won't be able to make it."

The words slide like icy blades from my lips. Anastasia arches a brow, turning to smile thinly at me.

"Oh, I'm sorry, *sweetie*, but I actually wasn't inviting you."

My brow furrows in an exaggerated frown. "Oh, well, *that's* weird…"

"*Serena*," Kristoff growls quietly, his hand hardening at my back.

"What's weird, exactly?"

I smile at her. "Well, it's just weird that he's invited."

She frowns. "I'm not sure—"

"It just seemed like it was a cunts-only party."

Anastasia stares at me, half in amusement, half in cold fury.

"Kris, I'm not sure I like your date here."

"That's okay, I'm *quite* sure I don't like you," I smile sweetly, before suddenly, Kristoff grabs my arm, pulling me away.

"My regards to your father, Anastasia."

My smile turns to fury as he pulls me away like a petulant child, dragging me across the ballroom until we get to an arched doorway to a side hallway.

"Let me go!"

"What the *fuck* was that?" He snaps, whirling us and pinning me to the wall as he looms over me.

I glare at him.

"*Nothing.*"

His eyes roll.

"Tatiana—"

"*Oh! Kristoff! You should neeeever underestimate me. Oh Kristoff, you're soooo sexy.*"

His eyes hold mine coolly.

"Are you finished?"

"Oh fuck you."

He smirks, and the rage comes roaring out harder.

"Sorry, I just didn't realize how far away from your fucking type I was."

"I… my *type?*"

"Blonde?" I snap. "Tall, beautiful, cunty as fuck."

He shakes his head, eyes narrowing.

"Tatiana, Anastasia and I—"

"Oh I don't *care*, Kristoff," I hiss through clenched teeth, looking away.

He's silent for a few seconds, still pinning me to the wall with his body.

"Are you jealous, *printsessa?*"

I clamp my mouth shut angrily.

"Tatiana, we're both adults—"

"Yeah? So go have some fucking adult time with fucking Anastasia—"

"As I said, we're both adults. *Surely* there are boyfriends in your past—"

"Yeah, keep thinking that."

I shove his arm away, whirl, and bolt down the hallway away from the gala.

You'd think by now, I'd be well aware of what happens when I run from him. You'd think I wouldn't be surprised when I hear the thudding pounding of his footsteps chasing me. But when I do, my heart leaps into my throat.

I bolt faster, whirling down another guided hallway and running as fast as the fucking heels on my shoes will allow. Which is not fast at all, because in a second, I'm shrieking as his hand clamps on my arm.

I gasp as he yanks me around, spinning me into him and then slamming me back into the hall of the dark, empty hallway. I glare up at him defiantly, seeing this hardened, piercing look in his eyes as they narrow at me.

"Are there boys from your past?" he growls quietly, intensely.

I look away.

"*Answer me.*"

My lips purse together.

"Tatiana—"

"*No*, okay?!" I snap. "No, there aren't. There's never been, before—"

I shake my head, tears stinging my eyes as I look away from him.

He goes still, his grip on my upper arms tightening slightly. And when I look back, he's got this haunted look on his face as his eyes burn into mine.

"That first time," he growls quietly. "When I chased you. When we fought, and I pinned you down and fucked you for the first time…"

My face burns as I look down.

"Were you a fucking virgin?"

I shake his hands off, push him aside, and whirl to storm down the hallway back to the gala.

"Tatiana."

At the corner of the hallway, I pause, shivering. I turn halfway back, my mouth tight as it locks with his.

"Yes."

I turn, flee around the corner, and run away back to the gala.

And for the first time ever, when I run, he doesn't chase.

26

A VIRGIN. She was a fucking *virgin* when I pinned her to the ground, ripped her pants down, and fucked her hard with my hand around her throat.

I stare down the dark hallway she's just disappeared around the corner of. My pulse hums in my ears, my jaw grinding.

Fuck.

If I'd known…

I growl quietly.

It would be a lie to finish that thought with "I wouldn't have fucked her." But if I'd known that was her first time, I might not have done it that way.

Roughly.

Brutally.

Choking her as I rammed every inch of my cock deep in her sweet little pussy.

It's not that I give a shit about whether or not she was a virgin when I had her that first time. The entire concept of a "first time" or any sort of sanctity in sex has never been something I've entertained.

Not with my training. Not when it was drilled into us in the Syndicate that sex was a tool or a weapon, rather than an expression of love.

I was fourteen when Mikhail locked me in a room with a woman easily twice my age and told me to "rip the bandaid off."

I don't remember her. I don't remember what she looked like, how it was, or what even happened. Because all I do remember is that I didn't want it.

I really, really didn't want it.

I didn't want it the next time, either. Or the time after that. I didn't want it when I was forced to do it with the rest of my training class looking on—all part of Mikhail's demented "conditioning."

Conditioning like twenty people watching you at your most intimate. Conditioning like trying to fuck with someone holding a gun to your head. Or while being waterboarded.

It's an open secret that Mikhail had other plans for those in the program who failed out. Young, pretty, would-be assassins, spies, and saboteurs who couldn't take Mik's brutality, but had been trained to be seducers and seductresses. Who had been conditioned to be sex robots for lack of a better word?

They got quietly shipped off for other uses. They went to dark places I've tried not to ever think about, to be the playthings of rich, inhuman pieces of shit like Boris Tsavakov and his ilk.

Or else, you stayed in the program. You learned to check out of your own head when it came to intimacy you didn't want, the same way you'd close off on a brutal physical conditioning run, or the exercises meant to simulate being drowned.

So, no. Sex has no sanctity in my reality. And I don't view virginity as a commodity or something to be placed on a fucking pedestal.

My eyes squeeze shut as my pulse hums.

And yet… why does the knowledge I have now, that I *was* her first, turn my blood to fire. Why does knowing that I and I alone have touched her like that, and tasted her, and felt her writhe and moan beneath me, taking all of me and begging for more, turn my cock to stone?

And why the fuck are you still standing here?

I grunt, snapping out of it and suddenly surging off down the hallway after her. I round the corner, prowling back out of the shadows into the crowded gala. My trained eyes sweep to the exits first. She's got a few minutes head start on me. She could have left the building by now.

But when I do another sweep of the ballroom, my jaw grits when my eyes land on the flash of red and black. They halt on the smooth curve of a neck my eyes and hands would know anywhere, and my gaze narrows.

She's by the bar. And she's not alone.

Molten lava surges inside of me as I take in the sight of Tatiana laughing, throwing her head back to giggle at something one of the two well-dressed, leering young men crowding close to her has just said.

Fuck. That.

I plow through the crowd like a shark through open water, heedless of who I push out of the way until I'm suddenly right at her side.

Her laugh instantly chokes off, and her face pales as she turns to me.

"Come with me."

Tatiana purses her lips.

"*Now.*"

"Now hang on, mate."

My eyes narrow as I slowly drag my gaze from her to the two fuckers she's been chatting with. One looks at me with horror and recognition in his eyes, his face paling as he slowly backs off. His friend doesn't seem to share his survival instinct.

I turn back to Tatiana and take her arm.

"Let's go—"

"I said hang the fuck on."

My jaw grinds, and a low rumble emanates from my chest. I slowly turn back to the dumber of the two of them.

"I think you should walk away."

He snorts.

"Fuck off, mate. Serena and us were having a lovely conversation before you barged in like—"

The terrified looking friend leans in, and I hear my name whispered into the moron's ear. His face pales, and his eyes widen in horror.

"Oh *fuck*—"

"Off. And never let me see you talking to her, near her, or even looking at her again. How does that sound?"

I'm thirty-five years old. I've lived a life, and I've had a few fleeting, not-ever-serious relationships before. But I've never once felt a possessiveness like this. Not with any woman, ever.

But with Tatiana, seeing her even talking to these two has something vicious raging inside. It has my beast slamming against the cage, wanting so badly to shed this tuxedo, and the manners, and the niceties.

It has me wanting to strip naked and chase her blindly through the darkness, to keep her all to myself.

The two younger guys staring at me nod quickly.

"Sounds good, sir," the slightly quicker of the two blurts. "Our sincere apologies. We didn't know she was with you."

"*Leave.*"

They almost trip over themselves bolting away through the crowd.

Tatiana snorts.

"What the fuck sort of macho bullshit was—"

She gasps as I whirl, grabbing her roughly and possessively by the hip as I yank her close.

"Let's get a few things absolutely fucking clear," I hiss darkly. "Anastasia Javanović and I *are not* and have *never* been a couple, or intimate in any fucking way you're thinking. Her father is Branko Javanović, head of the Javanović Bratva that she will one day inherit. *That's* how I know her, and what we've worked together concerning."

Tatiana swallows, chewing on her lip.

"Clear?"

She nods quickly.

"Great. And the second part is…"

She whimpers as my hand tightens, the other coming up to cup her chin. I tilt her face up to mine, the monster roaring at the bars inside as I fight to keep myself from ripping her gown off right here so that I can fuck her until she's screaming my name.

"The second part is, you are *mine*."

She trembles, but her eyes flash with that defiant fire of hers.

"You don't *own* me—"

She gasps as I whirl, grabbing her wrist and yanking her roughly after me. The crowd parts around us as I storm for a different arched doorway on this side of the ballroom. Through it, we march down another dark hallway, and around another dark corner before I stop, whirl, and slam her against the wall.

"I have you locked on a fucking private island as my own plaything," I rasp, inches from her mouth and relishing the way she shivers against me. "I very much *do*."

And then, like a bullet, it hits me. It's not that she was "untouched" before me that makes me want her even more. It's not that I was her first.

It's that I damn well will be her last.

My hand cups her jaw, lifting that tempting mouth of hers right before I crush mine against it. I kiss her savagely; punishingly. I kiss her like she fucking belongs to me, and I need to brand what's mine with bruises across her tender lips.

She melts into me, whimpering eagerly as my tongue delves into her mouth. I captivate hers, pinning her to the wall behind her as I claim her mouth. My blood roars in my ears. The need to have her, and to remind her that she's all mine, is almost overwhelming.

This possessiveness is an alien feeling to me—this surging need to make sure she understands that she's mine and mine alone. As is the need to make her know that I'm all hers.

But I like it. A lot.

I groan into her lips as my hand slides from her hip down her thigh. I grab a fistful of her gown, and she jolts, gasping sharply into my mouth as I boldly yank her the dress all the way up to her hip.

"Wait," she mumbles, pulling away from my kiss. "What are you—"

Her eyes bulge as my hand drags over her panties, slips into the top, and then slides down between her legs. My finger sinks deep into her slick little cunt.

"*Kristoff!*" She chokes on a gasp. "What are you—! People could—!"

Just as I sink another finger into her slit, my hand on her jaw suddenly moves up to clamp roughly over her mouth. And her eyes go fucking *wide*.

Her body surges again mine, and I feel her gasping moan of pleasure hum against my palm. My fingers curl deep, my thumb rubbing slow, pressured circles over her throbbing clit. Tatiana clings to me tightly, her eyes huge as her body trembles.

"You are *mine, printsessa*," I rasp, lowering my mouth to her ear and nipping at her lobe. "I found you. I took you. And you fucking belong to me and me alone now. And don't try and fight me on that, because I know damn well that it gets you wetter than you've ever been before. I know you *like* being mine—my captive. My plaything. My *fuck-toy*."

She moans a savage, guttural moan against my hand, her eyes rolling back in pleasure as she sags against my hand.

I slip my fingers from her pussy, but only so that I can grab her panties and yank them down to the side. Her eyes widen even more, and she gasps when I yank my belt open and pull the zipper of my trousers down. I pull my heavy, rock-hard cock out and drag the head over her inner thigh.

What's happening here suddenly seems to hit her. She scrabbles, her hand coming up to yank mine away from her mouth and flushed cheeks.

"*Kristoff*! People could hear—"

She whimpers as my hand clamps back across her mouth as mine finds her ear again.

"*Then you'd better keep quiet.*"

My knee shoves her thighs apart. My swollen head sinks between her slick lips. I grab her hip, and with one thrust, I bury every inch of my throbbing hard cock deep inside of her.

Tatiana *screams* into my hand

I grunt, hips flexing as I drag my cock out slowly, relishing every single millimeter of her silken wetness clinging so greedily to me. My glistening cock head slips out to rub over her clit, making her squeal before I sink back into her, hard.

Deep.

Mercilessly.

I grip her hip tightly as I fuck into her, pinning her to the wall at her back with each powerful thrust. She cries out under my palm, and I groan when I feel her teeth bite down against the heel of my hand.

But I keep thrusting—I keep fucking into her, without mercy. She moans and squeals louder and louder into my hand, shaking and trembling against me as I feel her sticky slick arousal drip down my balls.

"*Better be quiet,*" I snarl into her ear. "Lest someone comes around this corner to see you getting fucked like a dirty little cum slut. Begging for my cock with all these fancy fucking people milling around making bad jokes just around the corner."

Her eyes bulge as they roll back, her breath hot against my hand. Her fingers grip my shirt with a feverish energy, tugging me closer, wanting me deeper.

"Think of how scandalized they'd be, seeing you milking my cock like a greedy little girl, so eager to have my cum filling your little cunt and dripping down your thighs."

Tatiana starts to shake, her pussy rippling up and down my shaft as her legs begin to quiver. Her moans grow wanton and wild, loud against my clamped hand across her mouth. My muscles flex, the fire inside of me roaring to an inferno as I pound into her. My teeth find her neck, raking over the tender skin there and biting, leaving marks.

Leaving my claim on her skin, the same as I will with my cum deep inside of her.

Her body tenses, and clenches. And suddenly, as I drive in hard to the hilt and bite the spot where her neck curves into her collarbone hard, she erupts for me.

Tatiana screams into my hand, writhing and shuddering against me. She clenches and then goes slack, her body melting around me, until I can't hold back.

I'll never hold back with her.

I grunt as I sink deep, burying my mouth hungrily against her neck as my balls empty my cum deep inside of her.

My hand slides from her mouth. But before she can even take a breath, my lips sear to hers. Her hands push up my chest, her arms circling my neck as I scoop her into me.

"*Let's go home,*" I growl quietly.

Not "to my home." Not "to the island."

Just home.

Because as deranged as it may be, for the first time ever, my house, my sanctuary, and my island actually feels like one.

A home.

With her.

27

When it does happen, most people join the mile high club in the cramped restroom of a commercial flight.

I've just become a member bent over a teak-wood conference table with Kristoff's fist tangled in my hair as I exploded for him, forty-one-thousand feet above the Baltic Sea.

There's an animal savagery in the way we play. The way his fingers splay over my neck. The way he seems to both coax and demand the pleasure from me in using methods I know should seem devious or deranged. The way sex is a hard, full-contact sport between us—my submission versus his dominance.

The way his dark, prowling demon that I always know lives deep inside of him seems to roar to the surface in terrifying and yet darkly addictive ways.

And yet afterwards, like now, it's as if the pressure simmers off. The roaring, prowling, bloodthirsty beast that's been slamming at the cage bars slinks back to the shadows. It's there—it's always there. But after it's satiated, it goes back to lingering in the background. And it's then that a sort of possessive tenderness takes its place.

I curl into his chest, sitting naked on his lap, covered with a blanket as the jet soars back to Finland from the party.

Finland. That's where I've been living for the last three months, I've just learned.

His fingers trail small delicate patterns across my shoulder and the nape of my neck as I breath in his scent, and exhale against the skin of his neck.

"Why didn't you do it that day?"

His finger halts in its lazy drawing. I swallow as I lift my head, raising my eyes to his.

"I mean—"

"I know what you mean."

I chew on my lip as his icy blue eyes swallow me whole.

Why didn't he kill me.

"I told you, I just couldn't."

"Yeah, but… why?"

He draws in a slow breath before his other hand slips between us. I shiver as his knuckles brush against a nipple—still sensitive from his teeth and fingers—before he finds what he's after. I swallow as he draws the ring on the little chain around my neck up so that we're both looking at it.

"My ring?"

"I know it's not the same one," he says quietly. "But it looks exactly like one I once got for someone, as a gift."

My heart winces at the sudden sting I wasn't expecting.

He didn't kill me because I reminded him of some other girl.

I start to drop my gaze, but his hand on my neck suddenly slides around to cup my cheek and jaw, keeping my eyes raised to his. He shakes his head.

"It was a gift I once bought for my sister."

Relief floods into me, coming hand in hand at the desire to roll my eyes at myself for giving in to where I went with that.

"I didn't know you had a sister."

"I know."

His lips curl a little at the corners. But there's a sadness to that half smile that brings questions to my lips I won't ask.

"She died, young."

He shifts, twisting his shoulder towards me and pointing to a red rose I've noticed as part of his swirl of tattoos there. Beneath it, two years—like bookends of a life.

She *was* young.

My heart sinks. I slide my hand up his chest to his fingers, entwining mine with his.

"I'm sorry," I whisper.

Kristoff looks away out the window at the passing darkness of night.

"I grew up poor as fuck. We had some money when we were still in Russia, but when my mother and I left, we came to the UK with nothing. We lived in this shithole in Liverpool, and my mom cleaned big houses on the other side of the city. I was fourteen when the man I told you about, Mikhail, came into our lives."

He shakes his head, a darkness creeping into his eyes.

"All I wanted to do was fight, hang out. But then Mik—"

He sighs.

"But then Mik came into our lives, and everything changed. He started dating my mother, which was always weird because he had a ton of money. But it was what it was. They got married fast, when I'd just started at his training academy for the Ghost Syndicate."

My eyes dart to his. No words are spoken. But I can see him seeing me swallow the fact that the man who sent him to kill me is his *stepfather*.

"They had my sister soon after they got married."

I swallow, leaning in to kiss his chest.

"What was her name?"

"Her name was Nikita," he says quietly. "My Nik-nack."

I cling to him tighter, viscerally feeling his pain through my own heart as my fingers entwine with his—*wanting* this pain, if only to suck it away from him.

"Mikhail and my mother barely lasted two years. But when I was in my early twenties, he came for *her*."

I shiver as our eyes lock.

"Your sister."

He nods.

"I tried to fight it, but my mother never let go of Mik. She was forever under his spell. Christ, she never even signed the divorce papers even when he'd been gone for years."

I curl tighter against him, my brow furrowing.

"What did he want with her? Your sister, I mean?"

"To recruit her, the same as he'd recruited me."

My face falls.

"He wanted his own biological daughter to train as a killer?"

"Mikhail is a psychopath. And I don't mean that colloquially. He's a manipulative, cruel, single-minded narcissist. He gets what he wants, *always*. And in this case, he took my sister into that deranged program of his and…"

His jaw grinds as he looks away again, his pulse thudding heavily under his skin.

"And he let her die."

I choke, the horrible pieces coming together jarringly.

"He brought her into that fucking place, he pushed her too hard, and he let her fucking die. She was fifteen."

"I'm so sorry."

I turn in his lap, straddling his waist as my arms circle his neck. I kiss him deeply, but this time, it's not a sensual or fevered kiss.

It's a kiss that says, "I see you, and I'm here for you."

"I walked away from Mikhail after that. Mik, the Syndicate, all of it. And I never looked back," he mutters quietly. "Until he dangled the one thing in front of me he knew would have me diving head first into hell."

His eyes meet mine, a sadness and anger in them.

"I had *nothing* to do with what happened to your father—either with Jana implanting herself into your lives, or his accident. I have no play in Mikhail's power games to try and take the Balagula family by force. And the only reason I took the job of…"

"Killing me."

"Yes. I took it, after years of not even speaking to Mikhail, because they offered me the location of Nikita's final resting place."

My heart breaks as I stare into his eyes in pain and horror.

"I agreed to take a life, so that I could properly grieve and bury the one taken from me."

"Kristoff…"

My eyes tear as I hug him tightly, feeling his powerful arms circle me. His hand slides up into the back of my hair, the warmth and strength of his body surrounding me.

"I'm so sorry," I choke against his shoulder as I cling to him.

"You have nothing to apologize for, *printsessa*. You didn't kill her. Mikhail did."

"But her resting place… you didn't kill—"

He pulls back, shaking his head with a wry smile.

"You're dead, remember?"

I smile a crooked, sad smile back.

"So he gave you Nikita's final—"

"No. Not yet."

My face caves. "Kris—"

"I made a choice, Tatiana," he growls heavily.

I shiver as his hand tightens possessively in almost a sensual way in my hair, keeping me close.

"I *will* get what I was promised. But I made a choice. And I chose you."

I'm falling into him, choking on the sob as his lips crush to mine.

"I would always choose you, my printsessa."

We just sit there, locked in each other's arms and kissing, until the lull of the jet engines begins to pull me to sleep.

"Kristoff?"

I've been thinking about the last few months. I've been replaying everything in rewind, going from now, back through the island, the first blindingly hectic chases. The plane where I was blindfolded and bound. All the way back to the morning he caught me.

And something's just stuck out to me.

"Yes?" He murmurs, kissing the top of my sleepy head.

"How close was I really to that cliff? I mean when I tried to run from the car that first day."

He's silent. And suddenly, I can feel his chest hitching with a snickered laughs.

I whip my head up, staring at him as my jaw drops.

"*Please* tell me there really was a cliff."

Kristoff just grins.

"Oh you *motherfucker*!"

I smack his chest as he laughs, pulls me close, and slams his lips to mine.

28

Maybe leaving solitude to rejoin society is a good thing from time to time. But the second we're back on the island, I'm ready to give it another three months before we interact with anyone else again.

Part of that feeling is that I never felt free when I was out there "in the world." And here, acknowledging the dark irony of it, I do. And yes, part of it is that out there, I need to hide. I need to be someone who isn't Tatiana Fairist, because Tatiana Fairist is dead.

And maybe she is, in a way.

I'm not that girl anymore. This place has changed me. Being freed from the life I knew as a reluctant Bratva princess looking down the barrel of arranged marriage. *He's* changed me.

And that's the biggest part: Kristoff.

The reason I'm more than content to just stay here is him. I could spend… well?

I could spend forever here with him. Just being with him, and kissing him, and running from him. Here on this island, our dark sides combine. I thrive off the thrill of being hunted, and the adrenaline rush of the run along with the flashes of memory from my gaps that come back with it. And he feeds off of that.

Together, we're a circle. A two-group food chain of sorts.

I feed off his darkness.

He devours mine.

Two weeks after our excursion to Vienna, I'm waving from the end of the dock as Kristoff roars across the lake in the boat. I've been seeing it in his eyes, though he's freakishly good at hiding it.

The fact that I may be dead to the world, without any responsibilities to answer to. But he's not. He's got a job, and a boss. He's got friends, presumably. And the boy, Misha, who he jokingly refers to as his little brother.

When you're "dead," those things can stay on the outskirts, "out there." But when you're alive, there comes a point where you can't ignore life anymore.

Kristoff's just hit one of those un-ignorable parts, and now has to make a quick overnight trip to Germany for a business thing. I've told myself a thousand times it's going to be fine. I've rolled my eyes at myself for being mopey that there's *one day* in almost four months of being with him daily that he won't be here.

But still, there's a twinge of something when I watch his boat skim over the lake to the far shore. A looming sensation like I won't ever see him again.

I roll my eyes, shivering as I hug myself.

You fucking dork.

But still, I watch until he's out of sight on the far shore before turning and walking back up to the house.

Our house.

For the first time in months, I make and eat dinner alone. And being alone comes with unexpected mind-games, too. I find myself, for the first time in months, actually wanting to look into how the world has viewed the death of Tatiana Fairist. I want to see if Lyra, or any other vague acquaintance from college, has posted about me, or misses me.

But I won't. I can't, in any case. I know it's too risky to log into any of my old accounts or social media things from here.

So instead, I finish my dinner and then retreat into the library to crack open my latest adventure escape—Lewis Carroll's *Through the Looking-glass, and What Alice Found There*. But less than half an hour later, I set it back down on the couch next to me, my brow knitting as my lips twist.

Goddamnit, I miss him.

I stand, padding barefoot through the house and out the kitchen door. The weather is turning a little colder than when I first got here. But I love the slight coolness the nights have been getting recently. For a second, I almost head back in for a sweatshirt or something. But instead, I just hug my arms around myself as I walk down to the lapping shore under the moonlight.

I stare out at the almost still water, wishing it was choppy with the approach of his boat again.

Oh good God, chill.

I sigh, rolling my eyes at myself again as I turn and start to walk down the shore. I pick up a smooth stone and skip it across the water before I keep walking, getting closer to the boathouse. I kick at a clump of dirt with my bare feet as I walk past it, until suddenly, something catches the corner of my eye.

I stop suddenly, my heart leaping in my throat as I whip my head around to look at the little boat pulled up to the shore, moored to the far side of the boathouse in the shadows.

A grin creeps over my face.

That sneak.

But then, another feeling aside from giddiness creeps over me.

Lust.

There's a fantasy Kristoff and I have talked about, once or twice. One that pushes the boundaries. One that pushes sanity, even. And makes me question just how fucked up I really am if this is something I want, and actually desire.

In the fantasy, the chase isn't just me "escaping" as I've done countless times before to run into the night. It's not just him "chasing" me, as *he's* done countless times before. Because that's just our dark game.

But in the fantasy, it feels *real*.

We've never talked through the logistics. Just some of the pieces of what it would entail. Of him surprising me—like for real surprising me, somehow. Like jumping out at me when I least expect it or something. Or one idea we touched on was that in our next excursion to the real world, he'd grab me somewhere and "kidnap" me again.

The point being, to tap into that primal, depraved fear-arousal that was there the first time he took me, and then chased me.

But it's all been vague. It's all been fantasy.

Until now.

My pulse thuds as I stare at the boat. His whole business trip thing was a play to leave, only to come back and surprise me. Part of me pouts that I've just spoiled some of that surprise, like I've discovered the unwrapped Christmas presents in the closet. But my pulse still thuds.

My skin still tingles.

And my heart still lurches chokingly into my throat when I hear the soft snap of a twig behind me.

I whirl, shaking and feeling an electric chill creep down my spine. And when I see him—sweet *Jesus*.

A war of pure desire swirling with abject fear explodes through my core.

He's dressed in all black, standing there menacingly in the shadows of the tree line, staring right at me.

Through a fucking *mask*.

My pulse hums under the surface, my breath quickening as my heart quickens.

Black boots, black pants, a black flack jacket, a black fucking *mask*—fuck, he even has a freaking knife in his hand.

I shiver, my eyes flitting to the side, gauging the angle to see if I can make it to the trees before he—

"Run all you want, little bitch."

My world turns to ice. My eager grin vanishes as my heart seizes.

The man standing in front of me in all black, with a gun, *isn't fucking Kristoff*.

"I'll still catch you. And *then*, we'll have some real fun before I bleed you out."

My gut reaction is to scream, or cry, or just collapse and beg for mercy. But, I don't. Something stops me. A voice. A power inside, overriding the pre-programmed flight or fight response of evolution.

It's Kristoff. The power and the sudden determination I feel inside is Kristoff. It's months of running from him. Months of training with him. Months of realizing myself with him.

And suddenly, something hardens in me. My eyes narrow at the man across from me, and my teeth grit.

I will not die like this.

I turn to my left and spring forward as if to make a run for it. But in one fluid motion, just as he makes a play to bolt after me, I pivot—a trick I've pulled on Kristoff in dozens of chases. I whirl, and I spring to my *right*, instead.

It's not much, but suddenly, I have a fighting chance.

"You little bitch!" The man roars as he charges after me.

But I can barely hear him as I crash into the trees. All I can hear is the crash and snap of branches. The terrifying, adrenaline-soaked roar of my pulse. The ragged panting of my breath as I charge headlong through the trees.

He's coming after me. But he's not Kristoff. He's not *me*, and he doesn't know this island like I do. I twist hard to the left, bolting for a specific spot. It's a trap I've tried to spring on Kristoff before, but it's always failed with him, since he knows this place better than me.

I'm betting the man chasing me does not. In fact, I'm literally betting my life on it.

"Run run, little bitch!"

The snarled words rattling through the haunting, dark woods make me gasp; fear gripping my throat.

"Run away, *Tatiana*," he cackles darkly. "I'll get you. And when I do, I'm going to use those pretty tears of yours for lube."

That horrible gut reaction to cry or scream sinks it's claws deep into me. I choke out a sob as I fling myself through the darkness. But I push on. I keep running.

I have to keep running.

And then a second later, as soon as I see the familiar stump, I just jump on instinct. On memory.

This is the trap.

At one point during Kristoff and I's hunter-prey games through these woods, I found a small stream that cuts through part of the island. It's not big, but at a certain place, it cuts deep through a hilly rise in the trees, creating a sudden trench of sorts.

That's what I jump over, hearing the terrifying crash of a body slamming through the trees right behind me.

"Come out and play, you little cun—"

I hear the scrabble of feet skidding into space. I hear the choked grunt, the gasp, and then a sickeningly wet gurgling sound.

And then suddenly, the woods are silent.

I stop running. My ears are ringing, and my muscles quivering. Swallowing feels like sandpaper as I caught, turning to let my eyes stab into the darkness.

My pulse thuds like a hammer at my chest.

Slowly, I walk back the way I ran, back towards the sudden trench. A slight and sudden choked gurgling sound has my heart leaping into my throat. But then it's gone. My face is ashen as I step to the edge and glance over.

Oh fuck.

He's dead. Or, he's about to be. The man in the mask who was just chasing me with a knife has slipped over the edge of the trench and landed twisted against the far side with that very knife embedded in his throat to the hilt.

My eyes bulge, the color draining from my face.

There's a lot of blood. A *lot* of blood. A flash of something hits me, but I shake it off, focusing and telling myself to breathe.

It's over. I'm safe.

I'm safe.

I swallow, standing with every intention of running back to the house and locking myself in one of the bedrooms until Kristoff gets back.

When suddenly, the silence of the forest is shattered.

By a ringtone.

My gaze snaps down into the trench. Next to the now clearly dead attacker, a cellphone is lying in the pine needles. The blueish glow of the screen casts ghastly shadows across the dead man's face as the ring tone blares into the night.

Slowly, I turn and climb down into the ravine.

My hands shake with adrenaline and fear as I reach for the ringing phone. I don't even know what the hell I'm doing, or what my plan is. But I don't have time to contemplate it too hard before I'm tapping the answer button and bringing the phone to my ear.

"Is it done?"

A sensation like knife sinking into my gut and twisting bites into me. A cold chill creeps up my back, turning my face pale as the sick roils in my stomach.

The voice on the other end is Jana; my stepmother.

"Hello?" she snaps. "I said, is it *done?*"

Without even thinking, I grunt in the lowest tone I possible can. Jana audibly exhales.

"*Good*," she mutters with almost a glee in her voice. "Good. Kristoff's in Berlin, but I'll deal with him myself. He'll learn to fall in line."

My heart thuds in my chest, my pulse slugging like oil through my veins.

"Fuck him for trying to sweep this himself. Keeping her there, seducing her, I'm sure, to get his hands on what's mine."

A coldness sinks into me. A horrible, twisting sensation snarls in my gut.

"Anyway," Jana says dismissively. "Thank you for your work, Ansel. Leave her body somewhere he'll see, yes?"

I swallow.

"Ansel."

I make a grunting sound again. But even I know this one fails. I'm too cold. I'm too dizzy. I'm too feeling like I'm outside my own body, watching this whole horrid thing play out.

The phone goes absolutely silent as the seconds tick by.

"Who the fuck is this?"

I swallow.

Suddenly, Jana starts to chuckle.

"My my *my*… it's you, Tatiana, isn't it?"

I can't answer. I can't breathe. Cold, abject fear and horror sinks into every part of me, nailing me to the ground beneath my feet.

"I'm impressed," Jana purrs. "Is Ansel dead?"

Swallowing feels like sand. But I do, clearing my throat.

"*Yes*," I rasp.

"*Hmm*. Curious. Well, my dear, now you have a choice to make."

I blink as Jana sighs.

"Meet me, and I'll arrange for paperwork for you to sign."

"Paperwork for what," I croak.

"The fucking *empire*, you stupid bitch."

My eyes narrow. Slowly, my body begins to unthaw. Because suddenly, I'm truly realizing who I'm talking to.

The woman who killed my father. Or the one who *had* him killed. The woman who slipped into my father's life while he was grieving my mother and seduced her way into his bed and our lives. All so she could destroy everything from the inside and take it for herself.

My dad and I were hardly close. But he was still my father.

Cold fury sinks into me as my lips curl.

"That's not happening," I hiss.

Jana sighs. "Well, *yes*, it is. Or I will hunt you like a dog to the ends of the goddamn earth. You can't run from me, little girl," she laughs. "You think he's there to save you, don't you? You think *that* is what Kristoff Zima is?"

My lips curl.

"You don't know what he—"

"I know he is *not* your savior," she laughs coldly. "This wasn't him *rescuing* you! This was making his own play for the throne!"

My pulse dulls. My eyes blur at the edges as I slowly shake my head.

"That's not—"

"Oh my God, you silly girl," Jana laughs a brittle, joy-less laugh. "There is *so much* you don't know."

My body trembles. My legs shake as a numb sensation starts to sink into me.

"I'll make this simple, Tatiana. Meet me, now, or I'll destroy you."

"Go to hell—"

"Kristoff was the carrot, you silly little girl," she sneers and then laughs again. "I mean, of all the trained assassins at our disposal, we send the ruggedly handsome one? Those eyes, those dimples, the tattoos? We send the hitman who makes women weak in the knees? The one who fucks like a god?"

My heart begins to unravel. My legs begin to go numb as my stomach drops.

"The *trained* operative, who excels at seduction and manipulation?" She snickers. "His job was never to kill you, Tatiana. His job was to *conquer* you. And judging by your reluctance to see that, I think deep down you know it's true."

Tears start to blur my eyes. My heart twists and wrenches, dying a thousand little deaths as my throat constricts.

No. No, no, no, no, no...

"What do you think a man like *that* wants with a sheltered little virgin?"

I blanch as she laughs a cold laugh.

"Oh and how do I know that? Because he fucking *told me*, Tatiana. Before he turned on me to try and take the Balagula for himself by seducing you."

"*Stop—*"

"The truth fucking *hurts*," she sneers. "Get used to it."

I lose my balance, reaching out to catch myself against the side of the trench as Jana sighs.

"Kristoff was one tool, little girl. I'm another. He was the carrot. I'm the fucking stick. Now, there's one way out of this where you live. Meet me, and sign over the Balagula to me, unequivocally. With you still alive, that fucking council of your grandfather's won't—"

"Go *fuck* yourself—"

"There is *one* fucking way you walk away from any of this with your heart still in your goddamn body, you little brat," Jana snaps coldly. "Sign the fucking—"

"You'll have to find me first."

She snickers.

"Oh, believe me, Tatiana, I'll—"

"Come and get me."

I hang up. Then I drop the phone to the ground, grab a rock, and smash it until it goes dark. I ignore the dead man in the puddle of blood, dirt, and pine needles as I climb out of the trench. Then I bolt through the woods until I get to the boat house.

Kristoff took the only boat. But the one that came with the man who just tried to kill me is still there, tied up in the shadows.

Then next time, be aware of your needs and surroundings before you make an escape.

I'm numb when I stagger back into the house. I climb the stairs in a cold daze, all the way up to Kristoff's room—which has been *my* room as well for months.

I don't take much. Just a small backpack from the walk-in, which I fill with a few light changes of clothes and some toiletries. I dress in jeans, a hoodie, and sneakers. Then I open one of the drawers on his side of the closet.

I lift out the Cartier watch and tap in the code I once watched him tap in. The panic room door slides open. Inside, I open an unlocked box on a shelf and pull out a gun and two spare mags, along with a few stacks of bills in both Euros and pounds.

Back in the closet, I open the watch drawer again. I don't know watches that well, but I'm guessing based on the house I'm in, on the private island, owned by the man who drives luxury cars and flies private jets that they're all valuable.

The whole drawer goes into the bag.

Outside, I run silently to the dinghy and untie it from the boathouse. I push off, climb inside, and then start the small outboard motor.

I don't look back. I don't need to see the place where I was toyed with. Gamed with. Where I was kept in a pretty little cage of the body and mind.

Where my heart was stolen and cut to pieces.

I don't ever need to look back.

I surge into the darkness as the moon glistens across the water.

Then, I'm gone.

29

Something's wrong.

It's a sixth sense that hits me before I even get close to the boathouse. But as I do get closer, my pulse suddenly explodes like napalm through my veins.

The front door of the house is wide fucking open.

I skip the boathouse. I just ram the boat full speed right up onto the shore before I lunge out. My gun is already in my hand as I sprint to the house, shouldering the open door almost off its hinges as I go crashing inside.

"Tatiana!"

I roar her name as I storm from room to room, but there's no answer. In the kitchen, I find a plate with the remains of what looks like dinner from the night before sitting in the sink. But nothing else. No morning coffee cup. No cereal bowl.

Nothing.

In the library, I find the copy of *Through the Looking-glass and What Alice Found There* that Tatiana's been reading.

But nothing else.

It's like she's turned into a ghost and fucking vanished.

At the top floor, in the expansive bedroom we've been sharing—a first for me, ever—there's still nothing. But when I move to the closet, my jaw sets.

The panic room door is ajar.

The spare gun and two mags I keep inside are gone, as well. So is about a hundred-thousand in mixed Euros and pounds.

So is a small backpack, some of her clothes and toiletries, and my entire drawer of watches.

My jaw sets. My eyes narrow wickedly as I whirl and storm back outside. My mind races through a thousand nightmare scenarios that all seem to fall on someone taking her from me. But there's no sign of struggle in the house. Nothing missing except her things, a gun, money, and a fortune in watches.

And her.

A low, simmering thought spreads like black ink over my thoughts. Because there's only one real conclusion here, and it's glaring right at me. Laughing. Mocking me. Mocking my idea that by some fucked up idea, what had here could be forever.

That she'd want to stay.

That she felt for me more than the thrill and lust of the dark games and primal sex. Like I do, for her.

That she wasn't just biding her time, waiting for a chance to escape.

My head whips around, eyes narrowing at the shore. But, the boat is still there, and there's not another one on the island. She can swim, but…

A cold hand grips my heart as I stare out at the inky black lake.

No way. She didn't try and swim for it. Which means…

She's still here. She's still on the island.

My eyes blaze as I whirl, searching, hunting, prowling as I stalk into the darkness around the house. Until suddenly, I see it.

A broken branch, near the tree line by the boathouse.

I stiffen, and a hungry, relieved grin spreads over my face.

That little *tease*.

We've half-talked about this—about upping the stakes. Making it all more real. About me surprising her. And now I know what this is.

She's engineered this. And goddamn, she did it well. She made it real, making it look like she ran from me, or was taken.

Now, I'm going to make it equally real when I hunt her down and make her moan into the forest floor with my cock buried in her pussy.

I set off through the woods, grinning maniacally and hungrily as I pick up the trail. I follow the broken branches, the fallen leaves, the trodden underbrush. When the tracks zig to the left, I grin.

I know where she is.

She actually almost seriously fucked me up with that goddamn trench ravine one time. I knew it was there—I know every damn square foot of this island. But it'd been a while. And I was distracted knowing my most favorite prey was sprinting through the woods from me, yet also aching for me to catch her and fuck her into submission.

I'd caught myself just shy of hurdling head-first over the edge of the trench and breaking my neck.

That's where she is—either where I'll pick up another changed direction in her tracks, or maybe, where she's hiding.

I slow to a creeping pace, slinking through the branches as I approach the little ravine. My heart pounds. My muscles clench, hands itching to rip her clothes off or find a fistful of her hair. To spank her bare ass red until she squeals for mercy.

To wrap my hands around that delicate throat and watch her eyes cloud with pure lust as I ram my cock deep and feel her come for me.

The moonlight glints through the trees off a slight peak of pale skin. My blood burns like diesel as I crouch, take a measured breath, and then pounce like a fucking tiger into the ravine.

Reality glitches, hard. The energy in my blood turns to ice, and suddenly, it's like I've been hit sideways by a fucking train.

It's not Tatiana hiding in the trench.

It's a fucking body.

I've seen more dead bodies that I can count. But the longer I look at this one, the more detached from reality I seem to get. It's as if my brain won't allow me to process this. It won't *let me* just blink this away.

But this is real.

Slowly, as if being dragged out of a pool of crude oil, everything fades back. I suddenly hear the dull background noises of the lake and the forest. I can hear and feel my own pulse hammering through my veins.

I'm aware of the lined look on my face and the cold sweat sheened over my back.

What. The. Fuck.

The body is blueish and bled out—obvious by the dark stains on the leaves and pine needles he's crumpled against. Also by the military-grade knife sunk to the hilt in his neck when I kick him over. I glance up at the lip of the ravine, then back down.

Tatiana didn't do this. Not directly, at least. He fell and landed on the knife.

But she led him here.

This was planned self-defense.

My head feels numb and heavy as I look down. There's a smashed phone next to the man, clearly hit with a rock, *after* it'd been dropped onto the bloody leaves.

That was her, too.

The only question now is *where the fuck is she*.

Back out of the trench, I catch her trail again. But it heads back in a similar way she came. I follow closely, every single sense I have tuned to a pin as I prowl through the darkness. Until I'm back to the house.

My eyes narrow as the events play out.

She was home. A man came in, or maybe caught her by surprise outside. But she ran, and she led him to that ravine, where he fell and bled out. She smashed his phone, came back here, and then…

Where did you go, printsessa…

The open space between the house and the shore and the boathouse is marred with my own footsteps from earlier. And it's been a full day. But something I missed before, being preoccupied by the wide-open front door, catches my eye.

It's a pink hair tie, lying in the grass, headed in the direction of the boathouse.

You've left a trail…

I bolt to the boathouse, scouting around the inside, but finding nothing. I stalk around the perimeter of the building, until suddenly, I spot it.

There's a scrape on the white paint of the boathouse pylon, on the far side from the house.

It's the rub of a rope that was lashed here.

A boat was moored here. The man's boat.

The pieces fall into place fast, making my pulse surge until suddenly, the whole puzzle is all there laid out in front of me.

But the image is horrible.

He came. He died. She took his boat. She *left*.

No message. No note. Nothing. Just like before when I was running through the house, she's gone—faded like a phantom.

I'm staring at near-still surface of the lake when my phone rings.

It's Jana. And I know before I even answer that it's no random chance that Mikhail's right hand is calling me at this exact moment.

"Where the fuck is she."

There's a pause, and then the grating, hateful sound of Jana's cold laugh rattles into my ear.

"She's gone, Kristoff."

I see red, even though I already know.

"Tell me where the *fuck* you took—"

"I didn't say I *took* her, Kristoff," she sighs. "I said she's gone."

"I'm never in the mood for you or your fucking games, Jana," I seethe through clenched teeth. "But trust when I say I am *beyond*—"

"Now, mind you, the plan *was* to take her," she purrs thinly. "But that plan changed when she killed my fucking man."

I sneer.

"Gloat if you want, Kristoff. She's still not there, is she? See, that's where the art lies with planning. To be able to switch gears, and switch plans at the drop of a—"

"Do not quote Mik's classroom bullshit to me," I snarl. "Where. The. *FUCK. IS. SHE*!?"

"*Away from you!*" she snaps. "And *that* is the plan that matters. She's away from you, where I can now find her myself."

I laugh coldly.

"You won't"

"We'll see. But you destroyed my plan, so now I'm destroying yours."

My brows knit. "What the actual fuck are you on about?"

Jana sighs a bored sigh. "Save us both the headache of arguing and don't."

"Don't *what*."

"Don't pretend you don't want the same thing I do, Kristoff. The crown. The throne. The Balagula fucking empire, which is worth billions. I went after it my way—"

"*Mikhail's* way," I spit. "You might be an evil, spiteful cunt, Jana, but don't try and tell me this is your master plan—"

I stop cold. The gears grind in my head, until a sudden awful, terrible truth materializes.

Jana snickers.

"Now you see it, don't you, Kristoff."

And I do.

The way she kept calling it "her Op." The way she kept hounding me to keep the intel between her and I, and not to "bother or involve" Mikhail.

The promise of Nikita's resting place came from *her*.

The orders to go to the Balagula house that day came from *her*. And the intel of the security detail, the guards and their firepower, the response time of the local law enforcement…

It all came from Jana. Not from Mikhail; *her*. She just kept mentioning that it was coming from Mik, *through her*. And suddenly, I see the whole thing for what it is.

This was a coup. Jana was already in place as Peter Fairist's second wife, and in line to be queen of a billion-dollar Bratva empire, so long as Tatiana wasn't in the picture.

And she made a move to sidestep Mik. To remove him from the chess board entirely. And I was the fucking pawn that helped her do it.

She starts to laugh as the silence ticks by.

"You see it now, don't you. I'm close to taking it all, Kristoff. All the marbles. All the cards. No more Mikhail and his bullshit. I had it all planned, until you decided to go rogue."

"I'll be sure to apologize profusely before I put a bullet through the back of your fucking throat, Jana."

She laughs coldly.

"Good luck. With that little bitch missing, she's as good as found by me, or dead some other way. You do know why she ran, don't you?"

My jaw tightens. Jana sighs.

"I showed her your cards, Kristoff."

"What the *fuck* are you talking about?"

"Oh, don't play hero to me, *bukavac*," she sneers. "You saw opportunity the same as I did! We may have gone at it differently, but I'd even say that my way was more humane. All I wanted to do was kill one little Bratva princess *brat* and be done with it. But you?" she sneers. "You decided to have some fun. You decided to have yourself a little plaything, and get the empire that way."

I stagger back, dropping to my knees as my heart begins to crack at the edges.

Oh fuck.

She didn't just run.

She ran *from me*.

And this time, it's not a game.

"You tried to destroy my plan," Jana spits. "So this is me destroying yours."

"There *was* no fucking plan!" I roar into the darkness.

"Well, my plan brought me happiness, Kristoff. And you burned it. This is me torching *your* happiness."

The world spins. My chest constricts as my teeth grind painfully.

"Oh, and before you threaten me with going to Mikhail… go ahead. I've made my play, Kristoff. The Balagula throne is *mine*. And pretty soon, I'll find that little bitch, and I'll—"

I hang up.

My pulse cools to a dark, molten, hateful thud. I stare out at the inky still blackness of the lake.

Not if I fucking find her first.

30

Two years later, London:

"Thank you for sharing your story, Theresa."

In my head, I think that might sound a *bit* more sincere to Theresa if there weren't eighteen other women saying it out loud to her at the same time as me. But, oh well. Besides, Theresa looks pleased, and she beams, thanking us all as she touches her heart before taking her seat.

Nneka stands next, clasping her hands together as she beams her radiant smile at us all. It amazes me that, *still*, her smile is always the first thing I or anyone notices about her. Not the scar on her jaw, by her ear, where her ex-husband struck her with a pint glass.

"Sisters, thank you to everyone who shared today. We share your pain. We share your triumph. We love you, as we love ourselves."

THE HUNTER KING

There's a smattering of "amen's" around the circle, even though the group isn't religiously based. A few others nod along. Monica, to my right, just smiles at me.

"Is there anyone who'd like to plan now to speak next week?"

Nneka lets her gentle gaze and calming smile settle on each of us around the circle. Monica's heal bumps mine.

"*You should*," she whispers. "If you're ready, I mean."

"I'm not."

She smiles again, though this time it's less encouraging and more of a "I share your pain and it's fine" kind of smile.

God, sometimes I really feel like a fraud here.

"Well, until next week then. If anyone needs anything, remember my phone is always on. I am always here for you."

With the meeting over, we all stand. Monica and Chella, who I think are also friends outside of the group, smile warmly as they approach me.

"Look, Harriet, no pressure, but we were thinking about going to get a glass of wine—"

"Or coffee?" Chella adds, a hopeful raise to her brows.

"Or coffee, yes!" Monica repeats. "Anyway, we'd love to have you if you'd like to join?"

It's not that she and Chella aren't perfectly nice women. Like Nneka, they both carry physical reminders of the pain and trauma they left behind with the toxic, abusive people they ran from.

Monica's right arm bears the myriad of dots left by her ex-girlfriend's cigarettes, which she'd stab out on Monica's skin when her mood soured. Chella walks with a cane, after her husband rammed her with a car when she tried to leave the first time.

And yet, they're both still smiling.

It's not that a drink—or several—with people I can call friends doesn't sound good. It sounds amazing, actually.

It's just that I can't.

Some of it is that feeling of being a phony. The other women who come to IPVS-Anon—Intimate Partner Violence Survivors Anonymous—come from real, horrible trauma. These women were beaten, sexually abused, and manipulated by husbands, wives, boyfriends, and girlfriends. They carry physical scars, or they flinch when the door to a meeting room shuts too hard.

No one beat me. No one assaulted me. No one snubbed out cigarettes on my arm or tried to run me over with a fucking car.

But I *was* manipulated. Gaslit. Lied to. Tricked. Played. Fooled. Toyed with.

Used.

Because I know now that all of it was a pretty, wrapped up tight with a bow, *lie*. I know now that all of our games, and moments, and ecstasy—all the ways I let go, and let him in, and dropped my defenses…

It was never about me. Or us. Or that feeling I thought I felt in my heart.

It was about worming his way in deep, so that he could use me to make a play for my family's empire.

It's not that I nakedly and unquestioningly believe what Jana told me that night on the shore of the island I thought was paradise. But once I was gone, and out on my own, I dug.

And slowly, so much of it began to make sense.

How he kept me "all to himself," which is another way of saying "isolating me." How he played into my every fantasy, knowing exactly what buttons to push, and how hard.

He could do that because he was literally *trained* to do that. For fuck's sake, he told me himself that the organization he was a part of trained it's initiates in seduction as a tool or weapon.

And I still let myself go with him. I *still* opened my legs and my heart and let him touch me where no one else ever has, physically and emotionally.

I've looked up his boss, too—Boris Tsavakov. There's not much on Kristoff himself online. But I've read enough horrible shit about the man he works for to see Kristoff for who and what he is.

So, maybe he never smashed a pint glass on my face, or anything like that. But emotional manipulation is still abuse. And when I discovered IPVS-Anon, it felt like a place I should at least come to once.

And honestly, if that's the only reason I came to the group, I'd probably feel better. But I'm also here for another reason: beyond meetings, IPVS-Anon is also a huge resource for women who've had to leave bad situations.

Women who need a place to stay, but don't have credit. Or money. Or they need a job, but they've been a housewife with no workplace experience for ten years.

Or they've had to change their names, and don't even have legal ID.

Yes, I'm here because it feels less alone sometimes to be around others who've had to run and leave everything. But I'm also here *because I ran and left everything*.

Because almost two and a half years ago, Tatiana Fairist died. Two years ago, when I found my way to London, I was like any of these other women at the meetings: no credit score. No bank accounts. No job training.

No official ID, even.

But IPVS-Anon was there, and it was a resource. So I used them.

Nneka herself introduced me to the lawyer who helped me "exist" again. They helped me get into the system, as my new name, and new identity. Another woman named Deirdre is the one who introduced me to a former IPSV-Anon attendee name Carly, who was willing to rent me the tiny basement flat in her Wandsworth apartment building.

And Becca got me in as a cocktail waitress at her friend's friend's pub, the Scarlet Hog, where I now bartend five nights a week.

I wish it wasn't there, but it is: the guilt. The feelings of being a fraud when I'm here. But it is what it is.

And what it is, is my new life.

I'm doing okay now with the bar shifts. But the cash I took from the lake house when I ran went quick, mostly just to get me to London in the first place. There was the truck driver who brought me—still shaking and dazed—from wherever I was in the wilderness of Finland to Helsinki.

From there, I paid a cargo ship captain—in cash, though he intimated there was another payment he'd have preferred—to take me across the Black Sea as an unregistered passenger to Stockholm.

I didn't sleep that trip, and my hand never left the gun in my bag.

In Sweden, I paid a pilot to take me in his single engine from Uppsala to Copenhagen, where *another* cargo captain took me all the way to Eastbourne, UK—for a whopping thirty-thousand pounds, once he saw the desperation in my eyes.

And beyond that, there's the money I've paid to random people around the world to act as decoys. The man in China I found in an anonymous dark web chat room who agreed to try and open credit cards under the name Tatiana Fairist for five-thousand Euros. The woman in Chicago who filled out an apartment lease application under that name, as well.

The people I paid to make hotel bookings, car rentals, cruises, and loan applications.

After all that, I was just surviving for a few months, watching my cash deplete and wondering when I'd have to start selling the watches, before I found IPVS-Anon.

"You know what?" I smile—a mask I've perfected over the last two years. It's a crafted smile, meant to hide the pain underneath.

The loss. The betrayal.

"I'd love to, it's just that I have a shift to get to."

"Oh! Yes, of course," Monica blurts. "Well, maybe next time?"

"I'd love that."

"Wonderful. See you next week, Harriet."

I turn to leave. But I jump a little as I almost crash into a small, middle-aged man with a smile.

"My goodness, I'm sorry if I startled you."

I recognize him as Pastor Seamus, the minister of the church which is good enough to let IPVS-Anon meet in its basement. We haven't spoken before, though.

He smiles at me.

"It's Miss… Quinton, is it?"

"Quimby."

"Right, of course. Harriet Quimby. My apologies."

His face lights up.

"My goodness, like the pilot who flew over the Thames?"

I stiffen.

"Yes, I… my mother was a big history fan."

He beams. "Marvelous. Well, Miss Quimby, a little bird told me…" he winks as he leans in conspiratorially. "It was Nneka," he murmurs with a grin. "Well, she mentioned that you're quite the runner. And I was wondering if you'd have any interest in helping to coach a local youth track and field club the church is helping to put together. We could always use knowledgeable athletes!"

Big, visible group activities. Yeah, that's a hard no.

"I'm *so* sorry, Pastor. I'd love to, I'm just booked up with work."

He nods with a smile.

"Of course. And no need to apologize at all. If things free up, though?"

"You'll be the first one I call."

He grins. "Lovely."

I TAKE a deep breath as I look up at the front of the pub. But it's not the Scarlet Hog. Contrary to what I told Monica and Chella, I don't actually have a shift right now.

My gaze drags over the place on the wall where letters once spelled "The Crook and Shanks Pub"—the dirty outlines the only thing remaining after they apparently closed a month ago. I drop my gaze further, until I catch my own reflection in the glass of the front door—my now dark-dyed hair pulled back in a high ponytail.

Another newness in my life. Another way to distance myself from the past. And him.

"Ahh, you beat me!"

I turn and smile as Camilla, the real estate agent I was emailing with all week, trots up smartly in heels.

"Nice to finally meet you, Harriet."

"And you!" I blink, grinning in surprise. "I'm... wow."

She lifts a brow. "Is everything alright?"

I shake my head.

"Yeah, no, sorry. It's just that I've been blown off by like three other agents over the last few weeks."

She sighs. "Men, yes?"

I nod, and she rolls her eyes.

"It's because it a bloody boys club, hon. They see your email expressing interest in purchasing or leasing a space to open a pub. But then they see the name *Harriet*. And I promise you, all they're thinking is that you're some bored wife of a hedge fund trader or something looking to start that doomed-to-fail bar you've just always wanted to open."

My brows furrow.

"You really believe that?"

"Oh, Harriet, I *know* that. Think of my emails this last week. How do they sign off?"

I frown.

"Best regards?"

"Best regards, *Cam*," she smirks triumphantly. "Not Camilla, Cam. As I said, it's a fucking boys club out there, especially in commercial real estate. So play their game better. Fake them and play off their bullshit."

I grin. "Yeah?"

"Oh, *yeah*. Like with you?" She looks me up and down and shrugs. "Try using Harry on your emails next time when you email those pricks. See how fast they respond begging to meet up on your schedule."

I shake my head. "*Yikes.*"

"Tell me about it. Now…." She fishes some keys out of her bag. "Shall we check out the space?"

It's empty and dusty inside. But I can see potential. Camilla sighs, smiling as she twirls around the bar space.

"Now, it would need some construction and work put into it to bring it up to par with the neighborhood. This is a trendy area now, and it's only going to go up. Which brings me to the less than happy subject of the *price*…"

She makes a face.

"The property owners feel it's a little too low. And they're looking to increase their ask by the end of the month, unless they get a serious offer."

I wince. The price is already *crazy* for this place. But… this is my future, now.

Harriet Quimby is my new name. I have dark brown hair now, and London's my new home. And it turns out, I *love* working in bars. I love the energy and the chaos. I love creating an experience for people to have a good time.

And I'm pretty damn good at it.

There's not a chance in hell I could afford this place with what I'm making at the Scarlet Hog. But, since I'm narrowing things down, I've just liquidated my last backup plan.

The watches.

It's been tough just sitting on them. But eleven wrist watches are easy to hide. A suitcase full of cash or a bulging bank account isn't. And it *would* be bulging.

I had the watches appraised two years ago when I first landed in London. There's not a one under ninety-thousand pounds. But the crown jewel is a super rare, stainless steel Patek Philippe that almost gave my appraiser a heart attack.

Because it's worth four million pounds.

And as of five days ago, through various back channels and underground circles my somewhat shady appraiser knew, it and the other ten watches have been sold.

For cash. Five and a half million pounds worth of cash, to be exact. Five and a half million pounds, hiding discreetly in a safety deposit box at the bank.

Yes, I stole from Kristoff's house when I ran.

No, I don't give a shit.

"So, I don't want to alarm you. But, if this space is really speaking to you, I'd make a decision soon. Before they bring the price tag up."

I nod, glancing around at the space, and seeing my future here.

"I could know for sure by the end of next week."

Camilla beams. *"Wonderful.* Now, I really need to show you the wine cellar, because it does come with the property, and some of these bottles and vintages will knock your socks off."

Later, my feet aching from walking all day, I plod down the stairs to my basement apartment. I really should go for a run or something, or maybe go train or spar down at the gym. But I'm exhausted, and I'm actually working a double at the Scarlet Hog tomorrow.

I shower quickly and make a peanut butter and jelly sandwich in my cramped little kitchen for dinner. But it's *my* cramped little kitchen. It's *my* crappy PB&J.

This life is mine. Not his. Not anyone's to mess with, or toy with. No one's to play seductive mind games with.

Harriet Quimby belongs to no one but herself.

Exhausted, I crawl into bed. I do what I always do—read a few pages of a book, put it to the side, and tell myself I'm free.

I tell myself I'm past it, and past him.

Then, I close my eyes, and I pretend I'm going to sleep a dreamless night. I pretend I'm *not* going to spend the entire night running from the savage and gorgeous monster hunting me through the woods. I pretend I won't wake up at least once, slick with sweat and desire, and still throbbing from the filthy, sinful ways he's just made me writhe and gasp in my sleep.

But every night, I know.

They're just lies.

Because I'm not past it. I'm not past him.

I'll never be over my demon.

31

"Aww, one more?"

I laugh, and for the first time in a while, it's a real, genuine laugh.

The two glasses of wine and the margarita I've had over the last two hours might have something to do with that. But hey, I'll take it.

I grin as I shake my head and my hands at Monica, Chelle, and Theresa, from group.

"I'd love to, really, but three is my absolute limit!" I giggle.

Today, finally, I decided it was time to stop hiding. I decided that pretty soon, I'm going to be the proud owner of my very own hip, swank, successful cocktail bar, in a very hip and swank neighborhood in London.

I might as well start celebrating.

"You're sure?" Chella pouts.

I grin, but I shake my head again as I stand. I reach into my pocket, ignoring the pleas from the other women to "just leave it, we'll take care of it." A lot of the others in IPVS-Anon think the fact that I've been coming for a year and a half and still haven't shared is because my demons and my darkness are so profoundly damaging.

That I'm so broken by the past that I still can't bear to talk about it, even in group.

Some of it is that I just don't have any interest in sharing. But the biggest part is that I *can't* talk about my past.

Not to them.

Not to anyone.

Because somewhere out there, a beautiful monster might still be looking for me. Jana might be, too.

My thoughts sour when her name enters them.

Obviously, the news doesn't cover the intimate inner power struggles of criminal empires. But, if you read between the lines, and know what you're looking for, sometimes, the *real* story presents itself.

That's how I know that Jana is now the *de facto* head of the Balagula family. The final nail was a small tabloid piece a year and a half ago, with a photo of two men holding a candle vigil on the steps of my father's old house—Matis Koschek and Igor Zavrazin, two of the most staunchly "traditionalists" on the Balagula family counsel.

The vigil was for *me*—Tatiana Fairist. And the fact that those two were now considering me dead as well spoke more than any direct article on the subject.

Jana won. She has the throne.

She can fucking have it.

"I'm sure, yeah," I sigh. "But thank you for dragging me out. I needed this."

It's the truth, too.

Monica beams as she gives me a hug.

"*Any* time, hon. We're always here."

I smile as I hug Chella and then Theresa, and then covertly sneak some cash onto the table to cover my drinks. Then, I'm out the door, into the night.

The Battersea bar we've met at isn't all that far from my Wandsworth flat. And it's nice out, so, I decide to walk. Though, barely a block into it, I'm already regretting that decision when I almost twist my ankle crossing an older, cobbled street.

I *never* wear heels. I have no idea why I put them on tonight.

It's not that late, but it's dark. And the streets are pretty empty. But I'm not worried. Over the last two years, I've trained myself, hard.

I work out six times a week. I have jiu-jitsu twice a week, and kickboxing on two other days of the week.

I also carry mace.

But tonight, I'm not worried about anything. It's beautiful outside, the moon is large, and the weather is still teased with warmth. I inhale and exhale slowly, feeling the buzz of alcohol and the glow of what I suppose is friendship.

It's taken two years of building this new world for myself. Maybe I'm ready for things like friends again.

Maybe I can finally put the final handful of dirt on Tatiana's grave and move on with this new life.

I cross the street and head down a side lane as I get closer to my flat. For a moment, I feel... *something* behind me. A force. A premonition. A gaze.

I shiver, whipping around as my hand darts into my bag for the mace. But there's no one there.

I knew there wouldn't be.

This is the last vestige of him I can't shake. The final mark he's left on me that won't seem to fade. The feeling of being *watched* or stalked after. As if his presence is still haunting my shadows, ready to pounce.

But he's not, and he won't. Not after this long. He's not even in the UK, from the few blips of him I've gotten from stalking other people's social medias. It's not like Bratva captains and assassins are exactly posting themselves all over Instagram. I'm ashamed to say, I've used a fake account myself to follow the boy he once talked about so fondly—Misha Tsavakov.

It's mostly sports cars, rugby, tattoos, and wild looking parties. But every now and then, I've caught glimpses—glimpses that send my heart lurching into my throat.

Because seeing him, even in a picture on the Internet on my phone, paralyzes me. And shatters me.

It makes me hate him and miss him all at the same time, until I force myself to toss the phone away and go for a run or something.

The last few times I've seen him in Misha's feed of pictures, it was places like Eastern Europe. Or Germany. Or New York.

He's not in London.

I'm fine.

And yet, those sometimes creeping sensation have grown more frequent, and more intense, over the last week or two. I feel that… *thing*, that power, around every corner and behind every tinted window.

But I know it's nothing. It's just me adjusting to my new world. It'll pass.

It always does.

I exhale, my body uncoiling as I turn to keep walking down the side lane. My fist unclenches from around the can of mace in my bag, and my chest loosens again.

You're fine.

I breathe again, relaxing as I walk on slightly wobbly heels down the lane, towards home.

And then I'm grabbed.

I scream, but a hand clamps roughly over my mouth. And for one awful, shameful, disturbing second, I wonder if it's him.

I *hope* it's him, and for a split second, my core surges with heat and excitement.

"Fuck baby, where you goin' tonight lookin' like this?"

Cold, naked, real fear stabs into me like a blade through the heart. My adrenaline screams, and my very skin shrivels.

It's not Kristoff. Not even close.

I scream again, but the hand clamps harder over my mouth. When I try it again, I wince as the man yanks me deeper into the alley and shoves me hard against a brick wall.

There's only the dim, flickering light of streetlamp out on the main lane. But with its horrific glow, I can make out the sneering, cruel, ruddy face of my attacker.

He grins lecherously as his eyes sweep down over the tank top and short skirt I'm wearing.

"Wot say you and me have a little fun, aye, luv?" He grumbles, his breath sour and heavy with liquor.

And suddenly, though I'm still half numb with the adrenaline, my training kicks in. His hand goes to shove between my legs, but before he can blink, I bite down *hard* on the hand over my mouth. And just as he's roaring in pain, my knee jerks up, slamming into his balls.

"Oi you little *cunt!*" he roars.

I twist away as his grip drops from me. I whirl, my hand shoving into my bag for the mace to finish him off.

And my heel breaks.

I gasp as the motion of my aggressive whirling spins me off balance and slams me into the ground.

Before I can blink, he's on me.

Cold, naked fear grips me, choking me as his big frame crashes into me. His weight pins me to the bags of garbage I've landed on. His sour breath stings my eyes as he leers close, his face a snarling mask of anger.

"Shoulda played nice, luv," he rasps. His knee jams between my legs, trying to pry them open.

I snarl, lashing out with elbows and fingernails. I catch his face, leaving vicious marks that drip blood down his face. But that only fuels his rage.

"Little *bitch!*"

I grunt as a heavy hand slams into the side of my head, stunning me.

Oh God.

I've trained for this. I *know* how to fight and defend myself. And well. But I've had some drinks. My heels fucked me up. I need one second to regroup and counter, but he's not giving me a millisecond.

I yell, slamming my knee up. But he dodges, catching it in the hip rather than his balls again. His hand claps the side of my head again, making me cry out as black spots dot my eyes. I hiss, shoving at him, trying to go for his eyes as I hear his belt jangling.

My bag is so close—it's *so* close as I jam my arm out to the side to try and snag it and the can of mace inside. But I can't reach. My fingers barely brush the handle, trying to hook it while the man's weight presses down on me, suffocating me.

"I was gonna shag you nice. But now I'm gonna make you bleed for fuckin' up my face, you little—"

His voice chokes out with a horrible gurgling sound. My gaze twists quickly from my bag to him face, and I freeze.

His eyes bulge unnaturally, and his face is turning a livid shade of purple. And there's an arm wrapped like iron around his neck, squeezing.

Suddenly, the weight is gone as the man is yanked back with a sharp jerk. I scrabble up, eyes wide, my chest heaving. My body still screaming with fear adrenaline as I watch the huge, hulking shadow grab my attacker in a choke hold, one hand wrapped around his head.

The shadow suddenly yanks, hard. There's a horrific cracking sound. My hand flies in horror to my mouth as I swallow the scream. My eyes go wide, face paling to white as I watch—and *hear*—the shadow snap my attacker's neck right in front of me.

The ruddy-faced man slumps dead to the ground, and the night goes still.

I stand there, panting, chest heaving, and my skin electrified with energy and fear. My eyes ring as the blood roars through them. And I just stare at the tall, dark, shadow.

He turns into the light. But I don't need it to know. I think I knew the second I saw the arm wrap around the other man's throat. I knew it before I was even attacked. I've been feeling it in the hairs on the back of my neck for a week.

It's him.

He's found me.

Kristoff turns, and the flickering light of the streetlamp glints in his lethal, ice-blue eyes.

"Found you, printsessa."

32

It's as if the whole world suddenly shrinks or disappears, until it's just the two of us. Like we're encased in a silent, still snow globe.

I've imagined this meeting a thousand times. I've dreamed about it; dreaded it. Hoped for it. Run from it.

But I, more than anyone, know there's no running from Kristoff. Maybe there is for a time, but in the end, like he always did, he finds me.

He catches me.

But this time, I won't be his prey.

I won't be.

My eyes narrow coldly at him, just as he does the same to me. His mouth is thin, jaw clenched tight enough to make the muscles of his neck ripple beneath his white collar. You can almost taste the tension hanging heavily in the air, crackling and flickering with a thudding electricity.

THE HUNTER KING

I swallow thickly as my eyes slowly drink him in.

Somehow, in two years' time, he's gotten even more attractive. Darker, more edged. More lethal looking. I shiver at the vicious lines of his jaw and the rippling muscles of his shoulders straining the tailored dark gray suit jacket.

His eyes are harder. That magnetic, captivating power about him seems stronger and darker, too.

And apparently, the way even being near him makes me feel has magnified and surged in the last two years. Because standing there ten feet apart from him, it's like I'm being pulled by invisible strings towards him.

Like I want to run, if only just to be caught. Like I want to hit him over and over just so I can kiss him after.

For the last two years, I've told myself I hate him. I've told myself he's the worst thing that ever happened to me.

Sixty seconds in to finally being in front of him again, and that house of lies comes crashing down.

I want to hate him. I really, really want to hate him, for all of it.

I just don't know if I can.

"How did you find me?" I finally blurt, shattering the silence throbbing between us.

His eyes flicker, lancing into mine and turning my knees weak.

"You assume…" he rasps.

Fuck, even his voice has morphed and magnified in power in the past two years. It seems even deeper now, and more edged in steel. The tone is more commanding, as if that was even possible.

"You assume that that wasn't always an inevitably, *Harriet*."

I stiffen. I try to stop it, and try to let it wash over me. But I fail, and he sees it.

"I know what you are," I hiss.

His eyes narrow slightly.

"You always knew what I was."

"I know what you *did*."

His lips curl.

"Enlighten me."

"*Stop it*," I spit at him, snarling. "Stop it. I *know*, Kristoff, okay?! I know you were using me to get to my family—"

"You're wrong."

I gasp as he surges towards me, closing the distance between us in a millisecond. I shiver as I trip backwards, grappling with a hand before I brace myself against the brick wall at my back.

My chest heaves, throat constricting as he looms over me, nailing me to the wall with those icy blues.

"You're in danger," he growls lowly.

My lips sneer.

"Get *away* from me. I can take care of myself."

"Like just now? Tipsy and walking around fucking Wandsworth in the dark by yourself? Cutting through alleys?"

His hand comes up as if to touch me—as if to cup my jaw, like he did a million times in our fantasy escape those years before.

But that was then, and this is now. And I'm not that girl anymore.

I'm something new.

I twist away from him, whirling as I grab his wrist and shove him towards the bricks.

"Stay the fuck away from me."

Kristoff braces himself with a palm against the wall, tensing before he slowly turns. His eyes stab into me over his shoulder, and when he turns, that hauntingly gorgeous and lethal look on his face throbs in the flickering light.

"That's not possible."

I gasp, adrenaline spiking in me as he lunges for me. But I block, dodging to the left and slamming his arm away. He lunges, but I duck, slamming my forearm out to shove him backwards, almost off his feet.

He catches himself with a scowl. But then slowly, his lips curl at the corners as those eyes land on me.

"You've been practicing, *printsessa*…"

My eyes narrow.

"Well as you said, maybe you *are* an inevitably. And this time, I was going to be prepared."

My jaw sets as I kick my broken heels off reach down to pluck them up.

"How did you find me?"

He rolls his shoulders, keeping his gaze locked on me as he fixes his collar.

"You don't sell three-of-a-kind Patek Philippe wrist-watches to black market collectors without it being noticed."

Shit.

I knew it was a risk. I knew the watch was rare, and that he may very well have people looking for it to hit a market. But I was careful. I even used a proxy and a fake company to sell it.

"And only through *one* proxy and dummy company?" He makes a tsking sound, slowly shaking his head as he grins coldly and hungrily at me.

"I taught you better."

"You taught me all sorts of things I never fucking asked you to teach me."

"I don't remember you complaining much."

"The word you're looking for is *coercion*," I spit. "Or Stockholm syndrome."

Kristoff's lips thin.

"You sound like a shrink."

"Yeah? Well I've seen enough of them after you."

His eyes narrow. So do mine.

"Why did you find me?"

"Why did you fucking *run?*" he hisses dangerously, moving towards me. I swallow, stepping back in time with his advance, keeping the distance between us.

Not because I'm scared of him.

Because I'm scared I'm not as strong as I want to think I am. Because even being this close to him has my pulse throbbing with heat. Even though I want to be furious, and curse him, and hit him… I also want him to knock my attacks aside and pin me to the wall.

I want to hate him.

I'm just deathly afraid I might horribly still love him.

"You know damn well why I ran."

He barks a cold laugh.

"Except I thought you were smart enough not to listen to Jana's poisonous bullshit."

"I was smart enough to see that I was being played, Kristoff!" I snap.

"Yeah!?" He snaps back. "But by who, *Harriet?*"

He's still coming towards me, and I'm still walking back. Until suddenly, I'm retreating out of the alley back onto the street.

"*Please,*" I choke, tears stinging my eyes. "Please just *let me go.*"

He laughs coldly.

"You stole six million pounds worth of watches."

"It was five and a half million."

"Then you were robbed."

"*You'd fucking know.*"

His eyes narrow as I sneer, shaking my head at him.

"You took so fucking much from me."

He barks a laugh. *"Please,* spare me. What I took away from you was that cage you'd locked around your true self. Around your true needs and desires."

"You *corrupted*—"

"Bullshit," he snaps harshly. "Those dark seeds and twisted needs have always been in you, *printsessa.* As they've always been in me. I just watered them, as you watered mine."

"The things you made me do, all just to—"

"Yes, that's it. I *made you,"* he sneers coldly. "The only thing I *made you* do, Tatiana—"

"That's not my fucking name."

His jaw clenches viciously.

"The only thing I made you do, *Harriet*, was ruin your panties with how *wet* you got waiting so fucking eagerly for the next time you could run from me and be a greedy little—"

My hand slaps hard across his face.

The reaction is instant.

I gasp, faltering back as he surges into me. His hands clamp like iron around my wrists as he shoves my hands behind me to the small of my back, pinning his hard body to mine.

My pulse *roars.*

My skin electrifies.

Horrible, treacherous, mortifying heat pools slick between my thighs.

"Don't," he rasps darkly.

"What," I sneer. "Hit you?"

I try and yank one of my arms free to do it again. But he's way too strong.

"No," he slowly shakes his head. *"Tempt me."*

Fuck...

Every nerve in my body aches for him. Every dark, hidden desire that I've spent two years burying and pretending I don't have comes screaming to the surface.

The need for him.

The need to be chased by him. And caught. And pinned down.

And *taken*.

"Oi!"

A man's voice shatters the throbbing silence simmering in the few inches between us. My head whips to the side, and I shiver when I see the two policemen approaching us, frowning in concern.

"Is there a problem here?" One snaps curtly, his eyes sliding from my pinned wrists up to Kristoff's grim face.

It's not like I think two policeman would stop a man like him. But it's clear this is too visible. And there's a body of a man he's just killed half covered with trash in the alley behind us.

And I know Kristoff understands that that gives me *all* the power here right now.

His hands release my wrists. He steps back.

I hate the pang of longing that hits me when he does.

"No," he mutters coldly. "There isn't."

The cops ignore him, turning to me.

"Miss?"

I'm still looking right at Kristoff, my eyes locked with his icy blues.

"No," I say curtly. "No, thank you. Just catching up with an old friend."

Kristoff's jaw ticks, but he says nothing.

The second policeman clears his throat.

"Where are you headed, miss?"

"Home. I only live a few blocks that way," I wave a hand in the opposite direction to where I live.

"We're going that way too, it would seem," the first cop grunts, eyeing Kristoff's size and the swirling, palatable darkness around him warily.

"Mind you stay where you are, mate," he grunts to the man I once shared a bed with.

The man I once opened my heart to.

The man who had all of me.

Kristoff's face darkens, and his eyes flash. But he smiles thinly as he holds his hands up.

"As she said. Just catching up with an old friend."

"Are we through catching up, then?" The first cop says coldly.

I swallow. "Very much so."

Kristoff's lethal gaze stabs into me before I force myself to turn, walking away with the two policemen.

Like before, I can feel that energy tingling in the hair on my neck. I can feel that darkness swirling after me. I can feel his eyes piercing into my very soul.

Only this time, I know it's not my imagination—my twisted nightmare or forbidden dream.

This time, I know it's real.

We round the corner, and the feeling diminishes. But only a little. Because deep down, I know he's right.

I can run from him all I want.

But him catching me isn't just a fantasy.

It's an inevitability.

33

SHE HID WELL.

I'd be impressed if I wasn't already almost overwhelmed with the swirling maelstrom of fury, resentment, and barely contained desire currently surging through me.

She hid well. But now, I've found her. And this time, she won't be running away from me again. She might think she is. In fact, I'm almost sure she believes that, because I could see it in her eyes before she conveniently slipped away from me, chaperoned by the two policemen.

I could see her already trying to puzzle through how she'll run this time. How she'll evade me, and how she'll change her name and her hair to hide from me.

But I won't be allowing that to happen again. As I told her, when it comes to her running and me chasing, my catching her isn't a probability.

It's an inevitability. A certainty as set in stone as the tides, or the fucking sun rising.

It took two years this time—two years of me turning over every fucking rock. Two years of me chasing down a dozen fucking bullshit leads—kicking down some shithead's door in China who opened an Amex card under Tatiana's name. Scaring the shit out of some woman in Chicago who'd submitted a rental application as her, too.

None of them led me to her. But the scent of a trail is still a trail. Even in her attempts at throwing me off, she only succeeded in doing one thing:

She kept that furious fire inside of me roaring.

She kept me focused.

She kept me on the hunt. And now, I've found my prey. Again.

Back in the darkness of the hotel penthouse I'm staying in, my eyes narrow as they stab into London night.

London. She's been in fucking *London* this whole goddamn time. Not hiding under a palm tree in the middle of the desert. Not huddled in a shack in the Siberian wilderness.

London. There are a million CCTV cameras I could have swept to find her, I just didn't know where to look.

But now, I've found her. She's right down there somewhere in this glittering city.

It was the watches that ended up being her undoing. The night I realized she was gone, I put a dozen people on that— the kind of people who float in the murky world beneath the surface. People who trade in stolen art, or forgeries. I mean it's not like she'd be able to go to fucking Christies if she wanted to trade them for cash.

And so a week ago, when one of my people came to me with a proof of sale of the ultra-rare Patek Philippe watch she'd taken, I finally knew.

I finally had her. And now, I've found her.

She's grown up.

My jaw grits tightly.

She's grown up, grown stronger, grown bolder.

Grown more beautiful. More captivating. Those eyes and those lips could bring me to my knees and make me break every rule I had two years ago.

I'm pretty sure they could fucking kill me, now.

I exhale slowly against the glass of the penthouse, glaring at the city.

A lot of things are different now, two years later. Jana now openly and publicly leads the Balagula Bratva. There were a couple of holdouts on the family counsel who were still waiting for Tatiana to be found before declaring the transition of power.

Jana waited them out, and then hit them with the very blood and hair I'd delivered into her hands. After that, the throne was hers.

Knowing nothing was as it seems is bad. But knowing you were a pawn is worse.

I've waited from the shadows to see if Mikhail would ever start a war with his niece and former second in command. But there's been nothing. On the surface, you'd think he'd given up, thrown in the towel, and slunk back to his own schemes and organization.

But I know Mikhail. And he most certainly hasn't thrown in any towel at all. If he's hidden, it's because he's a fucking shark, lurking beneath the surface to strike at the first drop of blood.

But fuck them both. Mikhail and Jana can cut each other to pieces for all I care. I've only been tracking them to see if they'd ever lead me to Tatiana.

To *Harriet*.

They never did, but Harriet, or Tatiana, or whoever the fuck she is now, is in more danger than she knows.

I'm not the only one hunting her.

I've risen higher in the Tsavakov empire. I command more resources now, and I've used those to set up a network of spies. The Ghost Syndicate is a no-go, obviously. Mik's people are far too trained, and too conditioned, and too brainwashed to be infiltrated. But the Balagula was ripe for some well-placed eyes and ears.

Jana is looking for her. She has to. Because her crown and throne, and arguably her life, depends on it.

She hasn't found her yet, or even come very close at all. But she's actually closer to her prey than she knows.

Currently, Jana is trying to expand the Balagula empire into the UK. Into *London*. She's actually living here at the moment, in a well-guarded penthouse on the south bank that hangs out high over the Thames.

Even with her resources, she's not half the tracker and hunter I am. Given enough time, even a room full of monkeys with typewriters will theoretically write the works of William Shakespeare.

Sooner than later, Jana is going to realize the loose end she's been looking for is right under her fucking nose.

My eyes close. I breathe in, filling my nose with the faintest lingering scent of Tatiana still clinging to my clothes and skin. Breathing in the lingering sting of her palm against my face.

She hid well. But as I said, I'm not a chance.

I'm a fucking inevitability.

Two goddamn years away from her have hardened me in ways I never was before. They've made me more guarded, more brutal, more unflinching. When she first knew me, I was trying to leave the monster in me behind. I was trying to exorcise the specter of the *bukavac* from my soul.

When she met me, she only fed that monster.

When she ran, he smashed free of his cage. And now, he's caught her scent again.

Mirror mirror on the wall, I'll find the Fairist one of all.

And this time, I'll swallow her fucking whole.

I whirl from the glass, surging through the darkness of my hotel room back out into the inky blackness of night.

It's time to take back what was taken from me.

34

I can't breathe.

When I slam the door to my flat shut behind me, I sink against it, gasping. The room spins, black dots floating through my vision. I drop to the floor, hugging my knees to my chest as a heated shiver ripples up my spine.

He found me.

Two years of hiding. Two years of muddying my tracks and sending up false flags all over the world to throw him off. Two years of remaking myself and rebuilding a life that's been taken from me twice.

The first time was when he took me.

The second time was when my blinders came off, and I saw him for what he was.

What you thought he was.

Because for the first time in two hard, angry years, a flicker of something close to doubt creeps into me. Seeing him face to face again…

It's shaken me. And it's knocked hard at the foundation of my firm belief that all I was to him was a pawn in a play for my family's empire.

Tonight, for the first time in two years, I looked into the eyes of the man who once stole me and then stole my heart. I looked deep into those terrifying and beautiful, hauntingly lethal, ice-blue eyes, and I didn't see the smugness or the malice I've spent two years imagining I'd see there.

I just saw pain. I saw truly real, brutal, shattered pain. And it's smashing down every single belief I've clung to like a life raft for the last two years.

Of course, I've had those dark moments late at night, wondering if any of it was true. Of course, I've doubted running at all, and fallen into that spiral of wondering if it's really true that his goal all along was the empire, not me.

But after running, going down that hole to its end might've killed me. And besides that, every single scrap of information I've painstakingly gathered over the last two years points to Jana telling the truth.

Until tonight, when the whole house of cards began to shake.

I draw in a ragged breath, brushing the back of my hand across my eyes as I climb to my feet. I stagger into the small bedroom and swivel my gaze to the wall.

If anyone were to see this, they'd think I was insane. *I* think I might be insane. But I've needed this.

One entire wall of the bedroom is covered with computer printouts, maps, and newspaper clippings, with decidedly crazy-looking bits of orange string connecting some to others. At first glance, it looks like the ravings of a lunatic trying to prove that moon people secretly run the world, or some other insanity like birds as a species being a government cover-up.

But my "crazy wall," as even I call it, isn't conspiracy theories.

It's a hunt.

Slowly, I slip out of the skirt and tank top and into yoga pants a t-shirt. My eyes slide to the wall of madness again.

In one corner, I have everything I've collected on Jana. Clippings of her at gala events well-known to be host to numerous heads of Bratva families. A printout of a blog post by a guy who actually tries to follow the inner politics of crime families, almost like a true-crime serial.

Pictures of her and my dad's wedding.

Another section of the wall has information about my family's council. And another section hosts a bunch of stuff on the Tsavakov empire and family—on Boris, and his heir Misha who's currently a third year at the prestigious Oxford Hills Academy. Boris himself seems to be an insanely well documented piece of shit. But there's really nothing on Kristoff.

Other groups on the wall are dedicated to other Bratva families, and any connections they may have to Jana as the head of the Balagula. And then, at the center…

The biggest mystery of all: The Ghost Syndicate, and the utterly invisible Mikhail Arakas.

He's the center point to all of this—Kristoff, Jana, the takeover of my family's throne. The plot to have me killed. And yet, the organization's name couldn't be more appropriate, because Mikhail is a *ghost*.

He doesn't exist. He isn't in a single dark corner of even the deepest parts of the dark web. There's no pictures of him. Nothing. But there *are* whispers here and there, if you look hard enough, of the Ghost Syndicate.

Rumors, mostly. Assassinations. Political upheaval. Vicious corporate takeovers, and violent family power-shifts.

I exhale slowly as my eyes drag over the whole wall, until finally, they land on the one blurry printout from Misha Tsavakov's Instagram, with a familiar, chiseled face sightly in the background.

It's the only picture I have of Kristoff. It's the only way I've seen him for two years. Until tonight.

Until *he found me*.

I swallow thickly as an alarm sound starts to wail deep inside my head.

Two years. I made it *two years*. And now, I need to run again.

I squeeze my eyes shut, trying to bury the pain of knowing I have to leave everything again. The group meetings. The cocktail bar. My new name and life.

All of it. And this time, I need to burrow deeper. I need to hide better, and never, ever let him find me again.

Because I don't trust myself with him. I don't trust that I'll survive colliding with Kristoff Zima again.

My pulse thuds as I grab a bag from under my bed. I'm numb as I start to throw things into it, sucking back the tears before they can fall.

My phone rings, jarring me. I glance at it, and the scowl. It's an "unknown" number. Which always just means a scam or sales call. I silence the phone, toss it on the bed, and go back to shoving clothes in my bag.

The phone goes off again, but I ignore it. Then again. And then again. And then again, until the panic starts to ripple through me. I shiver as I snatch the fucking thing off the bed and angrily jab the answer button.

"Who the hell—"

"Hello, Tatiana."

I go cold, instantly. The voice is robotic and clipped—like it's someone using one of those voice changing things kidnappers use in thriller movies. But even with the flat, mechanical tone, it's still sinister sounding.

It still just sounds like magic.

"I heard you were looking for me."

The world goes still. I swallow again, sucking in a breath as the walls begin to close in.

"Who the hell is—"

"My name is Mikhail Arakas."

My ears ring. I stare, suddenly cold and scared as the looming silence on the other end of the line throbs into my ear.

"Perhaps you've heard of—"

"I know who you are," I choke, my throat constricting as my body goes numb.

"Of course you do. Now, I need you to listen to me, *very carefully*."

35

On my wall, the big middle section labeled "Mikhail" just has a big sharpie-drawn question mark.

Now, I'm talking to the man himself. Even if his true voice is being obscured by the robotic, deepened voice altering software, or whatever he's using. I know it's him. It's like I can feel it, like a malevolent force seeping over my skin like poison.

This is the man who destroyed my life. The man who killed my father and tried to have me killed.

"What the fuck do you want?" I seethe, hatred scouring through my veins as my eyes narrow at the question mark on the wall.

The robotic voice of Mikhail Arakas chuckles deeply.

"I do hope you're listening, Tatiana, because I don't like to repeat myself."

"And I don't like to be talked down to."

"I don't much care what you like or don't like."

My lips purse.

"You've been lied to, Tatiana."

I bark a cold, mirthless laugh.

"That is amusing to you?"

"It's obvious to me. And besides, you're late to the party. Your friend Jana already told me about—"

"I'm not talking about Kristoff," Mikhail growls in that robo-voice. "I'm talking about your former stepmother, and my former second in command. You and Kristoff have both been played."

My pulse hums in my ears, my breath quickening.

"What are you saying?"

"Jana wasn't just my second in command, my dear."

"She's also your niece. I've heard this story."

"Good for you. But she was also my second-best student, in addition. She was trained for years to lie as necessary. To stab in the back when it's demanded of her. To seduce, to use any and all weakness as a weapon. And two years ago, she used a moment of chaos to take what was not hers to take. When your father was killed—"

I wince. My heart wrenches into a twisted knot, and it feels like I've just been punched in the stomach.

It's not like I haven't been told that the "accident" that killed my father wasn't accidental at all. Kristoff told me as much two years ago. But to hear it from the mouth of the man who ordered it is… painful. And brutal.

And hateful.

"*Fuck you—*"

"Be silent," he snaps. "Mourn on your time, not mine."

I squeeze my eyes shut. "You *motherfucker—*"

"As I was saying," he barges on. "When your father was killed, the plan was to have you strategically married in order to cement *my* claim over your grandfather's empire."

I bark out a laugh. "Let me guess. *Strategically married* to *you?*"

He's silent for a few second.

"Interrupt me again and there will be consequences, Tatiana."

My teeth grind.

"Those plans fell apart, however, when Jana saw an opportunity to take what was mine for herself. Your family's empire."

I snort. "She can fucking have it."

"Unfortunately, I'm not interested in your position on the matter."

My eyes narrow to slits. "*Too fucking bad.*"

I'm a second away from ending the call either the normal way or by smashing the phone against the wall, when his voice grates out coldly.

"Hang up this phone and there will be consequences you are *not* prepared to deal with."

"I disappeared from you people once, I'll do it again."

"And then again? And again, and again?" Mikhail's robotic voice chuckles in this horrible, rasping tone. "Because this isn't going away, my dear. And if you run this time?"

"*What*," I snap. "You'll do *what*. You've already taken—"

"I'll shoot Kristoff in the heart."

I swallow. A cold blade drags down my back as my heart clenches.

"Why would I care—"

"Don't. Your emotions towards him are pathetically clear to me."

I swallow, shaking as I stumble back to sit on the edge of my bed.

"I'm going to need you to do something for me, Tatiana. Ahh, but don't worry, and don't cry foul just yet. Because first, I'm going to do *you* a favor."

"What?"

"I'm going to kill your stepmother."

My brows arch as I shiver.

"But after that, you're going to do as I say."

"And what are you going to say?" I hiss.

"You will cease this ridiculous business of being a barmaid and skulking around the dark web looking for information on me and my organization to put up on your wall of insanity."

I swallow thickly.

"You will end this fake life you've set up for yourself, and you will take up the mantle you were born to take up."

I slowly shake my head, shuddering as I rake my teeth over my lip.

"No, I—"

"I wasn't asking," Mikhail barks abruptly. "The family structure won't let anyone but the designated heir dictate who leads. Your grandfather's high council is still—despite all outward appearances, and despite Jana currently sitting on the throne—too loyal to break that. For them to throw her out, you need to make the fact that you are alive known."

I smile thinly.

"Ahhh, I see. So, you *need* me," I sneer.

"Yes, I do. But before you get clever or quippy, let me remind you that *you* need *me*."

"For what, exactly."

"Kristoff's life."

A stabbing feeling pierces my chest. I wince, the breath leaving my body as my face pales.

"His life, as well as your own, I should add. You are valuable to me so long as you play the part. If you choose to not, you rapidly become a liability. And I don't tolerate liabilities, Tatiana."

I suck in air, the walls closing in on me as I tremble on the edge of the bed.

"What happens if I do everything?" I choke in a whispered tone. "If I make myself known, and then take the throne?"

"You immediately use your powers to throw out the council, bring me in, and then abdicate your throne, leaving me alone in control of the empire. And if you do all that, exactly how I ask, I will let you and Kristoff live. You have my word."

Cold malice digs into me, clawing at my heart as I slowly shake my head.

"Why on earth would I ever fucking trust your—"

He laughs.

"You trusted a professionally trained liar like Jana when she told you Kristoff wanted to use you. And I'm the one you have reservations about?"

My throat closes. My heart rips.

Mikhail chuckles quietly in that monotone, robotic rasp.

"You've always known deep down it wasn't true, Tatiana. You just knew if you *didn't* believe it, it would all have been for nothing. You would have killed your own happiness, and fled that island two years ago for nothing but a lie. And you've spent two years running from that bitter truth."

It's been two years in the making. But finally, my heart breaks. It just shatters to pieces as big, silent tears roll down my cheeks.

"I told you Jana was the second-best student I ever had. The best was Kristoff. I know him as if he's my own son, and he *never* wanted your family's empire."

The room spins. My vision swims.

"Now get me what I asked for, Tatiana. Get me my fucking empire, or I'll burn your world to the ground."

36

I STUMBLE OUTSIDE into the night choking for air. I turn, lurching through the night, sucking in breath after breath as every nerve in my body screams. Every synapse in my brain shorts out.

Every lie I believed, and every one I kept telling myself because I knew I was in too deep to believe anything else comes flinging at me like thrown knifes. The blades rake my skin, ripping me apart and flaying me open to the naked truths grinning back at me.

Kristoff never wanted your family's empire.

I choke on the sob as I lurch down my block. I ran for nothing. I believed the lie, and I left the only paradise I've ever known.

The only love I've ever known.

The screaming panic and suffocating realization is almost too much to bear. Tears roll down my cheeks as I stagger block after block, my heart shredding to pieces inside of me.

And then the hair on the back of my neck stands up. That dark, powerful feeling creeps over me. The sensation of being watched.

Of being stalked.

Of being hunted.

I suck in a breath of air, choking back a sob as I veer down another street. The sensation grows, tingling over my skin and arresting my pulse. I stumble towards the dark, somewhat sketchy park at the end of my street.

Maybe I'm insane. Maybe I've *always* been insane.

But somehow, I know.

I just know.

I step into the park, my pulse jangling and my nerves humming as I leave the lit sidewalk behind. Step after step, my heart beats faster and harder, as the shadows close in around me. Until finally, about a hundred paces down the dark footpath, I come to a stop next to an empty bench.

And I close my eyes.

"I know you're here."

My words tumble into the inky blackness around me without echo. Without response.

I clear my throat, trying to swallow my heart back into my chest.

"I know you're with me, right now."

I take a shaky breath, filling my lungs before I take one of the single biggest leaps of faith in my life. Then I open my eyes and stare deep into the night.

"I'm going to run."

The air is still, and all I can hear is my own heavy breaths and my own thudding, molten pulse.

"And you're going to chase me."

My eyes close. I'm shaking.

"Because I need you to catch me."

And then, I run. I turn, and I just bolt as fast as I can down the barely visible, dangerously unlit footpath.

My thoughts scream into the front of my mind as I question my own sanity, and wonder if I'm being an idiot. If I've gone off the deep end. They scream at me to fucking stop, or better, to turn and run until I'm locked in my little basement apartment, back to my little world as the new me.

Except suddenly…

I hear it.

I hear the sound of footsteps. The crunch of shoes on gravel. The sound of a runner pounding heavily down the footpath behind me.

Rushing towards me like a homing missile.

And my entire body explodes with the sudden rush of adrenaline. I choke on a scream, blinding bursting forward as my nerves scream at the peripherals. My lungs burn, my feet pound hard against the footpath, and every cell in my body jangles as if there's a blade poised millimeters from my skin.

I run harder than I've run since that first chase through the dark on the island.

A hand plunges from the darkness next to me and grabs me by the throat. And it's so sudden and jarring that my brain goes numb, and my vision goes black for a moment.

And then, reality rushes in.

The hand grabs me tight, whipping me off my feet. I choke, whirling around through the air before I'm suddenly pinned hard against the rough bark of a tree at my back.

The clouds clear. Dim, blue moonlight illuminates the haunting lines of his chiseled face, the dark shadows in the hollows of his cheeks.

The lethal beauty of his icy-blue eyes.

Time freezes for half a second. And then suddenly, his powerful hand still wrapped around my throat, his mouth slams to mine.

And the world explodes.

It's a punishing kiss. A brutal kiss.

It's the venomous antidote to the bottomless pit I've been drowning in for two years.

And for the first time in two years, I finally feel the feeling I've been craving ever since I ran.

I feel caught. Captured. Possessed.

And it feels like home.

37

AFTER TWO FUCKING YEARS, it's not that I'm kissing her.

It's that I'm *devouring* her.

My lips crush to hers, a fevered urgency in both of our mouths and tongues as they meld together. I inhale the scent of her, my body hardening and undulating into her as if to drown itself in her. My skin feels electrified where it touches her, and my pulse thunders like wild fucking horses pounding through my ears.

My hands grip her face, keeping her seared to my lips as two fucking years of pent-up aggression, anger, desire, ache, pain, and want come rushing out. She clings to me, whimpering as she balls my shirt in her fists and rocks her hips into me.

And the kiss says it all. The kiss says she knows now that we were both pawns. That both of us were played, and then played off each other. The fever in her lips and the broken urgency in the sobs she chokes back as she gives herself to me tell the story we don't need to use words for.

I want to scream at the two fucking years lost. I want to tear my fucking skin off at the theft of my—of *our*—happiness. Two years of her hiding from me. Two years of her hating me. Two years of her running from the memory of us.

But finding her again was always going to happen.

We aren't chance.

We're the inevitability.

And not distance or time could shatter that.

My pulse roars as my hand slides into her hair, grabbing a fistful of it. She whimpers, gasping as I pull her head back and move my mouth to devour her neck. I bite, suck, rake my teeth over her skin as she shivers and melts into me.

Her nipples pebble hard through her t-shirt against my chest. The heat between her thighs as I grind myself between them turns me to fire.

And her.

My hand shoves her t-shirt up as she frantically yanks at the buttons of my shirt. I win the race, and she cries out as my mouth hungrily devours a pink, pebbled nipple. My tongue swirls over the little point, dragging cries of pleasure from her lips as she all but rips my shirt open.

Her hands press against my chest, gripping, as if clinging to me. My mouth moves to her other nipple as her hands drop to my belt.

Panting, pulse racing, muscles aching from a run. The moonlight and the night cloaking us, the shadows of a tree pressed to her back.

This is our element. This is a dance we know so well that two fucking years wouldn't ever erase it.

She whimpers as I pull away and suddenly twist her around. Heavy, panted moans fall from her lips as I press her roughly to the tree and drag my mouth over the nape of her neck. My hand fists her hair, pinning her there as I cup her breasts from behind and drag my teeth across her neck.

My hand slides over her ribs, down over her caved stomach, and then sinks deep into the waist of her yoga pants.

"Kristoff…"

Feeling how goddamn wet she is shatters the last of my restraint. I snarl into her shoulder as I bury two thick fingers in her pussy, curling them deep as my palm grinds into her aching clit. I reach between us with my other hand and yank her yoga pants down to her thighs.

My zipper is next.

She moans when I let my bulging, swollen cock spring free against her ass. I bite the soft lobe of her ear, rubbing her clit as I fist my cock. My knee shoves her thighs apart as far as they can with the yoga pants and her panties tangled at her thighs. My slick, swollen head pushes between her sticky, greedy lips.

I ram in to the hilt with one thrust.

And suddenly, it's like time hasn't passed at all. We're just still back there in the woods of my island. I've just caught her after a chase and pinned her to a tree like I've done a hundred times to bury myself in her heat.

My cock saws into her, my abs crashing into her ass I fuck her from behind. My fingers rub her clit, and my other hand grabs another fistful of her hair. My lips and my teeth drag across her nape, her jawline, her ears, groaning as I lose myself in her.

The images of that night, when I lost her, come flooding back. I know she was deceived, but there's a piece of me that still holds so fucking much resentment for her leaving. For her not believing in me… in us.

And suddenly, I want to punish her for that.

I grit my teeth, groaning into her ear as I ram my cock into her, hard. She whimpers, her body jolting and quivering as my pace grows hard and more savage. My fist tightens in her hair, and my hand drags wet fingers from her pussy up to her nipples. I take one between them and twist, dragging a deep, guttural cry of pleasure from her lips as I fuck into her hard.

"Oh… fuck… Kristoff!"

"You thought you could fucking run from me," I rasp darkly into her ear. Her pussy clamps down hard around me, somehow getting even fucking wetter at the rough, edged tone to my voice.

"You thought you could escape me? That I wouldn't find you, as I always do? That I wouldn't *hunt you*, and pin you to the ground, and *fuck* this little pussy exactly how I please, because it is *mine* to fuck?"

My hips crash into hers, my cock swelling so fucking hard inside of her quivering pussy. Her moans grow louder and more desperate, her legs shaking as she clings desperately to the tree.

"Did you think I wouldn't go to the ends of the fucking earth to make you *beg* for my cock again, *printsessa?*"

I plunge deep, the choked, whimpered moans from her lips spurring me even harder.

"Fuck me!" She cries, shaking as I pound into her. *"Please, please fuck—Ah!"*

She moans as my palm swats her ass, my teeth gritting as I thrust into her.

"You think I wouldn't go through Hell itself to find this greedy little cunt and fuck it like I know damn well it's been dying to get fucked? That I wouldn't put you on your knees and watch you swallow my cum like a good girl."

She's almost incoherently whimpering now, her nails clawing at the tree as I plunge my cock into her pretty pussy over and over. My hand spanks her ass until it's red and raw, until her pussy is dripping down her fucking thighs.

"This is what you've fucking craved, isn't it?" I snarl into her ear as I sink deep, my fingers pinching her clit.

"This is what you've ached for, for two fucking years. To be hunted. To be chased through the fucking dark like the prey you are, only for me to catch you."

I ram into her.

"Only for me to trap you, and take you, and fuck you like a good little cumslut against a tree with your panties at your thighs and your pussy so fucking wet and eager for me. My own little personal fuck-toy, desperate for my cum."

Her moans are guttural and almost otherworldly. I know pushing her like this takes her to that dark, forbidden place that ignites something in her. That frees her.

And I know she craves it as much as I do, like she always did.

I'm her poisonous cure. She's my venomous antidote.

It's how it was, and how it always will be. And not even two years could erase that law of the universe.

My cock pounds into her, my muscles coiling as I thrust deep. My fingers rub her clit and yank her head back by the hair to let my lips and teeth drag across her jaw. My hand slips to her neck, my fingers wrapping around her throat.

She jolts, her mouth going slack and her pussy rippling tightly around me.

"This is how you come for me," I rasp thickly into her ear, my cock grinding deep. "Utterly and completely *had* by me. Whimpering like a greedy little girl with my fat cock buried in that eager pussy and my hand around your throat. Panties at your knees, tits out. Begging for it. Begging for *me*."

The world blurs and darkens at the corners. Her body clenches, quivering… tipping at the very edge of that drop.

"This is how you come for me, *printsessa*."

The match light, the gas catches.

"*So be a good little prey and fucking* come *for me.*"

The world explodes.

She screams as my hand clamps hard around her mouth, the other still wrapped around her throat. I bite down hard on her shoulder as I sink my cock to the hilt in her quivering, clenching, greedy pussy.

And I let go.

My cum spills into her, choking me as I pin her hard to the tree. I keep myself there, relishing the way her body melts around me as she comes with me. Drowning in the thrill of the chase and the capture. Of the hunt and the catch.

Of having *her*, finally, after two years without.

She twists in my arms. I slip out of her as I twist her around, cup her jaw, and sear my lips to hers. Her legs spread. My hands grip her ass, lifting her before I sink back in.

I'm not even close to being done with her.

I'll never be done with her.

38

THE TEARS COME LATER. After the reality of having him again, and kissing him, and touching him… it's after that that the magnitude of what was lost hits me. And I cry for the time that was taken from us.

In his bed in the top floor, penthouse suite of the Berkeley Hotel, I cling to him. I hold him like the wind, or time, or disaster might rip him away from me. And I cry into his chest.

For the years taken. For the ways we were played. How I let Jana's poisonous lies into my veins.

"*Don't*," he murmurs quietly, wrapping his muscled, inked arms around me. "Jana was one of Mikhail's top students. She spent years training to hone lies into lethal weapons. She's a master of manipulation."

I cling to him, twisting my head to kiss his bare chest.

I swallow.

"He called me."

Kristoff stiffens.

"Mikhail?"

I nod quietly.

"He wants me to come forward and claim the throne."

A growl rumbles in Kristoff's chest. "And I suppose after that, he wants you to dismiss the counsel and bring him in somehow?"

My eyes close as I nod.

"Yes."

"How?"

I swallow.

"He said something about marriage."

I shiver at the intense and possessive way Kristoff's hands suddenly tighten on my skin.

"That isn't happening."

"Kristoff… he said he'd kill you."

He's still for a second, but then he chuckles darkly.

"Let me worry about Mik."

"Kris—"

"He's not going to kill me."

"How do you know he—"

"His pride won't let him."

I frown, twisting to look up at him.

"I was Mikhail's prized pupil. The best he ever had. I was his machine, for years." He shakes his head. "He won't kill me because he's too pleased with his creation. His monster."

I shake my head as I kiss his chest.

"Stop it. You're not—"

"I was, though," he murmurs darkly, his face dipping into shadow as he looks away.

My gazes slides up his arm to his shoulder. It lingers when I realize he's got some new ink—new tattoos since the island.

And then another thought prowls out of the dark mist into my head.

It's been two years. He's grown even more devastatingly, lethally gorgeous. Even his body is stronger, harder, more grooved. He's got new tattoos.

My chest constricts as I start to sink into the dark thoughts of wondering what else was "new" in the last two years.

Or who else.

I startle when I realize he's looking down at me, his eyes piercing mine.

"Tell me," he growls.

I shake my head and look away.

"Tatiana."

I close my eyes.

"Did you ever find anyone else to chase over the last two years?"

The room is quiet. His stroking fingers go still on me.

"Tatiana, two years ago—"

"Look, I don't have a claim or anything," I choke. "I *left*. I ran. I—"

"Two years ago, I laid eyes on the only thing I ever wanted to hunt and chase again," he growls quietly. "So, *no*, *printsessa*. There hasn't been anyone else. There couldn't be."

The tears slide down my cheeks. But these ones aren't so much tears for the pain of time lost. They're broken, happy tears, for the man returned to me.

The only man I ever wanted. The only one I ever let in.

I shake the tears away.

"For *two years*," I choke quietly. "For two years, you didn't—"

I gasp as his hand slides lazily around my neck, cupping my jaw and twisting my face up to his.

"*You are all I want*," he growls thickly.

I shiver as his other hand slides down my front, between my breasts, over my stomach, and down lower. His powerful hand boldly cups my bare pussy, one finger dragging heavily up through my lips, eliciting a whimper.

"*This* perfect little pussy is all I want."

His finger curls into me, sucking the air from my lungs.

"Did any other fucking man—"

"*No*."

I shake my head, panting as he buries a second finger into me.

"*No*," I choke. "I ran from the only man I ever—"

His mouth crushes to mine, devouring my lips as he suddenly rolls us over in the sheets. I whimper as his mouth falls to my neck, his fingers driving into me as his thumb rolls my clit.

"I need to ask you one more thing, before."

I nod, panting, trembling as his fingers stroke against the spot just inside.

"Are you Tatiana or are you Harriet?"

His fingers pause. My lip sucks between my teeth before I swallow.

"Tatiana Fairist died a little over two years ago."

My eyes drag to his, locking with his gaze as the words leave my lips.

"My name is Harriet."

"Pleasure to meet you, Harriet," he rumbles. "I'm Kristoff. And I'm going to pin your knees to your chest now so I can fucking devour this pretty little pussy."

I manage to mumble a cheesy "the pleasure is all mine" before he does exactly as promised.

Then, I can't use words at all.

39

I don't emerge from the hotel room for another forty-eight hours. Literally. I spend two full days refamiliarizing myself with every fucking square inch of her body.

Two days getting to know Harriet Quimby.

A brunette-haired girl who tends bar now, who has her eye on buying a place to open her own spot in swank Camden. A girl who runs and trains at a gym almost every day. Who takes jiu-jitsu and kickboxing.

A girl a little more hardened by the world. A little less naïve. A girl who's built her own new life.

But for all the changes, she's somehow even more captivating to me.

And for all the changes, she's still decidedly *mine*. And this time, I won't be letting her go.

When I do finally step back into the real world, it's to go collect some things of hers from her flat. Harriet wants to come with me, of course. But I convince her to stay and pamper herself back at the hotel.

She's smart enough to get the real reason I want her behind a locked hotel room door, with one of my men—who she doesn't know about—stationed out in the hallway.

Mikhail.

But we both pretend it's so she can soak in a tub and nap to her heart's content.

At her Wandsworth basement flat, I find the suitcase she told me about, half packed from two days ago when she ran out of her place. I pick up where she left off, stuffing in clothes and toiletries.

I pause at her underwear drawer, a smirk on my lips. It's full of plain, boring, completely devoid of sexiness panties.

I *like* that she's spent the last two years wearing panties not meant to be seen. Or removed by someone else.

Of course, that's going to change now. And I make a note to spend an absolute goddamn *fortune* making sure nothing but silk and lace touches the intimate places of her body again.

I stuff a few pairs into the suitcase, and then my grin widens when I see what's buried at the bottom of the drawer.

A thick—though not as thick as *me*—life-like toy cock, with vibration control buttons at the base. Beside it, there's a wide leather collar with adjustable notches.

My jaw grinds as my cock thickens. She uses this alone, to choke herself just a little, while she fucks herself with this toy.

I groan as I finish packing her stuff, so that I can get back to her and do exactly that to her.

And then suddenly, I'm whirling as I yank my gun free and level it at the men who've just walked into the apartment behind me. My pulse thuds, and my eyes narrow to lethal, vicious slits.

"Hello, Kristoff."

My teeth grit. A fury surges like wildfire through my body.

"What the fuck do you want, Mik?"

I haven't seen him in more than six years. Not since before Nikita died.

Before he *let her* die.

He's aged obnoxiously well. Just shy of sixty, the man is still built strong, still with most of his hair, though silver now. A silver, close-cropped beard covers his jaw beneath dark, shark-like eyes.

Mine narrow.

This man was the closest thing I had to a father for years. He legally *was* my father for a time, for the two years he was married to my mother.

And yet he was as much a demon as my biological dad.

Actually, he was worse.

Military-level training of the sort exacted on us in Mik's training academy is designed to be brutal. Combat conditioning is hard no matter how or where you train. But with Mik, there was always a sadistic coloring to it all.

He *enjoyed* trying to break us. He *liked* pitting children against each other in vicious combat.

With him, it wasn't that the results were worth the brutal methods. To a man like Mikhail, the brutal methods were simply *enjoyable* to him.

I survived because I was determined that nothing would break me. I'd think of my mother, and my new baby sister, and I would block out everything else. I would swallow what I had to. Endure anything. Destroy whatever was ordered of me to destroy.

But others didn't. Others broke or were broken.

Or were killed.

Like Nikita.

I exhale hatred as I grit my teeth and stare down the barrel at him. Mik just raises his brow. It's then that I realize he's not alone. A younger man I don't know stands slightly behind him in a wide, militaristic stance.

"Oh, I think you're perfectly aware of what I want, Kristoff."

My mouth thins.

"Who's your fucking friend?"

"Ahh, yes. This is my new second, Decker."

"Yeah? So which widowed Bratva king are you going to have him go seduce for you, Mik?"

Mikhail smiles benignly. Decker glares at me.

"So," the older man sighs. "You found her. I knew you would."

"This is done, Mik," I rasp dangerously. "It's *done*. Go play politics with someone new. She's out."

Mikhail clicks his tongue against his teeth, shaking his head.

"I'm afraid that isn't possible. She's the key to this entire—"

"And I don't. Give. A. *Fuck*," I spit.

His brow furrows.

"For all your strengths, Kristoff," he muses. "You were always shit at hiding emotions."

"And you were always shit at being a father."

He just looks at me, unblinking. Uncaring.

"Let me put this in ways someone as broken as you can understand," I mutter. "You come near either of us again, and I'll fucking kill you. And I will go to the ends of the *earth* to destroy everything you have first."

My eyes narrow as I take one step closer to him, leveling the gun at his forehead.

"*Don't* test me on this one, Mik."

I shut the suitcase on the bed and grab the handle before I turn back to the both of them.

"This is done, and I'm leaving."

I lower the gun, shouldering past Mikhail and then his new second to step into the hallway.

"Curious, isn't it?"

Keep walking. Keep fucking walking.

But I don't listen. I stop, glancing back at him coldly.

"What's fucking curious."

He grins.

"How a rich, pampered little Bratva princess manages to learn jiu jitsu at summer camp."

I stiffen. His grin curls deeper.

"I never would have guessed that hand-to-hand combat was part of the schedule of tennis and tea at rich-girl summer camp."

I stare at him coldly, my nostrils flaring.

"I bet she's an exceptional shot, too. Isn't she?"

"Whatever the fuck you're getting at—"

"You know what I'm getting at, Kristoff," he murmurs quietly. "You've suspected for years. As you did back on your island with her. You *know*, Kristoff…"

I shake my head, a numbness creeping over me.

"*No*. That isn't possible—"

"She was one of my best students."

The words hit me like a blade to the gut. I choke, blinking, sucking back the rage and the swirling confusion. I want to scream in his face to shut the fuck up and get the fuck out of my head.

But he's right.

It *is* a thought I've had. Something I picked at in the darkest parts of the night. A little thread that unraveled just a little bit more with each chase through the woods on the island. And a little more each time she fought me like she'd been sparring for years.

Every time she picked up a gun and shot targets like she was Doc fucking Holiday.

"Oh *please*, Kristoff. Stop insulting your own intelligence by denying it. You know. I know you can see it."

He smiles cruelly at me.

"Where do you *think* she learned to fight. To shoot. How to twist your emotions and your lust for her into a weapon she could use."

The knife twists, choking me.

"*Fuck you—*"

"You know it's the truth, Kristoff. Summer camp?" He laughs. "You believe she learned four different kinds of hand-to-hand fighting at rich girl *summer camp?*"

He scoffs.

"You throw her in a dark room and put a knife to her throat, and I guarantee, she could break down a rifle and reassemble it in under two minutes."

I swallow thickly, but then my eyes narrow.

"I looked into her eyes when she fought me, Mik," I hiss. "When she shot a target clean through the middle on her first try. She wasn't hiding shit. She was—"

"She wasn't hiding anything, Kristoff, because it was hidden *for her.*"

He sighs.

"It was a new idea stolen from the military when you were still in the academy. But I tried to develop it with later trainees. They call it acute trauma neural conditioning—"

"Hypnosis," I snarl darkly. "You fucking *hypnotized her.*"

I know what the fuck he's talking about. ATNC was an experimental and mostly theoretical conditioning developed by the Russian military in the nineties. The idea was to use extreme violence and near-death experiences to fucking *hypnotize* soldiers into burying their trauma.

They'd waterboard them or pin them underwater until their brains thought they were dead as part of the conditioning, so that they could keep on fighting without even remembering the fact that their buddies had been blown to shit right next to them the day before.

…Or so that a teenaged girl could forget that she'd been trained to be a weapon.

A girl who was later told she'd been at summer camp. A girl who was told the gaps in her memories were from a fucking *boating* accident.

I wince, the flash of a memory from two years ago ripping into my consciousness—one where I'm lying in bed with her as she tells me about the accident. How she'd been told she'd fallen into the water and was kept under by the boat rocking against the dock. How she still had night terrors sometimes where she was being pinned under the waves.

I want to scream. I want to tear Mikhail apart with my bare fucking hands.

Harriet never went to summer camp. There never was a boating accident.

She was a weapon in Mikhail's nightmare academy, and then she was fucking *drowned* to make her forget it.

Blinding, painful white light flashes in my head, sending me reeling as I grip the doorframe tightly.

"Not just her," Mikhail says casually. "There was a whole class of students who'd come from privileged families—Bratva heirs, the children of warlords and tyrants. The goal was to train them to be lethal killers, and then bury that very training, erasing it from their very minds as if it never happened." He sighs. "Of course the next part was to be able to *awaken* that training later. That's where I struggled—"

"You're a fucking monster, Mik," I rasp coldly. "You trained *children* to be fucking killers, and then tried to hide—"

"If you're looking to hurt my feelings, Kristoff, I can promise you, you're wasting your time."

I level my gaze at him.

"You know what? You're right." My eyes narrow. "*Everything* about you and your bullshit is a waste of my fucking time."

I whirl, shaking, my muscles quivering as my hands curl to fists. I need to get to her. I need to wrap her in my arms and tell her I'm going to protect her, and destroy everyone who had a hand in what happened to—

"You two seem so good together."

I stiffen, my eyes closing. My jaw grinds as I glance back at him.

"Have a nice life, you piece of shit."

I step out of the front door to Harriet's apartment.

"It's a shame, though."

I squeeze my eyes shut, paused with one foot out the door.

Don't.

I *know* he's trying to get inside my head. I know this is one of his games, because it's *always* a fucking mind game with Mikhail.

But then I engage him anyway.

"What's a shame, Mik?" I snarl, turning back to him.

Something's wrong.

He's too triumphant looking. Too pleased with himself. And far too willing to let me just walk away from this conversation.

"*What* is a shame?" I repeat.

Mikhail inhales and exhales slowly. His shoulder lifts casually as he shrugs.

"Munich, two and a half years ago."

A cold blade drags up my spine.

"The hit you did a month before you were sent after Tatiana."

"I'm leaving, Mik," I snarl. "I'm not listening to any more your fucking bull—"

"Oh *surely* you've put the place and time together before this, Kristoff." His eyes glint wickedly, his lips curling triumphantly.

My brow furrows deeply.

"I killed Werner Köhln, a federal cabinet minister."

My mind flashes back to that day—me laying on the roof of the Brandhorst Museum of modern art, my eye to the site of the long-range Ruger precision rifle. The crosshairs leveled at the black town car barreling right towards me down the *Türkenstraube*.

Breathing in, exhaling. Knowing that the target—a cabinet minister trying to push through some new border budgetary measures that would have constricted black market trade via Poland—is sitting right behind the driver.

Knowing the car and all the windows are bulletproof—with the exception of the windshield, which is only rated up to small arms fire.

It won't stop a caliber of this size, with this power, with this piercing tip, from this range.

I remember being angry that I'd been sucked back into this world. That'd I'd been forced back into my *bukavac* role.

But also knowing I'd storm hell itself if it meant finally laying my Nik-nack to a proper rest.

I remember exhaling again. The trigger pulls, the gun recoil slams into my shoulder. The windshield of the car spiderwebs and splatters red with the driver's blood. The round is designed to pass right through him and into Warner. But even if it vectors, he won't survive the aftermath of this. The car is traveling way too fast, and with the driver dead against the wheel, it careens wildly.

Exactly as planned.

If Werner isn't dead by the bullet, he's about to be by the car itself.

The town car veers into the sloped wall of meridian. The front side tire hits first, catapulting the whole car up into the air and flipping it twice before it hits the side of a stolen dump truck I parked there this morning with a dull crunch.

The gun barrel swivels. I center the crosshairs on the underside of the car as I chamber the incendiary round.

There's a chance Werner wasn't hit by the bullet. There's an even smaller, though possible, chance that the head-on collision with a stationary truck at ninety kilometers an hour, upside down, didn't kill him.

But when the incendiary round pierces the gas tank, and the whole mess goes up in a roaring column of flame, his fate is sealed.

And I'm one step closer to laying Nikita to rest.

"You seem so sure about that."

I blink, staring coldly at Mikhail as I slowly nod.

"He's *dead*, Mik. It's public record. Werner Köhln died in Munich on—"

"Werner Köhln was shot in the back of the head in a parking garage. A staged mugging."

His eyes narrow, and his glinting, shark-like smile cuts deeply across his face.

"He was killed roughly three minutes before you put a bullet through a car windshield and into Peter Fairist's forehead."

The air leaves my lungs. The floor wobbles under my feet.

No.

My mouth opens, though no sound comes out.

"You used your old contact in Munich for the intel on that hit, didn't you? Ziegler, was it?" He smiles. "I know it was Ziegler, Kristoff. You know Ziegler and I are good friends, actually."

My lungs feel heavy. The air feels too thick.

"Maybe this will help."

I'm numb, the roaring in my head almost deafening as Mik passes me a tablet with a news article from two years ago open to it.

One that details a car crash, in Munich. Right by the Brandhorst Museum on the *Türkenstraube*, which was under construction.

One that talks about the driver losing control and flipping the car over the meridian, into the side of a dump truck. Where the car then caught fire and exploded, killing the driver and his only passenger:

The known head of the Balagula Russian crime family.

Otherwise known as Peter Fairist.

Otherwise known as *Harriet's fucking father.*

The room goes silent. My pulse twitches in the hollow of my neck. A low, whining sound hums in the back of my head like white noise. My brain glitches as my face freezes.

Of course I read years ago about Peter Fairist's death in a car accident in Germany. Of course, I heard the murmurings that his accident was staged, and part of a coup to take his throne.

I just never looked too deeply into it, because I was too busy planning my assault on the Fairist house. I was too busy ignoring my orders and kidnapping Harriet to the island.

I was too busy spending the next three and a half months losing myself in her.

I was too busy falling in love with the girl whose father I'd just murdered.

The roar in my head becomes deafening. It overwhelms me as my throat closes, choking me. The color drains from my face as I stare at Mik with a haggard, horrified mask stretched across my face.

"I wonder how much she'll enjoy your company once she knows you killed her dear father."

40

I don't even remember the drive back to the hotel, or how I survive it at the speeds I'm going. I stagger out of the car, leaving it half on the curb, ignoring the bellhop as I surge through the lobby doors

At the top floor, I stumble blindly out of the elevator and crash down the hall to the suite. My face is ashen, my heart twisted. My hands are fucking shaking.

But then I get to the front door, and something cuts me in two.

I get to where the suite doors are smashed in, with the man I had guarding her dead in a pool of his own blood on the foyer floor, and something breaks in me.

I drop to my knees, sucking in air I don't have to scream for her, or tear the place apart.

I already know she's not here.

My phone rings. I can barely see through the murderous red hate pounding through my veins and clouding my eyes. I'm shaking with rage as I yank the phone out and answer blindly, sucking in air.

"You sound distraught, Kristoff."

I roar. I literally roar like a fucking demon into the phone the second I hear Mikhail's voice.

"*When I find you*," I rasp like death himself. "It will be slow, Mik. I'm going to take my time slowly dimming the light from your fucking eyes, until the last thing you see is me pushing you into the darkness."

He's silent for a second.

"She's gone, isn't she?"

"*Run*, Mikhail," I choke. I pull my gun out, checking the clip as I lurch to my feet. "I want your blood pumping hot when I let it drip down your fucking neck—"

"Yes, very scary, Kristoff," he mutters. "But I can assure you, I didn't take her."

I start to storm down the hallway like a god of wrath.

"But I know who did. And I know where she is."

I stiffen.

"You're aware that Jana has been attempting to expand the Balagula empire into the UK, yes? And you're aware that she's been living here in London?"

"*Yes.*"

"Well…" he sighs. "She's the one who took Tatiana, Kristoff. And that's where she's got her. At her penthouse on the South Bank."

My eyes narrow lethally.

"If you know all this, why the *fuck* would you tell—"

"Because I want her *dead*, Kristoff," he hisses quietly. "And who else would I send besides the famous *bukavac*."

I shake with hatred and anguish, sucking in lungfuls of air as my eyes squeeze shut.

"If you want Tatiana, or Harriet, or whatever the hell you want to call her, Kristoff… that's where you'll find her."

He sighs.

"The question is, will she want *you* after she learns what you did to her?"

I close my eyes, shaking as my chest constricts around my black heart.

"And of course, there's the other question."

I don't answer, because I can't.

"Will *you* want *her* after you learn what she did?"

"*Mik—*"

"You've been looking to lay your sister to rest for years, Kristoff."

My mind glitches. My face tenses as I stare haggardly at the floor in front of me.

"Perhaps killing the person who killed Nikita would help you do that."

My eyes narrow as my pulse thuds like molten lead in my veins.

"*You son of a bitch—*"

"She was one of my top students. So exquisitely talented, and so deftly able to master anything we threw at her."

My skin turns to fire as my face freezes into a death mask.

Jana. It was fucking *Jana* who ended my sister's life in a training exercise gone too far.

And now, I'm going to cut her in two—

Mikhail chuckles.

"You think I'm taking about my niece, don't you?"

I flinch.

A warning light and a blaring siren goes off in my head.

No.

"Jana was a good student, but she was never my best."

Please God no...

"Nikita, now *she* was good. Better than Jana, yes. But still not the best."

My head starts to shake as my very soul starts to fray and crack at the edges.

No...

"The best student I ever had fought your sister in a training exercise and pinned her by the neck underwater."

The roar starts somewhere silent inside, ripping and clawing its way to my ragged throat just as he sinks the blade the rest of the way into my heart.

"The best student I ever had was Tatiana Fairist. And she drowned Nikita in eight inches of water when she was fifteen years old."

41

It isn't the first time I've been blindfolded and handcuffed.

But the last time, it was Kristoff. The last time, it was the start of an enormously path-altering new chapter of my life.

It scares the shit out of me that I have the same feeling now as I did then. That something drastic is about to happen. Something life-altering.

When it happened before, it woke me. *He* woke me up and pulled me out of the life that had been laid out for me into something wild and free. Something dangerous and dark. Something forbidden and depraved.

Something I didn't even know I'd been missing. But once I had a taste, I couldn't have imagined going back.

Now two years after losing it, I've found it again. I have *finally* found that balance of dark and light that balances so perfectly on the knife's edge of our connection.

And I'm fucking terrified that it's about to be taken from me again.

I try and block out the replay in my head—the crash of the hotel suite door. The man I didn't recognize shoving *another* man I didn't know through the smashed doorway and then shooting him in the head as he fell to the ground.

The sound of my scream as I bolted to the bedroom. The feel of uncaring, unfamiliar hands on me, grabbing me and slamming me to the ground.

When Kristoff catches me, my world turns to fire and aching need.

When it was someone else doing the catching, I wanted to throw up. I wanted to shrivel up and hide until I woke up. But this is no nightmare.

This is real.

I'm in one of Kristoff's huge t-shirts and a pair of his gym shorts. I'm barefoot, and I'm freezing. I swallow, shivering with my hands bound with a zip-tie behind my back. The blindfold blocks out everything but a thin sliver of light by my nose.

But even still, I know we're in an elevator when the doors ding shut and it starts to rise. I swallow thickly again.

"Where are you—"

I gasp sharply, jolting in fear as the man grabs the zip-tie around my wrist and yanks hard.

"I told you to shut the fuck up."

The elevator stops rising. The door dings open.

"Move," the man grunts. I tremble when I feel something cold and hard press between my shoulder-blades. A gun. The same one that just murdered someone in front of me.

There's hardwood floors under my bare feet. The man pushes me forward, down a hallway, until we stop.

When we first pulled up outside, and I was violently ushered from the car, there were several voices; the sound of men chuckling and snickering in my direction. Inside, there were even more voices, like a small group was present.

But up here—wherever "here" is—we're alone.

I focus on my breathing, not the gun at my back. Not the man I remember as cruel looking, with dark eyes and thin, pursed lips.

I hear beeps, like a code being punched into a keypad. Then a click of a lock. The man shoves me forward. I gasp, expecting to hit a door. But instead, I go tumbling forward into a softly lit, cool space.

I catch my footing and then tense as I feel the gun jam hard against my back.

"Please," I choke. *"Where—"*

"Oh, I don't think she needs to be tied up, now do you?"

I go absolutely cold. My blood curdles, and my heart drops into the floor when I hear her voice.

It's Jana.

It's the woman who slipped her way like a blade into my father's heart, and twisted there. The snake who slithered into our world and took him from me, before turning on *me* as well.

The woman who used both Kristoff and I as pawns, playing us and then playing us off each other, tearing us apart for two fucking years.

That is who sent this man to take me from Kristoff. And now I'm here, standing… somewhere, right in front of her.

"Release her."

"Ma'am—"

"I said *untie her*, for fuck's sake," she snaps.

I tense as I feel a blade slip between the zip-tie and my wrist. I have no idea who else is in this room. It could be just Jana, the guard, and I. Or maybe there's a small army of silent guards with guns on me.

But it doesn't matter.

When my arms are free, I already know I'm going for her. Army or no army, I'm going to kill this fucking woman.

The blade snips. A hand tugs my blindfold off. And I lunge.

Jana laughs as the man behind me grabs me by the collar of my t-shirt, yanking me back hard. But suddenly, training takes over.

I could somehow hold my ground sparring with Kristoff those years before on the island. But since then, I've been *religiously* training in jiu-jitsu and kickboxing.

You don't grab me from behind and expect nothing to happen.

As he yanks me back, I shove in the same direction, taking him by surprise. I crash hard into him, my elbows slinging back viciously to jab at pressure points on his ribcage. The guard groans, wincing in pain as I stamp down hard against his ankle, whirl, and slam a forearm into his throat.

He gurgles for air, his face bright red. But he yanks the gun up.

I'm faster, and I hadn't just been punched in the breathing pipe.

I grab his wrist holding the gun and pivot into him, keeping the barrel wide as I slam an elbow back into his solar plexus. I aim higher, and he screams as my elbow breaks his nose.

He also loses his grip on the gun.

In one motion, I wrench it from his hand, shove him back, and whirl to level it at his bloodied face.

My pulse thuds heavily. My chest heaves as I suck in air. My eyes dart around, quickly taking in the *gorgeous*, elegant penthouse.

And then, my gaze lands on *her*.

And she's smiling.

Jana grins as she slowly claps her hand, shaking her head.

"My *my*, someone's been training, hasn't she?"

My eyes flit past her, around the massive living room that leads to an open-air balcony surrounded by gorgeous pink chrysanthemums. It's just us. No army of guards. Not even a second one. Just me, the guard I just disarmed, and the woman who I very well may kill tonight.

And yet, she's just beaming at me, slowly clapping.

"*Very* well done," she purrs.

Her gaze slips past me, to the man I'm holding the gun to.

"You can leave us now."

Wait, what?

"Ma'am, I can't leave you with—"

"I said *leave*," she hisses.

The man glances at me, eyes narrowing as he holds his bloody nose. His eyes drop to the gun.

"I don't expect she's planning on returning that to you, you idiot," Jana sighs.

The guard glares at me once more, turns, and walks out of the very door he just shoved me through.

Then, it's just Jana and me.

I turn, my eyes narrowing dangerously as I raise the gun to *her*.

That's another thing I've been drilling in since the island. Since I landed in London, I've been taking the train out to one of the private ranges outside the city as often as I can.

Back on the island, I was a pretty damn good shot. Now, I'm lethal.

This is the very first time I've ever pointed a gun at a human, though. And I feel like I should be having a hard time swallowing that.

But I'm not. At all.

Jana smiles.

"I think we can probably lower that now, don't you?"

"Nope."

She shrugs. "If it makes you feel better."

"Shooting you would make me feel better, actually."

She shrugs, turning. I tense, baring my teeth as I step closer, jabbing the air between us with the gun.

"*Relax*," she sighs, rolling her eyes. "Can I get my drink without you shooting me?"

She gestures across the open concept penthouse to a glass of white wine sitting on the edge of an elegant white marble kitchen counter.

"No."

Jana rolls her eyes.

"You really do think I'm your enemy, don't you?"

My jaw clenches tightly, my eyes stabbing into her.

"Would I have really sent away my guard if I considered you an enemy?"

"Would you have really sent someone to shoot his way into my hotel room, pin me down, blindfold and handcuff me, and then drag me to your apartment against my will if I wasn't?"

"Well," she smirks. "Not *your* hotel room, now is it?"

My eyes narrow.

"Still falling for those charming baby-blues, hmm, Tatiana?"

"That's not my name."

She sighs.

"Right, right. It's *Harriet* now. How could I forget. Anyway, I'll grant that you and I have every reason to be enemies."

I bark a cold laugh.

"Is that amusing, dear?"

"Just obvious," I hiss.

"I don't think that has to be the case, though."

"Strongly fucking disagree," I spit.

She shakes her head, looking angrily away.

"Do you really not get that we're both pawns in this game? And the one pushing us all around the board just to amuse himself is *Mikhail*."

She swallows, anger clouding her eyes.

"Do you think I *wanted* to seduce your father?"

"Shut up."

"You think *that's* what I gave my childhood, my teens—my whole goddamn *life*—to Mikhail, to do with my time on this earth?!"

"Shut. *Up*."

"To try and get some grieving Bratva widower into bed, so that my *uncle* could steal his empire?"

"*Shut. Up!*" I scream, tears clouding my eyes. I step towards her, brandishing the gun as my throat goes dry.

"I'm as helpless in all of this as you are," she snaps. "Do you really not see—"

"I see a liar," I choke through clenched teeth. "I see a backstabbing snake. I see that Mikhail may have pulled the trigger, but you're the one who tied my father to the target and gleefully watched it happen. And for that, I swear to God—"

Jana starts to laugh.

I stare at her, shivering and unnerved by the sudden outburst.

She wipes her eyes, her lips curling wickedly.

"Oh you poor thing," she grins. "You haven't put the pieces together yet, have you?"

I swallow, nostrils flaring.

"They were all right there, waiting for you to look past your little puppy-love fuck-fest with Kristoff and connect together. But you just couldn't look past those big arms and those blue eyes, could you?"

"No more riddles," I snap. "*Enough*. What have I not put together—"

"That Mikhail didn't kill your father."

I blink, my heart thudding.

"And neither did I."

My lips curl as I drag my gaze back to her, leveling the gun.

"I'm going to enjoy—"

"Mikhail didn't murder your father."

Her smile simmers dangerously.

"Kristoff did."

Two words. It's just two words, but they slam into me like a train. I choke, blinking quickly as I stare at her.

"That's a lie."

She shrugs. "It's not. Here, over there."

She points to a side table, with a tablet sitting on it.

"Unlock it. There's no passcode."

I swallow.

"Just look," Jana says softly, her eyes holding mine fiercely as she smiles weakly.

I move sideways to the table, my skin shivering. I tap the screen and swipe, unlocking it to find a news article splashed across the screen.

I wince. I've read this headline before.

It's a screenshot of one of the newspaper pieces about the accident that killed my father—an accident that now comes with quotes around it, now that I know that it wasn't.

I've read all of these news pieces. How his driver lost control and hit a meridian, flipping the car into a truck, where it then caught on fire and exploded. And I've seen the horrible pictures. And even if my dad and I were never close at all, he was still my father.

And knowing that it was a person and not fate that took him from me cuts hard.

But I know what Jana is doing. She's trying to get inside my head. She's doing *exactly* the same thing she did to me two years ago.

I'm not buying it this time.

"You want me to look at this and somehow believe your bullshit that Kristoff was involved in this? Are you fucking serious?"

She smiles quietly. "Not that. The next picture. You can swipe now."

I swallow thickly, eying her. But then I drop my gaze and swipe to the next picture.

My chest constricts.

THE HUNTER KING

This one is screenshot of a police report, in German. I peer at it, trying to piece together the little vocabulary and few phrases I know in the language.

"This was the original cause of death report. But it was immediately pulled from the records and replaced with one signed by an expert declaring it a brake failure."

Jana smiles thinly, nodding her chin at the table.

"But that first report says something different."

My pulse hums louder in my ears.

"It says the driver was struck by a bullet that traveled through both him and the car seat to hit the man sitting behind him—your father—in the forehead."

My world goes numb. Pain clouds my eyes.

"It says the car *did* lose control after that, and did flip into that truck. But is also says they found an incendiary round fired into the fuel tank when the car was on its top."

No.

I blink back the sting of tears as my heart begins to clench.

"Swipe to the next picture," she urges.

And I do. This one chokes me, as it's a shot of the upside-down car, roaring with flames. It's my father's funeral pyre.

I start to look away, but Jana shakes her head.

"Look past the horror," she whispers. "Up higher, on top of that building. That's the Brandhorst Museum of modern art. It overlooks the street where your father died. *Look closer.*"

The world is buzzing in the peripherals as I zoom in. Until suddenly, I jolt.

There's a figure on the roof. A man, crouched down, holding a rifle. You can't make out the details, but he's right there, looking down at the burning car.

My face hardens as I glare up at her. "You want me to see this as fucking proof? Are you joking?"

She shakes her head no.

"Not proof," she urges. "More weight on the scale I already know you've got strung up in your head. I *know* you know what he is."

"What he was," I hiss.

She laughs. "The same place that made him made me," she sneers. "And trust me. That doesn't go away. That doesn't change. And you don't leave that behind. Not ever. And I'm telling you right now—not to hurt you, but to free you."

My heart thuds.

"*Kristoff* killed your father."

I stagger backwards, struggling to breathe.

"He pulled the trigger. *He's* the one who took your father from you."

Suddenly, there's the sound of gunfire nearby.

Above us.

My face pales, my eyes snapping to the ceiling.

"That would be the roof deck," Jana mutters casually. "And I suppose that sound would be Kristoff shooting my guards on his way to come rescue you."

My heart races as the shooting above us intensifies. And then suddenly, there's a crash and a loud thud. I whirl towards the big open glass doors leading out to a balcony full of pink chrysanthemums that looks over the Thames.

A man lies groaning and bleeding profusely on the ground, like he was just dropped off the roof above.

Or pushed.

He starts to get up. But a shot slams through the night, dropping him dead.

"He's here, Harriet," Jana says quietly behind me.

My pulse turns to fire. My throat closes as pain, fury, and betrayal erupts through me.

"Think about all the times he whispered little nothings in your ear," Jana purrs behind me. "Or undressed you. Or teased your body."

The tears bead in my eyes.

"All the times he said all the right things. Or fulfilled your every, darkest desires. All the times he swept you off your feet or put them behind your head while he fucked you."

A tear rolls down my cheek.

"And remember that *every single one of those times*, he knew."

She's right behind me, hissing the words into my numb ear as the gun grows heavier and heavier in my hand.

"He looked you right in the eye and smiled, knowing full well that he'd murdered your father."

She chokes.

"That's cold, even for me. How about you, Harriet?"

A figure drops lithely from the roof onto the patio. I stiffen, my heart wrenching in pain as he slowly turns and levels those piercing blue eyes at me.

"He knew, hon."

The words urge into my ear. Her hand slides down my arm, raising it.

"Look into his eyes, and you'll see the truth."

Kristoff's face is grim and lines. His nostrils flare as he starts to take a step towards the doors to inside.

My hand raises, and he falters to a stop. His brow furrows deeply.

"Harriet—"

"Is it true?"

My voice feels empty and hollow. It feels far away, like it's been buried alive, and it's calling through the ground.

His brows knit. "Harriet, listen to me—"

"Is it true?" I choke again.

"Whatever lies she's been poisoning you—"

"Is. It. Fucking. True!?"

I am death. I am vengeance. I am cold, broken, ripped apart from the inside *fury*. And the second his eyes lock with mine, and I see the haggard look behind them, I know.

And it breaks my heart.

He fucking knew.

"Yes."

The one word whispered from his lips is the last straw. The sob wrenches from my lips—not just a cry of anguish for my father, who he took from me.

But for our love. For the faith I place in him. For the trust I gave to him.

He murdered that, too.

My hand tightens around the heavy gun, my pulse thudding in my ears as the world shrinks and time stops.

"*Harriet*," he rasps. "Listen to me—"

"*Not anymore*," I hiss quietly.

His eyes pierce into me.

"Harriet, I love you."

"I hate you."

He takes a step forward, and it's like the trip-switch flicks.

The gun explodes in my hand. And in slow motion, I watch the man I thought I loved stagger back. His gun drops. His hand flies to his chest as he keeps staggering backwards.

His eyes raise to mine.

He hits the row of potted chrysanthemums. Then he trips backwards over the balcony edge, and he's gone.

My heart breaks. I mean it literally wrenches itself in two as a cry of sheer anguish shatters from my lips. I don't realize I'm running to the balcony until I'm at the edge, eyes bulging as I stare out over the dark of night with the lights of the city glittering over the Thames right below.

A few soft pink petals drift down into the darkness to drift upon inky black water.

But he's gone.

He's gone.

"I enjoyed that."

I'm numb as I slowly turn. So numb that I don't even really register that Jana is smiling as she aims a gun at me. I blink, and instinct has me raising my own arm.

She just laughs quietly.

"Oh, hon, you just had the one."

I blink.

"As I said, I did enjoy that little show. But I'm *truly* going to enjoy this."

She cocks the hammer back as she levels the gun at my head.

"Oh, and Tatiana? Or Harriet? Or whatever the fuck you're calling yourself now?"

She leers a sharp, poisonous, cruel grin at me.

"I lied."

I flinch. My head glitches.

"Kristoff didn't kill your father."

All I hear is thundering white noise; an overwhelming static in my very psyche. A high-pitched whine screeching into focus in my ears.

In slow motion, the gun falls from my hand. I turn to stare in absolute horror at the inky black water below.

"Kristoff didn't kill Peter," Jana snickers.

I slowly turn back to her.

Broken.

Empty.

Finished.

And done. I'm just *done*.

She smiles cruelly.

"No, your father—"

I see the massive, bubbling, churning fireball of the explosion rippling in the air behind her well before I feel it.

But then *oh* do I feel it. The inferno bulges out like a molten bubble, engulfing Jana before the blast punches into me, blowing my hair back, lifting me off my feet and hurling me backwards out into the darkness.

All I hear is a ringing sound. All I feel is heat, and the gentle pull of gravity as I sail out over the river. And suddenly, I *am* Harriet Quimby. I'm the real one, flying over the Thames.

But then, I'm not.

Then I'm falling, and flailing, and screaming, and sinking.

Drowning in the darkness as it drags me under.

Harriet and Kristoff's story continues in The Hunted Queen.
Find it here.

ALSO BY JAGGER COLE

Hunted Duet:

The Hunter King

The Hunted Queen

Cinder Duet:

Burned Cinder

Empire of Ash

Savage Heirs:

Savage Heir

Dark Prince

Brutal King

Forbidden Crown

Broken God

Defiant Queen

Bratva's Claim:

Paying The Bratva's Debt

The Bratva's Stolen Bride

Hunted By The Bratva Beast

His Captive Bratva Princess

Owned By The Bratva King

The Bratva's Locked Up Love

The Scaliami Crime Family:

(All standalone books which can be read in any order.)

The Hitman's Obsession

The Boss's Temptation

The Bodyguard's Weakness

Standalones:

Broken Lines

Bosshole

Grumpaholic

Her Rough Mechanic

Cherished

Captivated

Roping His Bride

Stalker of Mine

Hungry For Her

Wrapped Up In Her

Be Ours

Power Series:

Tyrant

Outlaw

Warlord

ABOUT THE AUTHOR

A reader first and foremost, Jagger Cole cut his romance writing teeth penning various steamy fan-fiction stories years ago. After deciding to hang up his writing boots, Jagger worked in advertising pretending to be Don Draper. It worked enough to convince a woman way out of his league to marry him, though, which is a total win.

Now, Dad to two little princesses and King to a Queen, Jagger is thrilled to be back at the keyboard.

When not writing or reading romance books, he can be found woodworking, enjoying good whiskey, and grilling outside - rain or shine.

You can find all of his books at
www.jaggercolewrites.com

Made in the USA
Columbia, SC
29 September 2022